Rake*ish*

LISA WELLS

RAKEish

Dedication
This one's for you PaPa.

This book is dedicated to Marvin Wells—best known as Big Papa or Dad. A man who taught me many invaluable lessons, the greatest of which is the importance of family.

I began writing *RAKEish* when my dad was hospitalized with an illness. Sadly, his health declined rapidly, and we never brought him home.

Since publishing my first book, I've dreamed of hitting the charts, a symbol of literary success, and sharing that triumph with my dad. I imagined his face alight with pride as my achievements were recognized on a grand scale. Unfortunately, he passed away before this dream could come true.

"Dad, I'll keep trying, so don't give up on me."

RAKEish

Blurb

You know what they say about Prince Charming—he's all charisma and arrogance until he falls head over heels right into the arms of his sworn arch-nemesis.

Psychologist Dr. Lux Stone is book brilliant, men clueless. Due to a massive glitch in a dating app's data collection, she's got the ego-bruising statistics to prove it. Unfortunately, when she vents by criticizing the advice given in a popular column on dating, it goes viral. Her boss demands she prove the author's advice is faulty or lose her dream job.

Scott Landshire, a prince by birth and a rake by design, has ditched the uptight shackles of royal life to become a Relationship Columnist at the fashion magazine, Naked Runway. When an opinionated psychologist questions his credibility—and his manhood—he's forced to prove her wrong or say goodbye to his platform, his visa, and his dignity.

Can this unlikely duo find love, or will their epic public battles crush their careers and hearts?

Get your copy of RAKEish now and embark on a delightfully chaotic enemies-to-lovers rollercoaster!

Contents

DISCLAIMER

Oh my...

Hello Book Boyfriend Connoisseurs,

I have a disclaimer for "RAKEish." My editor—whom I adore—advised me to cut a particular thread that runs throughout this royal rom-com. Normally, I adhere to her brilliant suggestions. And by normally, I mean ALWAYS.

But this time, I pushed back.

Some of you may wonder why my editor wanted it removed. The short answer—she considered it highly inappropriate. As for the long answer, I can't explain without spoiling a major plot point... but once you've read the book, I'm confident you'll understand.

For those of you who want to know the long answer, you'll find it at the end of the book...after the last chapter. I'm asking you to please read **my why** before you leave a review.

A bigger ask: "Even if you agree with my editor: please, *just let me have this one.*"

Your Book Boyfriend Creator,

Lisa Wells

RAKEish

Naked Runway's RAKEish

by Prince Scott Landshire

YOUR MONTHLY GO-TO-GUIDE FOR DATING IN THE MODERN WORLD

Greetings, Valiant Hearts,

As the revelry of last month's St. Patrick's Day festivities settles, I extend a warm hand to those marching onward from the trials of love, as well as to the fortunate souls who've met their perfect partner. To the latter, I jest, "When do we celebrate your union?" Curiously, I've unearthed that engagements in the United States tend to span an extensive three and a half years.

Pondering why, I recall the lavish balls of my homeland, where grand celebrations are orchestrated within mere weeks. Could this prolonged engagement be a trial of love's resilience, an opportunity for doubts to surface, or merely a pause for reflection? If so, bravo for such cautious deliberation.

However, heed my caution: such patience might spell ruin for a liaison with a rake, for whom restlessness, ennui, and allurements are inherent traits—woven into their very essence. Or, in my unique case, cursed by a vengeful enchantress centuries ago. This curse, a spiteful hex from a scorned witch against my ancestor, plagues my family's firstborn males, a testament to the perils of trifling with love.

Contrary to fairytale beliefs, no love can lift this curse. The true remedy, unfortunately, remains a mystery to us. My tales of fleeting romances in Manhattan are not for lack of desire for lasting love—as a certain radio announcer would have you believe—but to spare others from the curse's repercussions. My brief courtships are not whims, but a search for the one who might end our ancestral plight.

Setting aside my lament, let's celebrate a triumph—a reader's journey from fascination to love with a notorious charmer, employing strategies I've shared in these pages:

1. Be Unapologetically Fabulously Fashionable.

2. Master the Art of Wit.

3. Maintain an Air of Mystery

4. Create Memorable Moments.

5. Keep the Sizzle Alive.

This narrative stands as a testament to the power of our *RAKEish* philosophy.

Remember, you are someone's perfect someone, and while you're waiting to meet them, just know they are daydreaming about that moment, too.

Yours in the pursuit of love,

Scott Landshire / Your Royal Guide to Unconventional Romance.

Rake*ish*

CHAPTER 1

"Once upon a second glance." The phrase wobbled off psychology professor Dr. Luxury Stone's tongue like a cheating husband's confession in a couple's therapy session. She cleared her throat and repeated it again, only slower. "Once...upon a...second...chance."

She groaned.

Glance, not chance. Glance. Glance. Glance.

Who knew a five-word sentence could be so cumbersome? She wished she could blame this morning's continual butchering of the phrase on a sluggish Monday brain. She couldn't.

The culprit was a fat case of jitters.

She exhaled a breath, releasing her nerves, and repeated the phrase. "Once upon a second glance."

The quick double-tap horn toot of a taxi driver caused her to practically jump out of her thirty-one-year-old skin.

Geez Louise, get a grip.

If Manhattan had an official noise, it would be the sound of honking. Getting used to that ever-present racket had been the hardest part of adjusting to her life as a visiting professor at Columbia University.

Satisfied her vocal cords were ready for the day, Lux padded barefoot to her desk, muttering, "It's walk-the-walk time." The phrase sparked a new flutter of nerves, a stark contrast to her normal calm when going live with her show.

Today, however, she faced a daunting task: discussing a painfully personal topic. More humiliating than any of her previous public speaking misadventures. Even the time she'd taught a class at Missouri State University with the back of her skirt stuck in her granny-like underwear.

Refocusing, Lux blew out a breath, snagged the single pink Post-it stuck to her microphone, reread her scrawled show notes.

1. Speak about how flawed first impressions can be.

2. Move into the beauty of second glances.

That was it. Two broad bullet points. A far cry from last week's typed, printed, and laminated blueprint which had possessed thirty talking points.

Today's notes were miniscule because, unlike every other broadcast leading up to this one, she'd not spent a week preparing. Truthfully, she'd barely spent a couple of hours.

The topic had ambushed her late last night, an email notification cutting through the quiet. Its contents—a harsh reminder of her apparent invisibility on dating apps—had stung. Yet it was the catalyst for today's episode, pushing her to confront a societal obsession with surface-level judgments.

Lux's watch buzzed, snapping her back to the present. Exhaling, she reminded herself not to say *fuck* on air, slipped on her headphones, and hit the live button. "Wake up, Manhattan. You're listening to Monday Musings with Dr. Lux Stone," she began, her voice steady despite the whirlwind of emotions. "Go ahead. Rub the sleep from your eyes and curse the gods that Mondays insist on coming so quickly." She bit her tongue to keep from making a lewd comment about once dating a guy whom she'd nicknamed Mr. Monday for that very reason.

"Yes. You heard correctly. I'm not part of your dream. I'm real. It is indeed Monday, and you do, indeed, have to kick off those sheets, push the button on your coffee maker, and commit to adulting." Lux's own alarm had jolted her out of her restless slumber at three forty-five. Jolted because she'd been having a nightmare about the Prince of Manhattan. Ew.

"If you haven't yet opened your curtains or pulled up your blinds," Lux said, glancing toward her window, "you're in for a treat. It promises to be a beautiful spring day."

She pushed a button to play her show's jingle and glanced at the opened email on her computer screen. Subject line: HOW TO UN-DERSTAND YOUR DATING RESULTS! It was a correspondence from a dating app she'd signed up for on New Year's Day after making a resolution with a friend to do so. This in the hopes they would meet some nice guys to do things with around the city while waiting to meet the man of their hearts.

In short, the email explained men on dating apps aren't looking for personality-rich women.

In long, the correspondence revealed that over the last four months, 3,214 men (names included) had swiftly swiped past her profile image, dismissing her with a simple flick of the finger.

To add insult to injury, one of the swipers had been none other than Scott Landshire—the freaking prince of her nightmare.

A guy she'd met once and had hated instantly.

The jingle ended. "No rain in the forecast and highs in the low seventies." Feeling a yawn coming on, she muted her mic and took a quick sip of coffee. There might not be enough caffeine in Manhattan to keep her going all day. Then again, stimulants or not, her brain would never allow sleep when it could instead fixate on the email that had informed her that—when it came to men—she was invisible. As if her image contained the subject line: Nothing to see here, just keep on swiping.

Or at least that's what three thousand, two hundred and fourteen men must have told themselves as they judged her worth based solely on her profile image.

The knowledge of those rejections settled like a shadow draping over her spirit. While her brain knew she didn't need a man to be happy, her heart desired someone with whom to enjoy life's moments.

Her decision to share the results with this morning's listeners was one that required her to put aside her own humiliation for the greater good. As a psych professor, she had always made it a point to emphasize to her students that knowledge was powerful. But in this instance, it had crushed her spirit. And if it could do that to her, it could do that, or worse, to another.

If she could encourage just one listener to be okay with their appearance, one listener to decide today was the day they'd no longer twist their true self to fit another's mold, one listener to walk away from a bad situation, then it would be worth spilling her problem.

Not that the plan to share her results for the benefit of all made what she was about to do easy. God, no! It had all the markings of a topic that could go more viral than the infamous peek-a-boo granny-panty incident.

By nature, she strived to keep her failures private, her planners organized, and her vibrator fully charged.

But sometimes, nature had to take a backseat to the greater good.

Here goes my limping dignity.

She unmuted. "Now that you're awake, turn up the volume, because you won't want to miss a single word of today's show.

"I'm calling today's episode...Once Upon a Second Glance." She smiled as the title rolled correctly off her tongue. Practice indeed made perfect.

Once Upon a Second Glance gave today's topic the façade of a black-tie affair.

If only it were that civilized.

She always titled her broadcasts and her lectures and...well...lots of things. She was a strong believer in the value of titles. The right one would do the heavy lifting for you. The wrong one would sabotage your plans.

"Are you wondering what that title even means? Wondering if it's worth the brain power to figure out?" She spoke slowly so her words had a chance to soak into Monday-morning tired brains.

"No worries. I'll help you decipher." She readjusted her coffee cup. It had the words "KEEP TALKING. I'm diagnosing you" scrawled under an image of a therapist listening to her client. It was her favorite mug—not too big, not too small. In fact, now that she thought about it, she was holding this mug in her photo on the dating app.

"If hindsight is twenty-twenty, does that mean we should mindfully pay more attention to things or people we've dismissed at first glance? Should we make it a conscious practice to give things not one but two or even twenty additional glances before judging and moving on?"

The answer is yes, people. Absofudginglutely yes!

Three thousand, two hundred and fourteen.

"In a world where instant judgments and surface-level interactions reign supreme," she continued, "we must challenge these prevailing narratives. Our worth extends far beyond our physical appearance."

Mother had taught her this all too well. Not by good example—quite the opposite. Mother lived her life under the impression a woman should do everything in her power to remain beautiful. Beauty, according to Mother, was what kept a man in your bed. Well, that and knowing how to give a mind-altering blowjob.

No one had ever accused Mother of being parent-of-the-year material.

"As a therapist with a small private practice, I've witnessed the complexities of human nature firsthand, and I refuse to accept the notion that love can be won through superficial glances. Love begins upon a second glance. There is no such thing as love at first sight—just lust at first sight." Lux had purposefully lived her life downplaying her looks. When she won a man's heart, she would rest easy knowing his love was not all wrapped up in his admiration of her outer shell.

This way, when her looks faded, his love wouldn't.

"Think about it," she said. "How many times have you said or thought, 'if only I knew then what I know now?'"

As a rule, Lux lived by the edict *regret not*, which basically meant always look forward. After all, it's not like looking back would change the dysfunctional environment in which she'd been raised.

"I know it's Monday, and your brains don't want to think, so let me give you some examples of times a person might have wished they'd given another person a second glance."

Of course, her examples needed to focus on dating, since that's where she was headed with this show. "For instance, all you singles out there, think back to the last would-be-suitor who offered to buy you a drink or a cup of coffee, and you declined their offer because they were too big, too small, too tall, too short, too ugly." She paused as she silently counted to three, giving them time to recollect. "Now, I want you to imagine what might have happened had you taken a moment and given them a second glance. I shot down my guy in this scenario because he wore a T-shirt with the words: 'Why read when you can watch the movie?' to a Literacy Bowl event. My forever man will love reading as much as I do. That being said, given today's Once Upon a Second Glance topic, I can't help but wonder what if...?" She'd filtered through several what ifs on the dude last night while not sleeping. All but one of them ended with her deciding she'd been correct.

"For instance, what if he'd been wearing the offensive shirt because someone had spilled something all over him, and the bartender had offered him a replacement from their lost and found bin?" She rubbed at a kink forming in her neck.

"And before you scoff, let me point out in romantic comedies things like that could and would happen to thwart a couple from falling into insta-like, let alone insta-love. And, while I don't believe in the latter, I strongly believe that if funny meet cutes can happen in a book, they can happen in real life. Thus, I should have given him a second glance."

The realization humbled her already belittled self-esteem. She was no better than the gazillion men who'd swiped past her profile picture. Hell's fudging bells.

"If you're wondering what the why is behind today's topic, it's because of something that happened over the weekend. You see, I received not one, but two emails from a dating app I joined in January. The first provided me with the number of men who glanced at my profile picture and, in under one second, swiped not interested." She paused, swallowing the emotions welling inside of her. Emotions she could normally control, but on little-to-no sleep, they were all over the place.

"I'll be honest. That email was one gigantic ouch to my ego." And that had led to her second-guessing her long-standing stance to under-play her appearance until after she'd caught the heart of a guy.

"The other part of the unfortunate email listed the names of those men."

After receiving the information, she'd been pissed. The creator of the app would hear from her. After all, this list could cause irrevocable harm to an individual suffering from depression or low self-worth. She didn't care that the owner had immediately recalled it and sent out an apology. The damage had been inflicted.

"Hurt pride aside," Lux spoke succinctly into the microphone, "being dismissed as unworthy of another's attention—in under one second—caused me to toss and turn last night. During those awake hours, I reconsidered some of my past first impressions of people in general. Not guys trying to pick me up in a bar. Those times where I took one look and said no thank you." She glanced at her sticky note. Not that she needed to. She knew what was there.

"One person kept popping into my brain. His Royal Highness, Scott Landshire." It was one thing to be swiped out of existence by men she knew nothing about, but a totally different beast to have had it done by a guy she actively disliked. He'd joined the dating app in January as well and, ever since, had been reporting about his dating experiences in his monthly column RAKEish. A Guide to Dating from a Modern-Day Rake's Point of View.

Why RAKEish? From what little Lux had bothered to learn about the man, his deceased mom had nicknamed him her 'little rake' the day he had been born. This because of a supposed curse on the first-born males on his father's side to be unreformable rakes.

If it hadn't been for the fact Lux and Scott had both moved to Manhattan in the fall, he might not have ever hit her radar. It wasn't like she was a royal enthusiast or a reader of *Naked Runway*. Those were two things she had no desire to spend her free time pursuing.

But she did know of his move to the city because his arrival had caused quite the splash across many headlines. Including *Psychology Today*.

RUN AWAY PRINCE or PRINCE ENJOYING YEAR ABROAD?

THE PRINCE OF MANHATTAN TAKES JOB AT NAKED RUNWAY AS AN ADVICE COLUMNIST

"For those of you new to the city, Scott Landshire is a contributor for *Naked Runway*. Once a month, he updates his readers on the single life from a male perspective. My regular listeners are familiar with my opinion of the man." On more than one broadcast, she'd delved into why his column did a disservice to women. "His words of wisdom often linger at the corner of criminal negligence and reckless absurdity.

"My opinion of Manhattan's rake-about-town first formed when I had the not-so-decided pleasure of witnessing the prince in action soon after I arrived in the city. I had been standing outside of a club waiting to be admitted when he arrived in a limousine. Once he'd exited, he proceeded to make his way along the line of those of us waiting and made a production of choosing ten ladies to jump the line and enter with him." None of his choices had included ordinary women like

Lux. "In that moment, I lost all respect for him. A gentleman would have gone to the back of the line and waited his turn." Or at the very least, given his coat away to any one of the ladies in line wearing nothing meant to keep them warm.

He was exactly the type of man who'd made Mother into Mother. A woman who believed the sum of a woman's worth was all external. And, if the headlines about him were true, he was exactly like Lux's father. A man who thought women were disposable.

"I've decided to give Scott a second glance." She'd put it out into the universe. There would be no backing out now. "Not the man himself, but instead, his column." Well, maybe a little backing out. "In other words, I'll give his *advice* a second glance, even though I strongly believe his monthly ruminations are about as useful as a chocolate teapot sold as functionable. Next week, I will report back on the positives I uncover."

She took a sip of coffee and clicked open a different tab on her computer screen. An image of Scott's first column appeared.

RAKEish: A GUIDE TO HOOKING A MODERN-DAY RAKE.

What woman in their right mind wanted to hook a rake?

Sure, in historical romance novels, a high-society playboy with a propensity for scandal—or as Scott defined himself, a high-class charmer with a wild side—could be molded into husband material, but life wasn't a romance book.

"To be fair to Mr. Landshire, his column has glowing reviews. *Naked Runway's* readership has exploded ever since his first article."

The month she'd first unleashed her opinions, she had mocked his suggestions for pickup lines that would work on a rake—these for the women who had to do the heavy lifting to get a man's attention. You know, the ones not pretty enough, fashionable enough, sparkly enough to get noticed the moment they entered a room.

Last week, Lux had gone on a tirade about his advice to women to allow themselves to be hypnotized to better attract a guy. This after attending a show at a comedy club where a hypnotist had been the main attraction. A hypnotist with a raunchy act.

Her watch vibrated. She glanced at it and saw she had an incoming message from Mother. Ugh. Whatever it said, it wouldn't be nice. She took a cleansing breath and exhaled.

"I truly look forward to unearthing a nugget of good advice in one of his columns. Perhaps even his one on hypnosis," she said into the mic. "Not that I will change my mind about his stance on the subject. Truly, if a guy can't appreciate me for who I am, there's no way I'll agree to be hypnotized to make myself more appealing." Hypnosis was a tool to be used for good, not for laughs. And certainly not to get a man. "Though I'll peek a second time at Landshire's column in the spirit of today's topic—Once Upon a Second Glance—I'll never use hypnosis for romance." What was sad, some might. "But I will look for something good."

"If you're a fan of *RAKEish*, give me a call and let me know which of his tips you've found success with. But first, it's time for this week's sponsored ad."

She pushed the button to play a fifteen-second advertisement for tomorrow night's trivia fundraiser and picked up her phone to read Mother's message:

Why the fuck did you go and tell the whole world you're a dud at dating? Did you learn nothing from me? The one thing men want less than a plain Jane is a dull Jane. You've gone and made yourself both Janes.—Mom

Pain's grubby fist twisted her heart, causing her to grimace. By now, she should be immune to Mother's bluntness. According to the dating statistics, it would appear Mother had been right all along about the lovability of plain Janes. Sure, Lux didn't need a man to be happy, but she sort of wanted one.

A good one, that is.

Not a damn rake.

CHAPTER 2

Scott Landshire sat in the back of an SUV listening to Monday Musings with Dr. Lux Stone, while his driver drove him to work. Once again, the woman had mentioned him on her show. And once again, she'd done so in a derogatory fashion.

What in the hell had he ever done to her?

On a whim, he turned down the volume, pulled his phone out of his suit pocket, and dialed the number she'd just rattled off. It was time the two of them had a conversation.

"This is Monday Musings with Dr. Stone. Please hold."

He patiently waited, considering what he should say. He heard a click on his end of the line, and then her voice speaking into his ear.

"This is Dr. Lux Stone, and you're on the air. Who am I speaking to?"

"Good morning, Doc." Giving someone a nickname right out of the starting block was a flirting tool he'd often used on women. The implied intimacy tended to soften the response of even the wariest of them. "This is Scott Landshire, the man you love to hate. I've been listening this morning, and it dawned on me, what better man to help you out than me? If you've got a few minutes, I could help you with your dating profile."

There was a soft thud, as if the phone had been dropped. He waited. Nothing. "Hello. Are you still there?" Surely, she'd not hung up on him.

"Hello, Mr. Landshire." She blew out a breath straight into his ear. "What an unpleasant surprise. Is this your first time listening to Monday Musings?"

He ignored the insult. "On the contrary. I never miss an episode."

"I find that startling." The four words squeaked across the phone lines sounding like they had travelled through the chew toy of a pet Pitbull. Not at all like her normal self-assured tone.

"How else am I to know what I've done wrong if I don't listen?" His goal, he reminded himself, was to charm her into dropping her continual harassment of his column.

"You say that like you want to change," Doc said. "Do you want to transform from a rake into a romantic? Or do you just want the thorn in the side of your column to go away?"

He chuckled. "Just between us—and your dozen or so listeners—I'm gutted every time you attack RAKEish."

"Dozen?" she said, her voice more frozen steel then unaffected blasé.

"Too many?" he teased, glad to know she could be needled out of her calm demeanor.

"Mr. Landshire, my show reaches an audience of 1.6 million people. And in case you're math-challenged, that's more than a dozen. In fact, if you want to get down to the nitty gritty—"

"I'm always up for getting down to the nitty gritty—"

"It's 133,333 plus dozens," she said, ignoring his attempt at humor.

"I stand corrected. Your numbers are impressive," he responded.

"Thank you." Her words said one thing, her tone said *bite me*.

"Almost as impressive as the column I wrote on the art of pickup lines. May I suggest you start there with your second glance resolution? You'll find it in *Naked Runway's* February issue."

"I recall that issue. Your suggestions were archaic."

"And yet they work." Or at least they had until she'd voiced her opinion on them. An airing that, much to his annoyance, had resulted in Monday Musings bouncing out of its niche lane right into the traffic of mainstream popularity.

"That speaks more toward the type of woman you use them on than it does about my comment."

"And what type would that be?"

"The type with subpar standards when it comes to how evolved a man must be before she's willing to entertain the idea of having a drink with him."

"I must say, your ever-present need to hate on me is gutting." He liked to think of himself as a cheerleader for women's rights. Especially the one allowing them the freedom not to be thrust into an arranged marriage. A practice still going strong in Shiretopia where its future kings—like him—were concerned.

"If that gutted you," Doc said, "I could only imagine your reaction should you learn the content of the nightmare I had last night. A nightmare in which you starred."

"Why Doc, are you having dirty dreams about me?" Interesting. He'd not seen that coming.

"That is not what I said," she replied tersely. "And forgive me for even bringing it up. I'm afraid my brain is short-circuiting as a result of so little sleep last night."

"I'd much prefer to hear the content of your dream than accept your apology."

"Absolutely not."

He resisted an urge to push and instead took a different approach. "As you wish, but...I'd be lying if I didn't tell you that this rakish male brain of mine has jumped to the conclusion that if you're dreaming about me, it means—no matter how hard you bash what I do for a living— you secretly like me." It was a delightful deduction. Implying her public hate was a cover for her true feelings was sure to put her on edge. "From this moment forward, Doc, I will believe you have a massive crush on a rake."

"Don't be ridiculous," she snapped.

"I don't believe that's what I'm being," he said, biting back a chuckle. "And I bet your listeners don't either. In fact, I bet they'd love to hear your response. Do you, or do you not have a crush on me?"

"Trust me when I tell you this is a subject best dropped, for your sake," she replied.

His curiosity skyrocketed. "I give you permission to destroy my sake and tell your potential 133,333 plus dozens of listeners what it is you think I'm better off not knowing."

"Did you call for a reason," she inquired, smoothly changing the subject, "or may I hang up now?"

He laughed, amused she thought he could be easily moved to a new topic. "A change of focus can only mean one thing. Your dream was sexual in nature."

"Or it means, despite what I do for a living, I believe in the old tale, if a person retells a nightmare before breakfast, it will come true," she countered.

He'd never heard of that superstition. "It's quite convenient, this excuse not to spill the details."

"You should not push me. Once I accidentally tested the superstition, and it came true." Something in her voice had shifted. Like he'd forced her to recall a memory that pained her to do so, or she'd realized she'd allowed him to get under her skin and was pissed. His money was on pissed.

"Once, you say?" She was a doctor of psychology. Surely, she did not believe she caused something bad to happen to a person.

"Not that it's any of your business, but I repeated another before breakfast to test the results, and it also came true."

"That was quite brave of you." The doc had a fanciful side. He would have bet his bejeweled crown she did not. What other surprises did she hold?

"Not really. I was just curious."

"I see. Well, I'll tell you what, Doc. If your dream was what I think it was, I can guarantee you it will not come true."

"Nightmare," she said firmly. "And it would serve you right if I did tell you so you could discover for yourself that all superstitions, crazy as they might sound, originated in someone's truth."

His curiosity grew. "Please, by all means, punish me with the truth."

"I'm not joking," she snapped. "Like I said, twice in my life, my nightmares have materialized after I relayed them before having ate breakfast."

"So, the scary quantity of two has turned an otherwise intelligent woman into one plagued with superstition?" he pushed.

"This coming from a man who believes he's the victim of a wicked witch's curse."

Touché. "Our family has five generations' worth of proof for our belief in the mystical. You have only two experiments for yours."

"While two is not much, it would have been criminal of me to continue the experiment all in the name of gathering further empirical evidence to back my hypothesis."

The woman was a glitchy scientific nerd. "I rather love being used by women in the name of a naughty experiment, so go ahead, lay this dream on me."

"Nightmare," she insisted.

How bad could it be? "Doc, I have a fabulous idea. I once dated a therapist who specialized in dreams. Why don't you reveal the content of the sex dream you had about me, and I will ask her to interpret it? In fact, I will write about it in next month's *RAKEish*." It would make for a great column.

"I'm more than capable of interpreting my nightmare that your penis fell off and you showed up at my door asking if I knew how to repair it." Her words were immediately followed by a loud gasp on her part. As if she'd shocked herself by speaking aloud the revelation.

He echoed the gasp. "Good God, woman." He reached for a bottle of water. This whole conversation had just taken a turn toward disaster.

"Pardon my vocabulary," Doc said, her voice full of dismay.

"It's not your vocabulary I'm worried about. It's your prediction. Take it back," he demanded, anticipating the endless ribbing from his colleagues if she refused. "Or better yet, admit you're messing with me because you don't like me."

"I don't have that kind of sense of humor," Doc said. "The demise of your penis is imminent."

"I insist you stop saying that. You're making it worse."

"I did warn you."

"Not hard enough."

"That's what she said," Doc replied.

"That is not very doctorly of you." Her unexpected humor softened his tone.

A huffed-out sigh, with undercurrents of dismay and distress, tickled his ear. "You're right. I'm tired and my mouth is taking advantage of my brain's inability to block it," she admitted. "Listeners, please forgive me for this morning's lapse in good judgment on my part."

"And do I get an apology?" he pressed.

"You do. Mr. Landshire, I sincerely apologize for telling you your penis is about to punch its last ticket."

"Please, stop saying *penis* followed by gloom and doom predictions."

She snorted, as if she wanted to laugh, but couldn't quite gather enough energy to pull one off. "On the bright side—for me, not you—I suddenly don't feel nearly as devastated about my situation."

And the sleep-deprived zingers just keep coming.

"And to think, I called in because I thought to apologize for being one of the men who'd swiped past your profile." He hadn't done so because of her image. Hell, he'd been on his phone and had barely been able to see it. He'd skimmed past her name in his quest to pair a newly single man with the ideal woman. A man he'd agreed to help because a fake fairy godmother, Ms. Birdie Faraway, had requested his help.

Ms. Birdie, the president of the Fairy Godmother Project, was quite the piece of work. She never took no for an answer. He'd tried. Not only that, but he was now being pestered by the dear to start up an offshoot of her program. The Fairy Godfather Project. Magic not required.

Doc cleared her throat. "Tell me, Your Majesty—"

"Your Majesty would be my father. You may call me Scott or Your Royal Highness." The reply was automatic. Most Americans, he'd discovered, did not know royal protocol.

"Tell me, Oh Great Rake of Manhattan, do you stand behind your dating advice? Or is it offered tongue-in-cheek?" She spoke distinctly as if she'd just gotten her second wind and was ready to once again slip into the role of professional psychologist, albeit a snarky one.

Or the wounded animal is coming in for the kill.

"I'm not familiar with that saying," he mused. "Is it equivalent to dick in hand?"

"I'm glad you have a sense of humor about your upcoming penile predicament."

He'd walked right into that one. "Not funny." It was damn funny.

"Too soon for dick jokes?"

There was that humor again. What other things would she surprise him with should he keep Doc off her stuffy game? "The way I see it, as long as your mouth is occupied with my dick, life is good."

"Touché," she said, after a beat of dead air. "And on that note, I do believe our time is up. Goodbye, Your Royal Rakeness."

Scott put his phone away, turned the volume up on her show, and settled back in his seat. He couldn't remember the last time he'd not been able to dazzle a woman with his charm.

A damn woman who'd predicted he'd soon lose his penis.

Rakeish

CHAPTER 3

FORTY-FIVE MINUTES LATER, SCOTT made his way through the bustling cubicles located in the trenches of *Naked Runway*, his brain replaying his conversation with Doc. He was late for a staff meeting, in part thanks to the number of people who had stopped him on the way to his office to mention they'd heard him on Monday Musings.

"What's today's pitch?" asked Lucy, a gorgeous redhead.

"Oh, you know—"

"Wait. Don't tell me," Lucy said saucily. "Let me guess. You're pitching an extended guide to spicing up your sex life with mood socks?"

He chuckled. At least it wasn't another penis joke. Mood socks had been the topic of last October's issue. His homage to the comeback of the mood ring. "Lucy, my love, it's this season's top ten perfumes that drive a man wild." The response rolled off the top of his head. He never preplanned before arriving at a pitch meeting. Long ago, he'd discovered his best ideas arrived at the last minute.

"Just men? Or will those perfumes work their magic on a woman as well?" Mandy asked, picking up on the conversation as he passed her cubicle.

He slowed to answer Mandy. "Absolutely, but don't waste your money. Your gorgeous smile is all you'll ever need."

Tom, a graphic artist, glanced up as Scott rushed past his desk, the hum of a graphic tablet filling the air. "I'd read that."

A chorus of me-toos rang out in the background as the sharp tap of Scott's newly polished shoes echoed around him. Shoes he'd learned to shine himself at the age of twelve. It had been a lesson in humility dished out by Mildred, his stepmother, after Scott had pulled one too many pranks on the Queen of Shiretopia during her and Father's first year of marriage.

Scott raised a hand in appreciation. "Thanks, everyone." He rounded the corner to the final hallway that would take him to the meeting where he would indeed pitch perfume if nothing else sprang to mind.

Or perhaps he'd go with Lucy's suggestion: An extended guide to spicing up your sex life with mood socks.

What would Doc have to say about an article on perfume that drove men wild? She'd despised the one he'd done on mood socks.

He could just hear her now stepping up on her broadcast soapbox and saying something pithy like: *Drive a man wild with your perfume, you have him for a night; drive him wild with your brain and you have him for life.*

Bloody hell. She wouldn't be wrong. On that thought, he stopped outside the doorway of the meeting room known as the Fishbowl, so called because of its four glass walls. He quickly counted heads. Eleven. Once again, he was dead last to arrive. Bollocks.

He yanked at the knot of his tie, plastered a smile on his face, and entered the lively conference room where stylish individuals milled around. The way they were talking and laughing and sipping beverages, you'd think it was Friday night and not Monday morning.

"Late again," Frankie Peterson, Editor-in-Chief of *Naked Runway*, snapped without even glancing in his direction.

"Sorry," Scott said. "I'm—"

"Must I continue to repeat myself?" Frankie pivoted toward him. "Apologies are for the lily-livered, Mr. Landshire. I have neither the time nor the inclination to listen to them." If her frigid tone hadn't properly indicated her mood, the sharp lift of her perfectly stamped brows emphasizing her cool disdain did.

"Lily-livered. Got it." He resisted making a statement of it never again happening because it would. People who scheduled anything of importance on the first day of the week puzzled him more so than the archaic rules that governed the life of royalty.

He took a seat next to Ziggy, the magazine's outlandishly fun fashion editor. The guy's personality and sense of style could only be described as flamboyant on steroids. And if that wasn't reason enough to befriend him, the fact Ziggy had more stories than Shiretopia's

Mother Goose librarian had sealed the deal. Last night, Ziggy had shared a snippet about the time the magazine's old editor-in-chief had been caught banging one too many of his employees in the breakroom and had been fired.

Feeling Frankie's gaze still upon him, Scott returned his attention to his boss. "Have I mentioned how lovely you look today?"

Her icy demeanor didn't thaw. If anything, it gave him freezer burn.

Scott offered her his best look of repentance. The same look he'd given Father so many times as a teenager after disappointing him with his antics. Antics usually meant to get under the skin of Queen Mildred.

Frankie drummed her dragon red nails on the table and studied him. "What won't happen again is your wearing red to a pitch meeting. Did you not read the memo?" She stared pointedly at his tie, which was black with row after row of tiny white dots broken up by oversized red dots.

America and its bloody love of memos. Or maybe it was just a Frankie thing. "I read the one that said ties were now required. I must have missed the one banning red," he said as he removed his tie.

Back home, Scott had had a butler who'd informed him daily of what he was expected to wear, where he was expected to go, and what he was expected to say at speaking engagements. Such was the life of the Ambassador of Goodwill. A role assigned to all future kings of Shiretopia.

While Scott didn't miss the hand holding, or the constant censuring, there were times, like now, he realized he'd still not picked up the habits of reading emails, or listening to voicemails, or arriving at engagements in a prompt fashion. Probably because he'd been too busy embracing his reputation as a rake. A title Mum had given him out of affection, but which had been later used as a weapon by Mildred.

Frankie's nostrils flared. "I do wonder how much longer you will be employed by *Naked Runway*."

Pushing aside thoughts of Mildred, Scott reached for another dose of charm. "Now, now, stop frowning." He turned to fully face his boss. "It would be so sad to see that beautiful face marred with Scott-induced frown lines." He'd used this line many times over the years to—if not melt away—at least soften his stepmother's anger. A woman who despised him and his American mum. "I promise to do better."

Frankie's lips briefly quirked before they flattened. She whipped her attention toward her assistant. "Jane, the meeting should have started ten minutes ago. Why has it not started? Must I fire you as well?"

Scott loved his job, but he didn't do it because he needed the money. He'd been Mum's sole beneficiary. And he didn't do it because of the bevy of lovely ladies the job placed at his fingertips, as he had a very un-rake-like rule against dating colleagues. He did it because he loved to write. A gift from Mum. She and Father had met while she'd been summering in Shiretopia, writing a novel. A romance. A passion she'd stopped pursuing once she and Father had eloped, thus saving Father from the arranged marriage that had awaited him.

"So sorry." Jane, a perky brunette with puppy dog eyes, rushed forward, and handed a wicker basket to the beauty editor who had the misfortune of sitting to Frankie's right. That spot, along with the one on Frankie's left were, without fail, the last two to be chosen. Scott always sat on one side or the other. "Okay, Frankie's Peons, phones in the basket. Let's begin our breath work," Jane said as the basket went around the table. "Inhale...exhale."

Scott relinquished his phone and passed the container to Ziggy. Then, while glancing at the others around the table, he inhaled and exhaled as told. Unlike him, everyone else had their eyes closed. Even Frankie. Scott smiled in appreciation at the collection of beauty.

The breathing continued for five in and out breaths. At least Frankie didn't require her peons to remove their shoes like the breathing scene in *How to Lose a Guy In Ten Days*.

"Open your eyes." Jane pointed toward the woman sitting on Ziggy's left. "Isabella, Frankie would like to start with you today."

Scott was intrigued by Isabella P. Chance. Partly because she was married to a guy with a frightful reputation around town, and partly because she had a mysterious relationship with Frankie, as in Isabella showed no fear toward the woman. None. Even Ziggy was terrified of Frankie.

"Of course." Isabella pushed back her chair and stood. She wore a man's white dress shirt tied in a knot at the waist, a black leather miniskirt, and stilettos. *Red*.

He chuckled silently. Were the shoes a power-move on her part, or had she failed to read the memo as well?

"I'm still working through my series on street wear makeovers," Isabella said.

"Of course you are," Frankie drawled as if Isabella had just announced she planned to dress the homeless for a charity function and then write about it. "Please, someone else go. Someone who is not trying to ruin our magazine with their mediocrity."

Isabella smiled prettily and took a seat all while semi-subtly scratching her nose with her middle finger. Even though she was the editor of the digital side, she still pitched for the hard copy side.

"I love that series," Scott whispered, leaning forward to see Isabella. "I'm glad there's more to come."

"Me, too," Annie, an editor who sat on the other side of Isabella, chimed in. Annie was a new mother, and as such looked bone tired, but oh-so-happy. She and Isabella worked closely together.

He made a mental note to send Annie flowers this month. Last month, he'd sent her a year's supply of diapers. It couldn't be easy being a single mom, and he felt compelled to make her life a little smoother. Of course, he sent the gifts anonymously. "How's the little one—"

"Scott, your mouth is moving. You must want to be my next victim," Frankie snapped. "Pitch already."

He cleared his throat in preparation to pitch the perfume idea, then recalled how he had imagined Doc would react to such a column. *With disdain.* Just once he'd like to have a column she couldn't hate.

Luckily, his brain did the thing his brain did and provided him with a new topic. "How to fall in love with the right per—"

Frankie flashed him her shut-the-fuck-up palm.

He cocked his head and waited. It was always like this when pitching to the woman.

"Jane, please explain the problem to Scott," Frankie ordered.

Jane, who'd taken a seat in a chair behind Frankie, popped up. "Scott, if you're not standing, Frankie doesn't hear a word you say."

Frankie sat next to him. She could hear just fine. "Right. I forgot." Scott stood. "I said—"

The palm again.

"Honestly," Frankie drawled, "that story is better suited for our February issue. Not our June. Do better."

She wasn't wrong; he'd have to pitch the perfume one. "My other idea—"

Frankie palmed him again. "Scott, I"—she drew out the word *I* like it contained twenty-five letters and multiple syllables—"will choose what you write next."

He raised a brow. This was a first. Frankie wasn't one to assign topics. She preferred to watch her editors and reporters sweat until they landed on an idea she didn't hate. "And that is?" Scott studied her for hints.

"I've been informed that the oh-so-blah Dr. Stone once again dissed your column this morning on her stupid little radio show."

Diss? Another new American word to research. "She's a nobody with a stick up her arse."

Ziggy chuckled. "Scott said arse."

Frankie tutted at Ziggy, cutting his amusement short. "This is not a laughing matter. Dr. Stone continues to bring into question the value of Scott's column. *Naked Runway* has spent a considerable amount of money and energy hyping Scott as the rakish prince who'd ditched his duties to come to America."

Scott gave Frankie a sincere smile. She might be an annoying boss, but she'd kept up her end of their agreement when it had come to pushing him as a rake to the public. He was banking on the publicity of his bad boy behavior to help his cause back home. "And I appreciate the fact that it is because of you and your faith in my column that *RAKEish* is a sensation."

"I've approached legal with the possibility of a lawsuit for slander," Frankie said in a no-nonsense tone. "If they contact you, inform them of the emotional suffering you've had as a result of that woman."

Scott stilled. While he wasn't a fan of Doc, he had no interest in seeing her in a messy legal battle. "A lawsuit may be bad optics," he said tactfully. "We wouldn't want social media to spin it that we are Goliath going after Cinderella."

"That is a lily-livered statement if ever I've heard one," Frankie snapped, slapping her palms on the table. "Should the threat play out in court, I'm certain our publicity department can spin the narrative in a direction that creates sympathy for us. For *you*."

Scott remained mute. What had he been thinking insinuating Frankie was wrong? The last thing he wanted was for Dragon Lady to go after his nemesis just to prove she was right.

"If we're going to threaten lawsuits," Ziggy said, jumping into the mix, "I would think we'd hold off and see if her prediction about the future viability of his penis pans out."

Scott cursed under his breath.

"This is the first I've heard about this," Frankie said. "Explain?"

Ziggy grinned like the Cheshire Cat that Scott had had as a child. "Dr. Stone told Scott she'd had a nightmare about him. When he asked her what it was, she told him she couldn't reveal the content of it because she'd not yet had breakfast. And according to her, there's a superstition that when one reveals a nightmare before eating breakfast, the nightmare comes true. But our boy Scott insisted she tell him anyway."

"Dear God, could you be any slower getting to the damn penis point," Frankie said.

"Her nightmare was that his dick fell off, and he sprinted to her door asking for help to get it reattached."

"Fuck," Frankie muttered, giving Scott a look of horror. "Keep me abreast as to the status of your penis, so I can keep legal informed."

This caused laughter all around.

"Please do, Scott," Annie said. "We all want to know the minute it happens. There might even be a pool going on the exact date."

Scott smiled good naturedly at his colleagues, while worried for Doc. The last person he'd want to have on his bad side was Frankie Peterson. "I can assure you my cock is not in danger of falling off, and Doc's views of me are skewed due to the fact she can't attract men. No one takes her I-hate-Scott game seriously. There is no need for a lawsuit...of any type." Animosity aside, he felt bad for the woman who'd been weirdly passed over solely on her looks, which weren't bad if you liked the earthy girl-next-door type. Not that beauty was everything, but it was a lot. Or at least it was in the beauty industry.

"If social media is anything to go by, and it is," Isabella said. "Why don't we lean into the whole fight between Lux and Scott? The last I checked, people are taking sides. There's Team Doc. And Team Penis—I mean Prince." She paused and winked at Scott. "While the memes concerning Dr. Stone are not flattering, right before I walked into the meeting, Team Doc was winning by a small margin as being on the right side of their conflict."

"She's winning?" Scott had to sit with that for a moment. He wasn't used to losing. "People believe my column is rubbish?" Was he letting Mum down with his attempt at honoring her love of writing? Would she be ashamed?

"Her students love her," Isabella told Scott. "They are going all in on her behalf."

"Interesting," Scott muttered. "The woman too uptight to smile in her profile picture is loved by her students."

"She is," Isabella said. "I'd be happy to dedicate some time on our *Naked Runway* podcast toward the hate battle between the two of you to help tip the polls in your favor."

"You want to purposefully fan the flames of a social media dogfight?" The idea made Scott aghast.

"I do love the idea of a good social media war," Frankie mused. "It could assist in our defamation lawsuit."

"But that's not what—"

"Scott," Frankie said, interrupting Isabella's rebuttal, "you will do a few posts defending your column and asking Dr. Stone to change her mind about you."

"How exactly do you suggest I make that miracle happen? Doc's opinion of me lives in quicksand. If it moves at all, it will be down, never up."

"That's what she said," Ziggy said into his hand, pretending to cough.

"Must I really explain?" Frankie asked.

Scott nodded. "I think you must."

Frankie rolled her eyes as if to say it was lonely being the only intelligent one among them. "Of course she won't change her mind. Instead, she'll stupidly double down, giving legal plenty of evidence with which to sue her for defamation."

He had to get Frankie off this whole idea of suing Doc. "What if the social media blitz ends up with me as the victor? Will you drop the threat of a lawsuit at that time?"

"You will not win, because our dear Isabella will inevitably fail in her endeavor to fix things."

A loud scoffing noise erupted from Isabella. "Says who?"

Frankie looked directly at her. "Darling, you're simply not that good at your job."

"Bite me," Isabella replied, before tearing her gaze away from Frankie and giving Scott a soft smile. "I've got your back. You can count on me."

Scott swallowed hard. He'd bet his left nut his whole life was about to blow up, and Doc would be collateral damage.

CHAPTER 4

WALKING TO WORK INSTEAD of taking the subway gave Lux-ury time to regroup her thoughts, something she greatly needed after this morning's on-air epic failure. Scott Landshire's un-expected call, combined with her no sleep situation, had thrown her bruised and battered psyche into a spiral of chaos, which had, unfor-tunately, resulted in her blurting things better left unsaid over the air, which had, super unfortunately, resulted in a swift social media fallout not even she could have imagined in her wildest pre-show jitters.

Her Monday Musings Instagram account had blown up after the show. Memes abounded, most of them hurtful. And much to her surprise, people were taking sides. Team Doc vs Team Prince. Which of them was right? One influencer had done a video explaining the situation for those who'd missed the show.

Could Scott's methods help a woman land the heart of a rake?

Or was Doc right, and his techniques were antiquated bullshit that would result only in some asshole getting away with his rakish ways while the woman lost her heart in the process of trying to fix him?

And that was truly what *RAKEish* boiled down to. Scott was portraying men who liked to play the field as the ultimate fixer-upper project. And by calling that type of men rakes he'd wrapped them up in a pretty bow, turning a fixer-upper of a shack into a fixer-upper of a castle.

She clenched her hands at the sheer ludicrousness of the whole column.

Two blocks from the campus of Columbia, her phone rang. "Hello."

"Hi, Lux. This is Dr. Marshall. The interview committee would like to meet briefly with you this morning. We will send a grad assistant to cover your first class."

Unease filled Lux's stomach. "May I ask what the meeting is about? Have you chosen your candidate?" She'd made it through two rounds of interviews for a tenure-track position which had unexpectedly opened when the professor she'd been filling in for had decided to make his sabbatical permanent. It was a dream job that would allow Lux to stay in New York. She'd not been expecting to hear from the interview committee until after the board had met. Unless...

"It is about the position." Dr. Marshall sounded even more stilted than normal. "But a decision has not yet been made."

"I see." Lux blew out a soft breath. According to her inside source, the committee had decided, and they were simply waiting for approval before telling Lux she was the chosen candidate.

"There are a few issues that need to be resolved," Dr. Marshall said.

Issues? A psychologist's word for problems. The committee must already know of this morning's on-air cluster. Why else would they want to meet? In no Ivy League universe was it okay for a professor to talk about penises before breakfast.

She had been such an idiot for not sticking to her original topic of conversation for today's show. One that had been completely overshadowed by the damn Prince of Manhattan's call in.

"Are you still there?" Dr. Marshall asked. "Did we lose our connection?"

"I'm here." Lux inhaled and exhaled deeply. "I'd be happy to meet with you. In fact, I'm almost to my office now."

"Excellent," Dr. Marshall said. "We'll meet in the conference room."

Fifteen minutes later, Lux sat in front of the interview committee, stress sweat perched on the tip of her nose waiting to fall.

"Lux, I'm afraid more information has come forward since we spoke on the phone," Dr. Marshall said. "Which leaves us with bad news."

"No foreplay or anything." Lux laughed nervously. "Just straight to the crux of the meeting."

Ms. Birdie, a community member—aka wealthy benefactor—on the committee, chuckled.

Everyone else around the table looked at Lux as if she'd just said *foreplay*.

Hell's fudging bells. She had. What was it with her and her mouth this morning? She'd already ridden the lack-of-sleep-excuse train once today. She couldn't take it for another spin. "I'm so sorry. That was quite unprofessional."

"After your show this morning," Dr. Marshall said stodgily, "the legal department received notice from Frankie Peterson at *Naked Runway* that a lawsuit was seriously being considered against the university."

Lux blinked. "On what grounds?"

"Your continued harassment of Scott Landshire and his column," Dr. Marshall replied, pushing his glasses up his pencil-thin nose.

"Not harassment," Lux said defensively. "I simply read his article and then point out its flaws to my listeners."

"The magazine believes you have caused irrevocable damage to their magazine by insinuating Prince Landshire's advice is bogus," another of the committee said.

"It is bogus." Lux laid a hand on her stomach where a bubble of acid had decided to frolic. "He spouts off nonsensical ways for a woman to land a rake, and he does so as if that would be a good thing. His methods aside, winning the heart of a promiscuous man is not a logical goal for a woman in this century."

Dr. Marshall cleared his throat. "I believe the tipping point for the magazine was when you made a threat of bodily mutilation to their reporter on this morning's episode."

The bubble in her stomach exploded and bile threatened to roll up her throat. She'd bet her planner collection Landshire had gone running to his editor after getting off the phone with her demanding they do something about her. "I told him about a superstition I believe to be true." What a crybaby. "And this only after he relentlessly pushed for me to tell him the contents of a nightmare I'd had in which he'd been present."

There was more laughter from Ms. Birdie.

"Did you have something you wanted to add to this conversation?" Dr. Marshall asked Ms. Birdie in a tone not quite approving.

The professor sitting next to Dr. Marshall laid a hand on his arm as if to remind him of Ms. Birdie's clout.

"Don't mind me," Ms. Birdie said, a smile playing havoc with her lips. "My sense of humor seems to be cavorting with my vocal cords today."

Luxury grinned. She liked the woman.

Dr. Marshall pursed his lips and turned his attention back to Lux. "Your dismissal was mentioned as a possible solution to avoid a lawsuit."

Lux's smile disappeared. "This over nothing more than my challenging the content of *RAKEish*?"

Dr. James, a woman sitting at the far end of the table, sighed. "Lux, you've made a habit of hating on his column and then doubled down and predicted the demise of a man's penis. That is not nothing." The woman had kind eyes.

"Not demise," Lux hedged. "I've read they can be reattached, and if done quickly, they have a decent chance of once again rising to the occasion."

Eyebrows went up on every single member of the committee.

Lux bit down on her tongue. The damn thing had to be exhausted from all its untethered frolicking. Should she try and explain to the committee that sleep was her superpower? She'd always been able to crawl into bed and fall into a deep slumber within five minutes only to awaken exactly eight hours later feeling refreshed and ready to conquer the world. As such, she'd had no idea her brain was prone to misfiring when sleep deprived. "I—

"Darling," Ms. Birdie interrupted, "I will be honest with you. I find this whole situation hilarious. And you remain my choice for the position at hand. Your students can't stop raving about you."

"Thank you," Lux said.

Ms. Birdie held up a finger. "That being said, if hiring you will cause damage to the university's stellar reputation, I cannot in good faith propose we do so."

"Exactly," Dr. Marshall said gruffly.

"In my defense," Lux said to Ms. Birdie, not daring to look at anyone else sitting around the table, "Scott insisted I tell him the contents of my nightmare even though I warned him of my belief."

"I see. I was not told of your warning." Ms. Birdie dabbed at the corners of her eyes with her handkerchief. "Even so, I do not believe that is enough to change the course of action we have decided upon."

"And that is?" Lux asked.

"Immediate termination," Dr. Marshall said.

Lux gasped and placed her hand on her chest. How would she explain getting fired on her resume? Never in her life had she been dismissed. Not even as a result of the panty debacle. Was she too young to have a massive coronary? "As in today?"

Dr. Marshal nodded. "That's what immediate means."

"I'll not be allowed to finish out the semester?" How had she'd gone from probable new hire to latest fire? "There are only three weeks left. Surely I could be allowed to finish out my contract and leave it at that."

Dr. Marshall shook his head sharply. "A grad assistant will administer the final and grade the projects. One of us will finish out your lectures."

A sob broke free from Lux's lips. She slapped her hand over her mouth to keep anymore from escaping. Too much had happened too fast. She'd been so busy planning how to use the dating information for the better of the greater good, she'd taken no time to grieve over the dating app discovery. And now she would have to add loss of job to the mix of bad news. "I can't believe this is happening. Am I allowed to fight your decision? I one hundred percent stand behind my view of *RAKEish*."

"Is it truly that bad?" Ms. Birdie asked.

Lux glanced at her searching for some sign the woman's mind could be changed. "He suggests women get hypnotized to change their shy ways into guy ways."

Ms. Birdie grimaced. "That does seem a bit extreme." She glanced at Dr. Marshall. "It is my understanding Ms. Peterson provided us with ten days to handle the matter. What if we gave Lux the opportunity to use those ten days to attempt to fix the problem before we dismiss her?"

"Is that even possible?" Dr. Marshall asked.

"I have no idea." Ms. Birdie folded her hands and laid them atop the table. "But Dr. Stone is a bright star. I bet she will come up with a solution."

Dr. Marshall frowned. "Lux, is this possible? Can you fix the problem to Ms. Peterson's satisfaction?"

"I'm willing to contact her and try," Lux said.

"Just to be upfront on this matter, I should tell you what I've told the committee. I own *Naked Runway*," Ms. Birdie said.

What? "Then you could get her to back down from the lawsuit," Lux said.

"I could, but I won't," Ms. Birdie responded. "I do not micromanage those I put in charge of my companies."

"Oh," Lux mumbled.

"That being said, I will tell you this." Ms. Birdie stopped and seemed to consider her words before speaking again. "Frankie is very much a hardass. It won't be easy for you to change her mind once it's made up."

"Oh," Lux said again. "Do you have any suggestions on how best to approach her?"

Ms. Birdie studied Lux for a second. "May I suggest you pitch her a fix that plays off the movie: *How to Lose a Guy In Ten Days*. I understand it's one of her favorites, which explains why she gave us ten days to fix the problem before suing the university."

Lux grinned. "I adore that movie." Anyone who loved romantic comedies couldn't be all bad.

"What I hear you saying," Dr. Marshall spoke directly to Ms. Birdie, "is that Lux has ten days to sufficiently grovel to Ms. Peterson. If she fails, you agree with our decision to relieve her of her duties. Is that correct?"

Ms. Birdie clasped her hands and settled them on the table in front of her. "I absolutely am not suggesting groveling. Ms. Peterson has a motto: apologies are for the lily livered. Dr. Stone must go to her with a strong proposal. If she fails, then yes, she will be dismissed. Lux, are you up for the challenge?"

"If I do this, if I get Ms. Peterson to back down from her threat, will the new position be given to me?"

"The possibility would exist," Dr. Marshall hedged. "If there is nothing more, this meeting is over."

Lux watched as they all filed out of the room before dropping her forehead onto the table. "How on earth will I pull this off?"

She remained there, lost in the void of the black tabletop, until an idea sparked. Taking a shuddery breath, she straightened up, ready to face her reality.

She grabbed several tissues from the nearby box and boisterously blew her nose while pondering the idea. It was riddled with holes.

Then again, it was the only one she had, and she had absolutely nothing left to lose.

Just how awful was Frankie Peterson?

CHAPTER 5

TUESDAY MORNING AT TEN, Scott Landshire rapped his knuckles against the polished mahogany door of Frankie Peterson's office. He had been summoned with an urgency that left little room for delay.

"Come in," Frankie's voice sounded from within.

Scott pushed open the door and stepped inside, a prepared remark about Frankie's latest mandate hanging on his lips. But the sight that greeted him halted his words mid-sentence. Frankie wasn't alone. The office, usually a sanctuary of high fashion and higher stakes, had an unexpected guest.

"Have a seat," Frankie's voice was sharp as she gestured toward a chair opposite her desk.

The woman sitting in the other chair across from Frankie's sleek, glass-topped desk stood and turned to face him. Doc. The very person who had become a constant prickling presence in his thoughts since her show had aired yesterday morning.

Her presence in Frankie's office was as surprising as it was intriguing.

"We meet at last," Doc said, her voice a smooth blend of professionalism and subtle challenge. She extended her slim hand. "I'm Dr. Luxury Stone."

Scott, recovering from his initial shock, stepped forward and took her hand. "Scott Landshire."

"Enough with the niceties," Frankie interjected briskly. "Sit already."

As they both took their seats, Scott assessed Doc.

Her confident posture was a sharp contrast to her dowdy appearance, a mismatch in the stylish and extravagant office where framed covers of the magazine's impactful fashion legacy covered the walls.

Frankie cleared her throat, drawing his gaze to his boss. She'd leaned back in her chair, the corners of her mouth twitching with a hint of mean amusement. "Scott, Dr. Stone came to me yesterday with a proposition to avoid our suing her employer for the harm she's done to your brand."

Scott raised an eyebrow, intrigued despite himself. "And what might that be? An admission of guilt followed by a heartfelt apology?" He laced his tone with a mix of sarcasm and genuine curiosity.

Frankie shook her head, a small chuckle escaping her lips. "Nothing so mundane. She proposes a challenge—to win your heart in ten days using the very methods you've advocated."

Scott almost laughed, mistaking the moment for a joke, but he stopped short. Frankie never joked around. Revenge, on the other hand...

He glanced at his nemesis. "That's quite the pitch. Very clever." The fact it was to happen in ten days meant someone had clued her in to Frankie's fondness for that movie. "Unfortunately, your pitch has a major flaw."

"And that is?" Frankie asked, her eyes gleaming.

"For my methods to work, there must be an initial spark between the two players." He glanced at Doc. "Do you feel a spark?"

"Everything about Your Royal Rakeness makes me spark," she replied immediately. "And I was under the impression I did the same for you, since you whined to your boss that I'd hurt your feelings and embarrassed you."

Scott narrowed his eyes at her accusation. "I most certainly did not complain—"

"Sparks. Excellent," Frankie interjected, clapping her hands in satisfaction. "We have the starting point for this to work."

Scott shifted his focus back to Frankie. "I must be frank and say there are no sparks. Not the right kind, anyway. What you're suggesting is equivalent to asking me to fall in love with a rock."

Frankie's lips tightened. "In that case, the challenge will be that she shall win the heart of a rake. Any rake. Does that work for you, Scott?"

Her easy capitulation worried him. She had an ace stashed away somewhere. He could only assume it was tucked away to help him win. Not that he would stand back and allow her to cheat on his behalf. "Do you have additional guidelines for us to follow?"

"Of course I do. First, the challenge will be titled: How to Win A Rake in Eight Days."

"Eight?" Scott said. "Why not ten?"

"Not that I owe you an explanation," Frankie replied coldly, "but because 'a Rake in Eight' has a nice ring to it. Now, if you're done interrupting, I'll continue. Dr. Stone will employ a series of techniques you've discussed over the past year. At the end of eight days, I expect a rake to be head over heels for her."

Head over heels was not necessarily love. "She can't successfully use my techniques without prior coaching," Scott said. "I suggest a month of coaching, followed by eight days of her executing them on a rake."

"I've read your column. Any monkey can execute them with very little guidance." No hint of a smile appeared on Frankie's lips to soften the coldness of her statement. "A month is absolutely out."

"I can assure you my methods may sound simple in theory." Scott struggled to keep anger out of his voice. "In practice, they take work."

"Are you implying Dr. Stone isn't intelligent enough to pull them off?" Frankie asked.

"Asshole," Doc said under her breath, but not so quiet he couldn't hear.

"Capturing the heart of a rake is nothing like capturing the heart of the everyday Joe." He spoke directly to Doc. "The rakes of Manhattan are sophisticated and are intrigued by cosmopolitan women. An amateur will never win their heart."

"That sounds like a *you* problem, Scott," Frankie said. "Figure it out. You've got eight days."

"And if I fail?" he asked, his jaw clenched.

Frankie's expression turned calculating. "I trust that won't happen."

"But if it does," he persisted.

She narrowed her eyes. "Then we will cease to publish *RAKEish*, and you're out of a job."

Of all the things for Frankie to threaten, that was the worst. "And if I succeed?" While his mother was an American, she'd never filled out the paperwork with the US Embassy for an official birth certificate. His father refused to give him any of the necessary papers so he could resolve the issue. Which meant his stay in the States hinged on his work visa, a precarious thread that now seemed more fragile than ever. He could not return home...not yet, anyway. "What happens if I succeed in teaching Doc how to win the affection of a rake?"

"For starters, Dr. Stone will leave her current position at Columbia and cease to broadcast Monday Musings." The coldness in Frankie's tone told him that was her real end game. A win she was gambling his future over.

"What is to prevent the doc from purposely sucking at everything I teach her?"

Frankie tapped her long red fingernail against her desk. "I will have spies watching your every date. Any indication she isn't trying, and the whole thing will be called off and the lawsuit will move forward."

Doc cleared her throat. "Being spied on wasn't part of my proposal. I have no desire—"

"Your desires ceased to matter when you viciously attacked the character of our star columnist," Frankie said. "And viciously attacked his manhood."

Doc stiffened. "Has anyone ever told you your manners are atrocious?"

"Not and lived to see another paycheck." Frankie smiled triumphantly. "Now, Scott, if there is nothing further you must leave, Luxury and I have an appointment with Ziggy and Isabella for her makeover."

"Already?" Doc asked. "Can't that wait until after Scott has taught me his methods?"

"I'm running a fashion magazine. I can't have my star columnist seen about town with a frump. It will taint his image."

"But—"

"Let's get one thing straight, Dr. Stone. When I agreed to your idea, it was with my own agenda in mind. Which means we will execute your plan under my guidelines. You asked for ten days, I gave you eight. Today, by the way, is day two. I will send you and Scott the schedule for your upcoming sessions. The first four days, you will be taught one of his principles of my choosing. The remaining you will use to reel in either him or another rake."

"My calendar—" Doc said.

"Clear your calendar or go back to your employer and tell them the pending lawsuit is now an actual lawsuit. Your choice."

Scott stood and faced Doc. She really had nice cheekbones. "It is sure to be an interesting week. May the best man or woman win."

"There's one more thing, Scott," Frankie said, forcing his attention to her.

"I'm listening," Scott said.

"We're in the business of selling magazines. I need this arrangement to go viral. I don't care how you make it known, but I want it known before the end of the day that your online battle with Dr. Stone will be resolved in person. Understood?"

Before either he or Doc could reply, there was a knock at her door and in swept Ziggy and Isabella.

"You summoned us, Oh Great One," Isabella said, eyebrows lifted.

Scott grinned at Isabella's impudence. He really would like to learn the story between her and Frankie.

Frankie ignored Isabella and glowered at Scott. "Remember, failure will result in dire consequences."

"Failure is not in my vocabulary," he replied before turning his attention on Doc.

"Mine either," she said, scowling.

He tipped his head toward her. "I look forward to our enchanting time together."

Lux's brow wrinkled. "I cannot imagine any time spent in your company will fall under the term enchanting."

He chuckled. "Until we meet again."

"Ooh. This sounds fabulously intriguing," Isabella cooed. "I hope someone is going to tell me what it is we've just walked in on."

"You'll have to take that up with the boss," he said, before strolling out of the room.

How in the hell had his life gotten even more complicated? Wasn't it bad enough to have to flee his country just to maintain the right to refuse an arranged marriage?

CHAPTER 6

L UX BREATHED EASIER ONCE Scott left the room. The man took up entirely too much space. Sure, she'd seen images of the infamous rake, had even seen him outside a club that one time, but up close and within cologne-sniffing distance, he was much more...everything. Way too handsome for his own good, and dear God, don't even get her started on—

"You, of course, are the lovely muse Frankie promised me I could transform if I agreed to drop everything and come at once." A person in RuPaul-worthy drag stepped forward and flopped their hand in front of Lux's face.

"Umm." Was the kissing of knuckles expected? Or had the trend gone from high-fives to limp-wrist-knuckles?

"I'm Ziggy—he, him." He stepped forward, grasped her cheeks, and tilted her head up, left, and right. Then he let go and took a dramatic step back. "A blank canvas waiting for a masterpiece. I declare you perfect for my talents."

"And what exactly are those?" she asked.

He framed his face with jazz hands. "Makeup."

She'd been afraid he would say that. "You can do subtle...right?"

"Subtle is for the timid." Ziggy tittered coquettishly.

"But—"

Frankie cleared her throat. "No subtle. Ziggy, Isabella, meet Dr. Luxury Stone."

"I'm so pleased to meet you," Isabella responded. "You've got the most beautiful eyes I've ever seen on a woman. Like emeralds. Your name, Luxury Stone, is pure perfection."

"Thank you." Lux had always hated her name. Probably because Mother had given it to her as a not-so-subtle reminder to Father he'd promised her luxurious stones in return for Mother ruining her body and birthing him a child. A child, as it turned out, he'd ditched along with his wife several years later.

"Do not befriend this woman," Frankie snapped. "She is the one who has made a mockery of Scott's column."

Isabella laughed. "Do you truly believe he will—"

Frankie held up her hand. "Enough of the chitchat. Dr. Stone and I have entered into an agreement that will save her from a lawsuit, one in which has Scott teaching her how to seduce a man with nothing more than body language and a turn of phrase. And after today's extreme makeover, the two of you will continue to do her makeup and clothes for the remainder of their arrangement. At no time will she be allowed to be photographed with Scott looking like she does now. If she is, I will fire you, as well as the entire Glam team."

Isabella winked at Lux. "Her bark is much worse than her bite."

"You, come with me," Ziggy said to Lux, before turning and flouncing out of the room in his hot pink Louboutin stilettos.

"You'll have to excuse Ziggy," Isabella said. She wore jeans and a white T-shirt, her hair pulled up in a messy bun. "He's known for his dramatic exits. I'm looking forward to designing your dating wardrobe."

"But of course you are. It's your one true talent," Frankie said dismissively. "Now, both of you, begone."

Lux trailed Isabella through *Naked Runway's* bustling corridors until they slowed to a stop outside a room that dazzled with a blend of glamour and practicality. Several people, already busily working inside, glanced her way and tossed her curious smiles.

"Hi," she said, feeling quite shy. Out of all the faces staring her way, not a one of them was ordinary.

"Everyone, this is Luxury Stone. We're to make her over. Frankie's orders." Isabella said. "Please make her feel welcome."

A chorus of hellos echoed through the room.

"Lux, you can change behind that screen." Isabella pointed toward a black and white divider. "This is for you to wear while you're being transformed." She handed her a lovely white robe. "Take everything off."

"Everything?" Lux questioned.

Isabella nodded. "Frankie has ordered us to make over your entire wardrobe. All the way down to your bra and panties. I have a runner ready to go and purchase you new undergarments."

"That seems a bit extreme," Lux said.

"Frankie doesn't do anything by half measures," Isabella said.

Twenty-minutes later, Lux, wearing the softest robe she'd ever had touch her skin, she thought it might be real silk, stood in front of Isabella, arms outstretched as the woman took yet another measurement.

"That should just about do it." Isabella took a step back right as a man sashayed up to them.

"I am Alberto," he announced. "I will transform your hair."

"Oh." Lux touched her bun. "Frankie said nothing about my hair."

"I am the most important part of the makeover," Alberto declared loud enough that several stopped what they were doing and glanced their way. He stepped forward, undid her bun, and ran his hands through her hair. "Your color... Are you a natural blonde?"

"I am." Mother had harassed her for years to dye her hair because it reminded her too much of Lux's father. Lux had never caved.

"Fabulous!" Alberto boomed. "I won't touch that. But the rest is screaming for a refresh."

Rude. Lux gave Isabella a beseeching look. "Where is Scott? Shouldn't he have some say in what you all do to me?"

Alberto harrumphed. "He has no interest in how the sausage is made. He's only interested in the finished product."

"Oh." Of course. Typical male.

"Darling, you are in excellent hands." Isabella handed Lux a mimosa. "I'd dare say, if Scott were here, he'd do nothing but get in the way with his low-cut cleavage ideas."

Lux took a sip of the drink, eyeballing Isabella as she did so. "On that, we agree."

For the next hour, Alberto washed, cut, and styled Lux's hair. Upon completion, he'd declared it his best work ever. She could neither confirm nor deny his boast, because she'd not been allowed to watch as he worked.

According to Alberto, she would not be permitted to see any of the results until her transformation was complete. On the bright side, he liked to chat as he worked. She'd learned from him that the room they were in was normally alive with top advertising models, persuasive photographers, and eccentric editors, but today, it had been set aside for the sole purpose of her transformation. He'd ended his chat with the words, "All in the name of helping their ever-so-popular relationship guru maintain his crown...so to speak." The way he said it made her wonder if there was bad blood between the two.

After meeting with Alberto, she was directed to a makeup station to wait for Ziggy, who had been whisked away earlier to handle a model crisis. In the interim, Lux observed Isabella's crew commanding the room. Arranged behind four laden tables, the assistants had everything laid out; fabrics cascaded over one, while another bristled with scissors, patterns, and pins. The steady hum of a sewing machine came from the third, and the last table was equipped with an iron and steamer.

Behind the tables, rows of garments dangled from rolling racks, all being tailored to accommodate Lux's fuller figure.

The atmosphere in the room magnified the clamoring shenanigans of Lux's brain. The biggest development of all being the excitement brimming inside of her. For her life, she couldn't figure out why that was. Intellectually, she wanted nothing to do with any of it, but somewhere deep within—it appeared—lived a girl longing for at least one rendezvous with the trappings of beauty.

The realization had had her stomach in a knot of conflict all morning.

I'm not doing this for a man. I'm doing this to prove it won't be enough. Sure, she would garner attention from men, but catching the eye of a player and winning his heart were two different things.

"Remember to breathe," Isabella said as she stopped by and held a couple of color swatches up to Lux's face, then scurried off toward the line of sewing machines.

"I've returned!" Ziggy's enthusiastic voice pierced the bustling atmosphere as he came to a stop in front of her. "Darling, you're a blank canvas begging for a masterpiece!" After picking up what appeared to be a painter's palette, he grabbed a fluffy brush with a pink handle out of an overflowing vase and then tilted his chin as he studied her face.

"I truly would prefer if you kept the transformation subtle," she said.

"Nonsense. Ziggy doesn't do subtle." As he spoke, his hands danced around her with a conductor's finesse, as if eager to begin. "Ziggy unleashes the goddess within!"

Luxury's stomach clenched, not just in anticipation, but also in resistance. This entire endeavor, while promising a newfound allure, sharply contradicted her belief that a man should fall for her genuine self, not an embellished version created by makeup and designer attire. Then again, it's not like she had a lot of choice in the matter. Necessity had brought her here, and like it or not, she would momentarily embrace a world she had always disdained and handle the fallout when it was over.

"As long as Ziggy recalls I'm more of a minimalist goddess," Lux said.

"Minimalist, maximalist, it's all about the essence, honey!" Ziggy replied, leading her to a chair in front of a mirror surrounded by lights. "Trust me, you're going to love this."

As Ziggy started working his magic, dabbing and brushing with the expertise of an artist, Luxury found herself relaxing. Each stroke of the brush was surprisingly soothing, a gentle nudge toward a world she had always viewed from a distance.

"Beauty isn't about hiding," Ziggy said after a bit. "It's about highlighting who you already are. And honey, you are fabulous!"

Luxury blushed. "That's sweet of you to say, but I know I'm not beautiful."

"Whoever told you that should be expelled from your life forever!" He wagged a finger as he spoke. "They obviously do not have your best interest at heart."

"On my thirteenth birthday, Mother said I should focus on personality since I inherited my looks from my father," Luxury explained.

Ziggy gasped. "Rude!"

This is not spill-your-guts story hour. "She became bitter after he left her for a younger woman," Luxury added, her voice softening with understanding. "Seeing me reminds her of him and the pain he caused. Studying for my doctorate in psychology, I came to understand how deep-seated hurt can lead someone to say cruel things, even to their own daughter. It's a way of coping, however misguided." The words flowed out of her as if he were the psychologist and she the patient. Did he have that effect on everyone?

Ziggy paused for a moment, his brush in mid-air. "It's a shame your mother's pain blinded her to your beauty." He spoke in a calm tone, not the exclamation-point one she'd grown accustomed to. For a moment, he continued working in silence. "Pucker your lips."

She did, and he swiped lipstick on them.

"There." He stepped back and eyed her. "Your cheekbones and eyes are your best features."

"But only if I emphasize them with makeup?" she asked.

Ziggy leaned in slightly, a mischievous grin playing on his purple lips. "Darling, makeup doesn't create beauty—it celebrates it."

"Oh." She'd never thought about it in that light.

"Your features are already there, stunning and real. Makeup is just the spotlight that helps others to see what's been there all along."

She hesitated. "But I want them to notice me without the makeup so that I know they've fallen for me, not my looks."

Ziggy paused. "Sweetheart, someone falling for you will always be about more than makeup or looks! It's about the sparkle in your eyes, the passion in your words, and the essence of who you are. Makeup or not, you are simply enhancing the beauty that's inherently yours."

If that was true, why had Father left Mother for someone younger and prettier? Intellectually, she knew the answer.

Father's actions were more about his choices and less about Mother's beauty or lack thereof. People leave for complex reasons, often reflecting their own issues or desires. It's rarely as simple as just chasing after a young, more beautiful face. True connections are built on deeper grounds than just physical appearance.

She'd spoken these words often during her private sessions, but her heart refused to buy in to the intellect.

"Isabella, she's all yours," Ziggy said loudly, abruptly ending therapy time without the customary five-minute warning, leaving Lux slightly discombobulated.

Isabella grabbed two dresses off a rack and rushed over to them. "Which do you like best?"

The gowns were exquisite. One blue. One black. "Are they both your designs?" Lux asked. "They're so lovely."

Isabella nodded. "I've been working on a line for my own show. You are going to showcase them for me instead. The publicity will be fabulous. Pick one and try it on."

Luxury chose the sleek midnight blue dress. Slipping into it, she felt how the fabric hugged her curves in all the right places. She longed for a mirror.

Scratch that. She didn't want a mirror. Seeing herself in a mirror, looking more fabulous than ever—Lux imagined it would be like the first hit of heroin. Lux did not want to become a beauty junkie, like Mother. A woman always in search of the next thing to camouflage reality.

Hell, if just wearing this dress made Lux feel bolder, she could only imagine the effect seeing herself in a mirror would have on her psyche.

Then again, she was a grown-ass woman with a sensible head on her shoulders. For the next seven days, she could allow herself to shine without worry of getting sucked into a lifestyle she wasn't interested in pursuing long term. Everything that was happening to her today was the means to an end. An end that would allow her to go back to her life as a college professor. With that thought firmly in place, she stepped out from behind the curtain.

"You are my new most favorite model ever," Isabella said, her voice filled with triumph. "I have never seen anything I've designed look more fabulous on a body than that dress does on yours."

Luxury blushed.

"With the way it hugs your curves and your expression, like you're in a suit of armor, I'm near tears. Scott won't know what hit him when he sees you tonight."

With every word Isabella gushed, Lux grew more confident in her mission. She could allow a rake to school her in the finer points of flirting. She was more than up for the challenge. She took a deep breath. "Thank you."

Others walked over to admire the new Luxury Stone, and one of them started a slow clap which grew into an enthusiastic round of applause.

"Thanks to all of you," she said when the clapping died. "I know I'm the enemy here in camp *Naked Runway*, and you're all rooting for Scott. Even so, I appreciate your taking the time out of your day to give me a makeover."

"All we ask in return," Ziggy said, "is that you promise to tell us if, and when, he comes to you with his ravaged penis asking for a fix!"

This caused a lot of laughter, laughter that released the nerves she'd been holding in her neck all day.

She was about to thank them again when the studio door opened. "Frankie has sent me to teach you how to walk in stilettos," announced an attractive woman. She held out a pair of killer nude heels.

Luxury glanced down at the sensible shoes she'd chosen from the ones Isabella had offered to go with the dress. "I'd much prefer—"

"It is my understanding your preference is of no matter," the woman said. "Put those on. Time is wasting."

Luxury did as she was told and immediately wobbled.

The woman handed her a skinny stick. "This is for balance until you've mastered the art of the runway walk."

"The what?" Luxury asked.

"Darling, do you not watch fashion week? One does not simply walk in stilettos. They glide. Watch me. You step, heel first, then toe, and then your back foot slides up, toe first, to take a step directly in front of the front foot."

"What?" Luxury asked, trying to visualize.

"Allow me to show you." The woman did a sexy walk, hips swaying rhythmically with each step.

"It looks harder than it is," Isabella whispered to Lux. "Just remember, heel, toe, heel toe."

Luxury took a breath and, at the age of thirty-one, prepared to learn to walk again.

Rake*ish*

CHAPTER 7

Two hours after meeting Doc in person—while unfortunately under Frankie's evil eye—Scott found himself once again summoned by a woman. This one just as terrifying but in a mysterious do-gooder way.

Ms. Birdie Faraway had sent an invitation via messenger for him to join her for afternoon tea. He hated tea but would never dream of saying no to, among other things, the corporate owner of *Naked Runway*, which was her least impressive title as far as he was concerned. He much more liked thinking of her as the President of the Fairy Godmother Project. It had *badass* written all over it...sort of like Doc when she was hiding behind her microphone and standing on her soapbox berating his column.

He couldn't help but wonder which was the real Doc. The dynamic, opinionated woman, or the woman who downplayed everything about her appearance as if she wanted to be invisible.

Arriving at his destination, he stopped and squared his shoulders before pushing open the doors of an establishment called Whispers of Java. He was five minutes late, something Ms. Birdie would frown upon.

As he stepped inside, the cozy, welcoming ambiance of the coffee shop engulfed him, and some of his stress from the day dissolved. With its warm, sun-kissed yellow walls—adorned with an eclectic mix of local artwork and vintage coffee advertisements—it would be the perfect place to slip away and get some work done. In no small part because it reminded him of his favorite coffee shop in Shiretopia. The place he, his best friend, and the woman Scott had been arranged to marry had first concocted the plan that had led to Scott leaving his country.

"Ah, there you are, my dear boy." Ms. Birdie beckoned from a corner booth.

He waved as he approached and leaned down to kiss her cheeks before sliding into the booth. "My apologies for being late, but Father called and insisted we talk."

She raised a brow in response and pushed a drink toward him. She was the only person in Manhattan who knew of the dilemma that faced him should he return to Shiretopia. "I took the liberty of ordering you today's special, the Spring Blossom Latte."

Scott eyeballed the drink, which was adorned with a single white flower petal. "Is it safe?" he teased. "Or did you have arsenic added to it when I failed to arrive in a timely matter?"

"Of course it's safe. I always wait for an explanation before deciding to poison young men," Ms. Birdie said with a touch of a smirk. "A call from your father is something you should never put off."

"My thoughts exactly." Scott wrapped his hands around the cup and glanced around. The space was a maze of mismatched tables and chairs, some plush loungers, and even a couple of loveseats that looked like they'd been plucked straight out of any one of the many quaint living rooms in Shiretopia. "Have you been here before?"

"This is my first time," Ms. Birdie said. "One of my former clients just opened it. Isn't it just the loveliest shop?"

"I would like to meet her interior designer. My place could use some touches of...warmth." He'd been about to say *home*, but to allow Ms. Birdie to know he was homesick didn't feel wise unless he wanted to become her next project.

She eyed him as if reading his mind. "Now that the pleasantries are out of the way, shall we get down to business?"

He pulled at his tie. What exactly was her agenda? Did he even want to know? "Does this meeting have anything to do with the Fairy Godmother Project?" The secret, nonprofit organization made things happen with money, influence, and connections instead of magic.

"You're such a bright young man."

He waited for her to expand. She didn't. Which she wouldn't, because confidentiality was a huge thing with her. "And am I right to assume you have another 'life-changing opportunity offer' for me?" That's how she'd framed her request the first time she'd asked him to assist in one of her projects.

Ms. Birdie's eyes twinkled with secrets and promises. "Oh, this is better than life-changing, darling. This is matchmaking magic."

He raised a brow. "Ah, so you've upgraded from fairy godmother to witchcraft."

"Nonsense," she declared. "My fairy godmother bag has all the tools I need. The witches of this world can keep their spells and curses."

He winced, recalling he was now under not one but two curses. The family curse and Luxury's prediction his penis would soon fall off. Not that he was concerned about the latter. It wasn't an actual curse.

Ms. Birdie reached across the table and patted his hand. "Stop fretting about stuff you can't control. Life has a way of working these things out."

The first time he'd assisted Ms. Birdie with a project, she'd asked him about his family curse. She'd been quite inquisitive, rattling on about a delightful woman she'd recently met—Molly Thorn—and how Molly could quite possibly assist in bringing the curse to an end if only she knew the name of the wicked witch who'd set the whole thing into motion.

When he'd queried Ms. Birdie on why she thought some random woman could help, she'd replied that it was on a need-to-know basis. And though it was his family curse, he didn't need to know. After careful consideration, he'd given Ms. Birdie the name of the witch, and then promptly forgotten about the conversation until now.

"Are you ready to hear why you're here?" Ms. Birdie asked.

"Yes, ma'am."

"Actually, I have two requests. The first concerns a damsel in distress..."

"Who needs rescuing?" he asked when she didn't finish the sentence.

"Oh, goodness no. What she needs is a little assistance in rescuing herself."

"I see." He trusted Ms. Birdie. If she said there was a woman in need, there was a woman in dire need. To get on Ms. Birdie's radar, things had to have gone terribly wrong in your life. "Happy to come to her aid." The moment the words left his lips, an uncomfortable thought struck him. "As long as her name isn't Luxury Stone." That was one damsel he could not help.

Ms. Birdie wiped the corners of her mouth with a cloth napkin. "I'm afraid that is exactly who it is."

"Then you've been duped," he said. "If ever there was a woman who didn't need a fairy godmother, it's her. She's quite capable of handling life on her own."

"Nonsense. If ever there was a lady in need of a sprinkling of fairy godmother hope, it's her. She may be strong and independent on the outside, but on the inside, she's fractured."

The only thing fractured about Doc was her ability to put together a decent wardrobe, and Ms. Birdie did not need his help in that arena. Besides, Frankie was taking care of that issue even as they spoke. He'd tried to drop in on Doc's makeover but had been turned away and told that under no circumstances would he see her before tonight's meetup. "I have a lot of phrases for Doc but fractured isn't on the list."

Ms. Birdie pursed her lips. "How can you say that with a straight face? That lovely girl is now the butt of hurtful internet memes thanks to you."

"Me?" he interjected. "She started it with her insufferable opinions about my column."

"But were they insufferable?" Ms. Birdie asked.

"Before you go any further," Scott replied, choosing not to argue the point, "you should know Frankie has pitted Doc and me against one another in a winner-take-all scenario."

"Oh, dear."

"Unless you have the power to veto the game afoot, it is not possible for me to be Doc's wingman in wisdom."

Ms. Birdie chuckled. "Very clever. I like that term. Do you mind if I share it with the rest of the staff of the Fairy Godmother Project?"

"Be my guest." He'd love to know how many were actually involved in the organization.

"Thank you," Ms. Birdie said. "Now, back to the matter at hand. I'm afraid—whatever this nonsense is with Frankie that you're talking about—it is my fault."

Scott stilled. "How is this your fault?"

Ms. Birdie went into a quick explanation of how she was currently serving on a hiring committee at Columbia University, and that was how she'd learned of Luxury Stone and the lawsuit. Then Ms. Birdie went on to explain how she'd pressed Luxury to go to Frankie and try to fix things. And how she'd warned Luxury not to apologize but instead offer an intriguing solution that included her proving herself correct.

"But I thought you believed in my relationship advice," he said when she had finished.

"I do. But I had a plan. One that will no longer work. It never dawned on me Frankie would set up a Hunger Games scenario where one of your careers survives, and the other doesn't."

"If that never occurred to you, you don't know Frankie Peterson very well. She's vicious. Can you get her to change her mind?"

Ms. Birdie frowned. "Part of her contract when she was hired at *Naked Runway* included a snippet in which I agreed not to interfere with her decisions during her first year on the job."

He sighed. "That's really too bad."

"There was a plus side to making that agreement. You see, when she made that demand, it opened the door for me to require certain concessions that worked in my favor."

"You're nothing if not shrewd."

Ms. Birdie waved off the compliment with the flick of a hand. "Tell me everything that was said in your meeting. Any little detail could assist me in fixing what I've unwittingly broken."

Scott took a sip of his beverage and then dove into the details of Frankie's plan.

When he had finished, Ms. Birdie smiled. "I can work with that."

"How so?" He and Doc were as incompatible as a mime and a karaoke machine. "Given my curse, there's no way I'll fall in love with her in that timeframe. And I can't imagine her capturing the heart of another rake that quickly, either." He exhaled a heavy sigh, the weight of the situation settling like a stone.

"Darling, I am not at all worried about the outcome for you. I believe in your techniques. Granted, they are sexist, and that is what gets under Luxury's nerves, but nevertheless, they work on rakes. She just needs to find one that falls in love with her at first sight. Which, I believe, is how most men like you lose their heart."

He ignored the *men like him* comment. "The chances of her meeting the one rake who is going to fall for her instantly are preposterously low. Let's face it, I'm playing on the losing team."

"Granted, the turnaround time we have is a wrinkle, but I'm quite good with an iron."

He rubbed the back of his neck. The conversation was giving him whiplash. "Then you are rooting for me and not Luxury?" That made no sense. "A moment ago, you hit me up to be her wingman."

"I am rooting for you, and you will be her wingman...in the sense that you will equip her with the necessary tools to win the heart of any man. Which is exactly what Frankie has asked of you."

"Not just any man. He must be gossip-worthy with a tendency toward scandalous behavior. And I'm still not following your logic."

"The confidence that will come from having a man like yourself declare his love to her will help soften the fall for Luxury when she loses her career no matter the outcome of your challenge."

"No matter? I'm still not following."

"After viewing all the social media buzz, her reputation is in tatters. As a result, I fear the hiring committee will be directed to cut our losses and go with our second choice for the position. And, as much as I'd like to fight them on Luxury's behalf, I'm not sure they would be wrong to do so."

He sighed.

"This is why I've decided to be an invisible fairy godmother to Luxury to ensure she has a soft landing, and your visible fairy godmother to ensure you win the challenge."

"That sounds like a fairy godmother conflict of interest."

"Not at all. With my help, you will still have your career when the challenge ends, and she will have love, with the side bonus of my helping her to find a new career. Win-win."

"Why are you going to so much trouble? There have to be other candidates waiting for a fairy godmother who are more deserving than either myself or Doc."

"The two of you may have made the initial mess that started this whole quandary, but I'm afraid my meddling exploded the mess. Thus, it's my sworn duty as a fairy godmother to clean it up."

Before leaving to meet Ms. Birdie, he'd checked his socials. He'd been tagged in two new memes. One was an image of Lux with the words written underneath: 'Just say no to ugly.' The other meme was a shirt-torn image of him and a group of women who were reaching for him like he was some damn rockstar they just wanted to touch. It had been an advertising stunt for *Naked Runway*. For *RAKEish*. Under it had been the words: 'Just say no to rakes.' The first had caused him to grimace, the latter to chuckle.

"You mentioned you had two favors to ask of me? What is the other?"

Ms. Birdie's eyes danced with a hint of mischief. "Darling, you'll be delighted to know, I saved the best for last."

He raised an eyebrow, skepticism running rampant within. "Considering the first favor was to help Lux, I'm certain the second will be better."

Her smile widened, exuding an enigmatic confidence. "Not just better. This one's a true game changer."

"Dare I ask?" he said, intrigued.

CHAPTER 8

TUESDAY EVENING, THE NEW and cosmetically improved Luxury Stone sat nursing a glass of water at the bustling bar inside newly opened Manhattan Mingles while waiting on Scott. He was supposed to have met her outside the doors but had sent a text saying he was running late. While she would have preferred to have entered the bar together, her damn shoes were not made for standing around, so she'd sucked it up and walked in alone.

Stilettos were sitting shoes if ever God had made sitting shoes.

She'd give Scott five more minutes. If he couldn't bother to show by then, she would ditch this joint, go home, shower, and do a reset back to Monday's Lux, Frankie be damned.

The magazine's editor-in-chief had stopped by to see Lux's transformation. After several seconds of eyeballing Lux, Frankie had shrugged and told the Glam Team—anxiously awaiting her accolades—'it will do.'

Then Frankie had told Lux where to meet Scott for their first official 'fix-the-queen-of-dud-dating' dates. This followed by an evil-eye reminder to Lux that *Naked Runway* had spies everywhere. If either Lux or Scott showed any sign of not giving their everything to the challenge, Frankie would declare them both losers.

Lux glanced at her watch. His five minutes were up. She stood and turned toward the exit. That's when she spotted the back of Scott's dark head. "It's about freaking time." She stayed in place and waited for him to spy her in the crowd.

Only he put zero effort into finding her. He was too busy talking and posing for pictures with women. When he took a black marker from a brunette and signed her flat stomach, Lux had had enough. Taking a breath of bravery, she exhaled and carefully heel-toed her way toward him, her new heels clicking against the polished floor of the upscale Manhattan bar.

The lesson in stiletto-walking had been an interesting one that had lasted two hours. In the end, she'd mastered the proper foot strike and had learned the art of placing each step in a straight line instead of allowing them to fall on two different pathways.

The extra hip movement...not so much.

The big reveal of the new her had come after Lux had successfully walked an imagined red carpet where at the end had been placed a shrouded, full-length mirror. Ziggy had stripped away the cover in a dramatic fashion and when Lux saw the new her, she'd cried.

Which had resulted in Isabella crying and Ziggy fussing at Lux not to ruin her makeup.

Mother had been wrong when she'd told Lux to work on her personality because she didn't have the face to keep a man long term. The face that had stared back at Lux in the mirror had been transformed from ordinary to extraordinary. It was truly amazing what could be accomplished with makeup.

Ziggy had played to the strength of her emerald-green eyes, intensifying their hue with carefully chosen shadows and liners. As he'd explained while he worked, the colors he selected were not just complementary, but were chosen from the palette of her irises, which deepened the green to a richness he called mesmerizing. He'd then framed her eyes with a hint of gold highlight at the corners, which he declared made the green stand out even more against her fair skin, like dew-kissed leaves against the morning light. From there, he'd meticulously brought definition to her cheekbones, creating an interplay of light and shadow that seemed to elevate her entire visage. On her lips, Ziggy had opted for a shade that was a whisper above her natural lip color, a soft, muted hue that enhanced without competing with the dramatic flair of her eyes. It was as if he'd chosen the barest hint of pink found on the inside of a seashell. The application was masterful—a matte finish that spoke of elegance and subtlety, giving her lips a fuller look that was inviting and touchable. This balance of bold and understated was a silent testament to the internal tug-of-war she faced—admiring the artistry, yet questioning the change.

While Mother's advice had been wrong on so many levels, Lux would still hold out for a man who fell in love with her intellect, her wit, her sheer tenacity any day over one who'd fallen for the enhanced curve of her smile or the sway of her hips.

Even so, Lux would be lying to herself if she didn't admit she loved the way it felt knowing she looked as good as any of those ladies draping themselves all over Scott. How would he react to the new Lux? Would he suddenly find her worthy of his interest, or would he have the same underwhelmed reaction as Frankie?

Almost upon him, Lux glanced down and was immediately distracted by what was surely too much braless cleavage. According to Isabella, bras had now been replaced by a new product on the market called CAKES. Grippy, nonstick nipple covers which were way more comfortable than a bra. Nonetheless, Lux didn't want Scott to think she was trying too hard.

Hell, she didn't want him to think she was trying at all.

Deep in thought about what she would do if one of her anti-nip-pleage thingamajigs decided to ungrip itself from a boob and fall to the floor, she plowed into a warm body that smelled like thunderclouds. Forgetting about her nipples, she searched for a solid surface to grasp for balance. Unfortunately, the movement resulted in the content of her glass going airborne—

Which resulted in an audible chorus of gasps ringing out around her. Then graveyards-on-a-Monday-night silence descended around them. It was either that or the blood roaring in her ears kept her from picking up on things like voices.

After a moment of mind-numbing shock, reality returned. She'd just spilled water on...she glanced up to see who. *Hell's fudging bells. It was him.*

Scott growled, grabbed her wrist, and yanked her into his body like a damn caveman, resulting in a shiver of trepidation sweeping through her. But one whiff of his cologne and the fear was replaced by her heartbeat going all swoony wonky.

Swoony! Wonky! Like a Victorian heroine on the verge of a fainting spell. All because a nice smelling thundercloud held her. How pathetic was that?

"It's been a while since a beautiful woman threw a drink on me," he said in a voice soft and teasing.

She stiffened. He had no idea who he held in his arms. If he did, no way would he have used that flirty tone. "I most certainly did not throw it," she said against his chest before pushing out of his arms enough to look up into his eyes. That's when he comically began the process of realizing the woman in his arms was the same woman who'd turned his smooth existence into one filled with potholes.

"Doc?" he murmured.

"Surprise," she said.

One second, his expression was a mix of tempered irritation; the next, his features were sliding all over the place as he shifted from one emotion to another.

His eyes, initially narrowed in annoyance, were now wide in sheer disbelief. It was as if his brain was frantically trying to reconcile the woman standing before him—this glamorous, composed figure—with the mental image he had of his known adversary.

About to make another snarky quip, she witnessed a flicker of something else—a brief, involuntary spark of admiration or even attraction. Of course, he suppressed it almost immediately. But she'd seen it—that split second where his defenses dropped and his true reaction slipped through.

His mouth, which had been set in a thin line, parted slightly, as if he were about to speak, only to find himself at a loss for words. The normally poised and confident man appeared momentarily disarmed, thrown off balance by her transformation.

Watching his composed demeanor unravel, even if just for a moment, gave her an unexpected surge of satisfaction. In that instant, she knew that no matter what had transpired between them before, tonight she had the upper hand.

"Doc," he said roughly.

"Rake," she said snippily—that was once she remembered to reply at all; the wonky swoony feelings were back. She tried to step away but his hold on her arms kept her from going far.

The cone of silence in the bar evaporated, and voices filled the void as she and Scott locked gazes in an apparent staring contest.

"Is that Dr. Stone?"

"Fuck yes. Wow."

"Oh, my God, I can't believe she did that."

"I can. Dr. Stone is a badass, and he deserves far worse."

"How do you figure?"

The conversations went on around them as Lux and Scott continued to lock gazes.

"Because of her, his penis is on borrowed time."

The last shattered Lux's trance. Would now be a bad time to inquire if all was still well...down there? Not because she wanted to personally know, but to put his fans at ease.

"Serves him right," someone said. "I heard he's the one who started the meme of her with the words 'Nothing to see here.'"

A tiny noise escaped Lux's lips. God, people were cruel on the internet.

Scott's nostrils flared, but he didn't deny it.

"Why would you do that?" someone said.

Tears filled Lux's eyes, and she rammed her tongue to the roof of her mouth to keep them at bay.

Horror flashed across his face. "I wouldn't. I didn't."

"Wouldn't you?" she pushed.

"Of course not."

She stared stonily at him.

He sighed. "Did you see the one about me standing in a hospital, wearing a hospital gown?" he asked her in a voice loud enough for all to hear.

"I saw that one," someone responded when she didn't.

"You'll have to be more specific," she finally said.

Scott didn't break eye contact with Lux. "The one where I was holding a jar that had my penis inside and telling the nurse it was my brain?"

Laughter ensued.

"The ones about you are all in fun," Lux said, keeping her voice low, swallowing back tears. "No one believes my superstitious prediction. The ones about me, though, are horrid. Everyone thinks I'm frigid because of that damn app and my big mouth."

He leaned in closer. "No one looking at you right now, Doc, will mistake you for a woman who is frigid." His eyes held hers, soft and earnest, as if he could chase away any doubts with his gaze alone.

The compliment brought on a fresh desire to cry, and she twitched her nose to ward off the tears.

He stepped back, released her, and gave her the most devilish smile a man had ever bestowed upon her. "What a delightful turn of events," he said as if they'd not just had a public conversation about memes.

"Delightful in what way?" She snuck a peek at the crowd and quickly surmised why he'd flipped switches. Phones were aimed at them. They were being recorded. Which of them worked for Frankie?

"I'm glad we bumped into each other," Scott said magnanimously. "I have an idea I wanted to run past you."

A gawker handed him a napkin, and he used it to wipe at his shirt.

"And that is?" she asked him.

"Listen up, everyone." He paused and winked at her before continuing. "As you are all aware, Doc here has made it a practice to question my viability as a relationship columnist."

"And with just cause," Lux said.

"Seeing Doc in the flesh—when she has obviously already taken a piece of my advice and had an extreme makeover—has given me a wonderful idea. Doc, I propose you go on a series of dates with me—dates in which you will choose a piece of advice that I've given in my column over the last nine months, and you will practice it on me. At which time, I will evaluate your delivery of the advice and advise you on how to improve."

At no time had she agreed to have her game critiqued. "I—"

"If—at the end of those dates—you're not able to go forth and slay the dating game by capturing the attention of a rake of your choice—something, according to you, you have not been able to do on your own—I will cease to write my column. Which, coincidentally, will result in my visa becoming invalid, and my return to my country imminent."

This set off a cacophony of conversation.

Was that last bit true? Or had he made it up for the sympathy vote? Knowing him, it was false. But the rumor was out there, and truth very seldom caught up to gossip. Now, if she won and proved his advice was shit, the whole of Manhattan would see her as a villain for sending their favorite prince back to Shiretopia.

"And if I set my sights on you?" she heard herself ask, wanting to say something, anything, to throw him off his high horse.

His jaw tightened. "That would be ill-advised considering, according to you, I will soon be tragically deprived of my glorious penis, to the eternal regret of ladies worldwide."

Her lips twitched. Well played. Someone had taught him to laugh at himself. Perhaps she should fill him in on the analysis she'd done of her nightmare. Then again, where was the fun in that? "What I'm hearing you say is you only enjoy sex if you get to come."

"Not at all." He looked her up and down. His expression not quite discernible. "But, in order for my techniques to work, there must be chemistry between two people. Are you implying you feel a spark, Doc?"

Gah. She'd walked right into this mess. Literally. "As long as you don't suck at kissing—considering other spark-like things that go on between a couple might soon be off the table for you—I don't see there being a problem on my side. And you?"

"Doc, has anyone ever told you it's dangerous to...*poke* a prince?" His voice rumbled out in a sexy European accent that did something to her knees.

"How dangerous?" She'd meant for that to have been an internal question.

He tugged her into his arms, tilted her chin up, and crashed his lips against hers in a bold, unapologetic kiss that sent a shockwave of heat through her entire body.

Once again, the patrons who were crowded around them faded into a hazy backdrop, the cacophony of voices and clinking glasses and recording devices melting into nothingness as his mouth moved over hers with a surprising tenderness that belied the force of his approach.

At first, she was too stunned to react, but then, instinct took over. Well, not instinct. Instinct said to knee him. Lust was what took over.

She kissed him back, her hands finding their way to his hair, tangling in the short strands as the kiss deepened. The world spun ever so slightly, and she became acutely aware of the heat of his body and the strength in the arms that held her close.

And what a kiss it was. A conundrum of sorts. Part challenge. Part surrender. Like their lips were receiving mixed messages from their brains on rather they should fight or dance.

Vaguely she realized her plans to take him down a notch or two had just taken an unexpected tumble as the startling chemistry zipped through her.

As Lux broke apart from Scott, breathless and with a newfound awareness of the Rake of Manhattan, the noise of the bar rushed back in. Searching his face for signs he'd felt it too, Lux saw a flicker of something like victory.

Crud. While she'd like to be upset at his arrogance, he wasn't wrong to look smug. She'd underestimated the power of physical chemistry on the heart. If she didn't proceed with extreme caution, it would be her heart at stake. Not his.

She swallowed her nerves, gathered her poise, and spoke. "All I have to do is go on a series of dates, try your asinine flirting tips on a man of my choosing—one who can hopefully kiss better than that"—definitely not on him—"and, if they fail, then you'll leave the country, and I'll never have to see you again? And you won't whine about it on social media when that happens?"

His cocky smile faltered a degree. "I won't whine about it. But if you find my tips get you the rake of your choosing, you must agree to admit as much on *Naked Runway's* podcast, as well as to your own audience, and allow me permission to document our experiment in my upcoming columns."

She yanked at the hems of her sleeves, still feeling the ghost of his lips on hers, and stood up straight as the boring arrow she remained despite her makeover. "Your Royal Rakeness, there's just one thing left to say."

"And that is?"

"Get ready to go down," she said, because even a boring arrow had a sharp tip.

Laughter ensued.

Lux glanced around. Why were they laughing at her? Even Scott. "What is so funny?"

Her question caused even more guffawing.

Scott took her by the elbow and led her away from the crowd. Once they were snugly tucked in a nook in the back of the bar, he said, "They're laughing because you invited me to go down on you."

Lux replayed her words. *Hell's fudging bells.* He was right.

If her dumping her drink on him hadn't already been viral worthy, her unintended double entendre certainly sealed the deal.

Frankie would be pleased as spiked punch.

CHAPTER 9

SCOTT'S GAZE SHIFTED FROM the crowd—now dissipated and going back to their business—to Doc, her blunder about 'going down' echoing in his mind. He couldn't help but worry what would unfold for her when she didn't succeed. While he had all the faith in the world in Ms. Birdie, even that darling busybody would have trouble helping Doc find employment at a university comparable to Columbia, given Doc's current reputation.

"What?" The profound disdain in Doc's deep green eyes as she stared back at him—eyes reminiscent of the finest emeralds, a stone as luxurious and captivating as her namesake suggested—made him wish for the freedom to reveal the truth about his exaggerated Manhattan reputation.

"What, what?" he asked, stalling while he continued to ruminate about the conundrum of a woman before him. Doc had more depth and facets than he'd originally given her credit for. This beauty was not a one-dimensional psychologist caricature. Not even a two-dimensional one. Hell, she might have more dimensions than all those in the establishment combined.

His gaze dropped to her mouth and lingered there, the memory of their first kiss still vivid in his mind. The way her lips had responded, both urgent and soft, left him craving another.

Doc shifted, a hint of pink coloring her cheeks. "Why are you staring? Do I have something on my face?" She reached up to touch her lips, now bare of their earlier glossy sheen.

"We can mark kissing lessons off the list of things I need to teach you to get the man of your dreams," he replied, deciding it was time to get on task.

"Kissing—check." Doc fidgeted slightly, the corners of her mouth twitching into an awkward smile. "I guess I'm not a complete disaster after all."

The vulnerability in her voice tugged at him. He wasn't used to being around women who weren't extremely confident in their sexual prowess. "Not a disaster," he agreed.

Her cheeks turned red, and the sight wrenched at something in his chest as well. Hell, if he wasn't careful, he would become completely mesmerized by the woman.

"What's next on Frankie's list of techniques for you to teach me? Or have I just graduated early from the Scott Landshire School of

Romance?" Her attempt at humor was a clear effort to mask her unease.

"It's not on the list, but we could add a lesson on inviting a man to go down on you." As he floated his outlandish suggestion, he watched Doc closely, not just for amusement but also to gauge her response. It was a test of sorts—he knew the dating world could be crude, and he wanted to see if she could handle herself against such bold advances. Or, at least, that's what he told himself.

Doc opened her mouth as if to retort, then seemed to think better of it, closing it again with an audible click.

"Did you want to say something?" he asked.

"Um." After a brief pause, she continued, her voice tinged with a mix of humor and nervousness. "I think I'll pass on that particular lesson. But thanks." Her fingers nervously toyed with the bracelet on her wrist. A clear sign she wasn't as blasé as she'd like him to believe. "Let's stick to the topics Frankie chose from your list of so many."

He chuckled. She must have gotten a good night's sleep last night, because she wasn't as easy to rattle as she had been on Monday. It was a small, yet significant, revelation about her character. She would be able to hold her own in their upcoming adventure.

A waitress stopped at the table. "What can I get for you two to drink tonight?"

"Whiskey on the rocks for me, please," he said, his voice carrying over the ambient noise of the bar.

The trendy-looking server turned to Doc, who paused for a moment before replying. "I'll just have water, thanks."

"Water?" Scott remarked, flashing a teasing smile at Doc. "We'll have to get you to be a bit more adventurous."

The server grinned, adding, "One whiskey on the rocks and one adventurous water, coming right up." Her eyes lingered on Doc for a moment, a genuine admiration in her gaze. "By the way, I absolutely love your new look, Dr. Stone. It's stunning. I'm on Team Doc all the way." With a supportive smile, she turned and disappeared into the crowd.

Scott studied Doc for a moment, fully taking in her transformation. "She's right, you know. The Glam Team have really outdone themselves. You look fabulous." He waited for a smile, some acknowledgment of the compliment, but her expression remained unreadable, puzzling him. Clearing his throat, he moved on. "My first assignment is to teach you pickup lines that work. They are key for landing the attention of a rake. And you can't steal his heart, until you steal his attention," he said. "Tell me, Doc, what is your go-to pickup line?"

Doc hesitated, her eyes darting around the room as if to make sure no one was listening. "Uh, how about, 'Are you a camera? Because every time I look at you, I smile?'"

"That's charming, but a smidge too wholesome for our target audience," he replied. "We need something with more of an edge to catch a rake's attention, don't you think?"

"Rakes aren't really a thing in Manhattan, are they?" she asked. "I mean, I get it. You're a rake because of the nickname your mom gave you, but Manhattan is not Shiretopia. We've evolved from the Victorian age of rakes and scoundrels and rogues," she continued. "If it's all the same to you, I'd prefer to set my sights on the heart of a college professor. Someone I can see myself falling in love with in return."

A college professor would be much easier to accomplish in the short amount of time they had. "I'm afraid that won't work. Frankie said rake, so rake it will be." Why was there a part of him glad to be able to give that answer? Was it because he didn't want her to find true love as a result of their time together?

She rolled her eyes. "What in the hell am I supposed to do with the heart of a rake?"

There was that disdain again, only this time in her voice, not her eyes. "I suggest you try loving him back," he said gruffly. "You might find he's a lot more appealing as a forever person than settling for the male equivalent of that glass of water you ordered."

"The very idea of entrusting my heart to a rake is repulsive." Her voice was sharp, each word an authentication to the depth of her aversion to men like him. "They're nothing but heartbreakers, trading in their partners for newer models without a second thought. "Just like my fa—."

Where was the romantic he'd assumed beat inside? "Just because a rake has enjoyed his freedom and broken a few hearts in the process, does not mean he's not lovable once he's admitted his feelings," Scott argued.

"Doesn't it?"

If he'd had any doubts before then, her scathing reply left no room for doubt about her position on the idea of falling for a rake. In her opinion, it would be the worst possible outcome to their adventure. And not just because it would mean she'd lost the challenge.

He collected his thoughts before responding. "Not every man who is labeled a rake is in it for the game, or because he can't settle on one woman. Some men are branded as rakes for reasons far more complex than a simple reluctance to choose."

"And which are you?" she asked.

As much as he'd love to set her straight, he couldn't. There was a nondisclosure agreement with his name signed to it back at *Naked Runway* that kept him from doing so. "Let's not get sidetracked," he drawled, forcing a smile to his lips. "Tonight, we're talking about pickup lines."

Her nostrils flared slightly. "Why can't I just say hello?"

"Hello is too plain, too vanilla. Rakes aren't intrigued by vanilla; they seek something more captivating. You need an arsenal of lines that are engaging, slightly daring, yet not off-putting," he explained.

"Sounds easy peasy," she replied, a touch of sarcasm in her voice.

He raised an eyebrow at the unfamiliar saying. "Not easy, but achievable with the right guidance," he said confidently. "Let's try another one. Do you have any more pickup lines?"

She shook her head, a wry smile on her lips. "I'm afraid I'm a one-hit wonder in that department. You might have to supply me with a few examples that have worked on you."

"Let's see." He smiled, recalling a memorable encounter. "There was one time when a stunning model from Russia approached me in a bar. She sat down and said, 'Let's be nothing tonight, because nothing lasts forever.'"

Doc's face contorted slightly in a grimace. "And that actually worked on you?"

He chuckled. "Context is everything, but yes, it did. I was more than willing to be her 'nothing' for the night."

"All right, I'll give it a try. What's another line I could use?"

He leaned back, a playful smile tugging his lips. "Then there was the time a striking redhead from Texas used this line on me when I sat next to her: 'Please, let's keep our distance. You look like the kind of guy I might make a bad decision for.'"

"And did she make that bad decision?"

He gave a nonchalant shrug. "I prefer to think of it as one she woke up feeling good about."

Doc let out a resigned sigh. "Fine. I'll give those two lines a try. But not on you," she quickly added, as if to set a clear boundary.

Why not him? "You can't use them on anyone else here, either. They've all seen us together. It might skew the results."

Doc looked as if she might argue but then shrugged. "It's been a long day, and I'm exhausted. I'll practice them tomorrow evening on some poor unsuspecting gentleman. Who knows, I might get lucky and land a rake right out of the starting block, and you and I can part ways."

The thought of Doc succeeding and leaving with another man twisted something unexpected inside of him, a feeling he couldn't quite name but couldn't ignore either. An emotion that lingered long past their evening goodbyes.

CHAPTER 10

The next evening, after another session in which the Glam Team transformed her looks, Lux met Scott outside of *Naked Runway*. Not that he'd noticed her yet—he was on the phone. Day three of their eight-day journey was already here. While she waited for him to finish, she covertly checked him out. Dressed in all black, he was by far the best-looking man she'd ever gone on a date with. Not that tonight was a date, but she had no idea what else to call it.

Laughter spilled out of him as he spoke animatedly. Not the sign of a man who'd quietly started panicking after he realized there was no way he would win their challenge. A conclusion she had assumed he would have come to after realizing last night that she was a water-drinking barfly with no game whatsoever.

He would have had a better shot at winning had he gone along with her idea of her landing a professor-like man instead of a rake. As it was, Scott was a sure loser.

A rake falling for Lux wouldn't happen. Made over or not, she just wasn't the type a bad boy fell in love with at first year let alone first sight. The pizzazziest thing about her was her freaking name, and God knew she'd never lived up to its potential.

Well, if not God, Mother knew.

Wearing shades and smiling as he listened to whomever was on the other end of his call, he didn't appear the least bit unnerved. Quite the opposite. The confidence oozing from his every pore practically shouted he knew something she didn't. Did Frankie have an ace in the hole for her star reporter? One that would guarantee his win? Like a patsy on the backburner ready to declare love to Lux should the need arise?

The thought caused anger to glob her throat like she'd swallowed an oversized jawbreaker. She tried to clear her throat, and the noise came out sounding like a creature about to attack.

Scott turned at the sound. "Whoa." His gaze did a slow intake of her...all of her. "I do like a woman in black leather pants and heels," he said when their gazes finally met again.

"Of course you do," she said in a weird voice. She cleared her throat again.

"Because you think I'm shallow?" he mused.

When she'd told Isabella that tonight's lesson would be on pickup lines, the perky blonde had insisted Luxury wear skintight leather pants. "Well, there's that, and according to Isabella, they are a nonverbal pickup line that work on all men...not just the bottom feeders."

"She's not wrong." Scott pulled at the collar of his turtleneck.

"Really?" Lux said, part incredulous, part not surprised. "They are as cliché as a stripper at a bachelor party."

His chuckle was all the rise she got out of him. "My intent was for us to walk to our destination, but I dare say your feet are not yet accustomed to those shoes. Shall I hail us a taxi? I gave my driver the evening off."

That was uncharacteristically aware for a rake. "I'll be fine. Besides, I need to practice my hip sways." She'd begged Isabella to provide alternative footwear for tonight's ensemble, but she'd informed Lux that no fashion icon would be caught pairing Givenchy leather pants and an Isabella P. Chance bodysuit with flats.

"Luckily, Velvet Vice isn't far from here," Scott said.

"I've never heard of the place." She fell into step next to him.

"It's an establishment Frankie chose. I've been there a couple of times. The clientele is interesting."

"How so?" With each step she took, she practiced pushing her hips out left and right.

"Think James Bond meets Dirty Harry."

"Techie, billionaire badasses meet thuggish, blue-collar badasses," Lux said sarcastically, and then stumbled when one of her hip punches landed against his body. "No stress there."

"You'll do fine." He held out the crook of his arm.

Lux reluctantly took it. Her mental energy would be better spent on running through her prepared pickup line. "Lay it out for me, Scott. What else is on the agenda prepared by Frankie?"

"She has me spending tonight and tomorrow night being your professor of seduction—"

"That's a fancy title," she teased, even as she recalled their kiss. Would there be more lessons in that arena?

"The final three nights will consist of you going on dates."

"With whom?"

"Hopefully men you've won over tonight and tomorrow night."

"And if there are none?"

"Then I will set you up with rakes I know."

That wasn't going to happen, but she'd fight that battle when the time came. "How will I pick up a man if you're with me on these dates for the next couple of nights?"

"I'll be there but not beside you. I'll situate myself to witness your attempts from afar so I can offer you feedback."

"Be honest, you can't really believe I'm going to capture a rake as a result of all this?"

"It could happen. I've been told rakes are known to fall into insta-love. One day they're playing the field, the next they are threatening to kick the ass of any man who looks sideways at their woman."

The term used to describe a certain romance trope caught her attention. "Do you believe in insta-love?" She glanced up at him, wanting to read his expression as she heard his response.

"We can feel other emotions instantly; I don't see why love should be excluded," he said with a genuine smile.

"Be still, my heart," she teased. "A rake who believes not just in love but the instant kind."

"My parents fell in love at first sight," he said, somewhat gruffly.

She stopped. "Then the curse has been broken? Why are you perpetuating the myth it hasn't been? Is it to get sympathy sex?"

"I misspoke. Father wasn't so much in love as enthralled. To this day, he swears it would have been love if it hadn't been for the damn curse. But Mum for sure fell the moment they met. And she said enthrallment from Father beat the hell out of love from any other man on the Earth."

His words gave Lux something to think about. Perhaps instead of searching for love, she should find herself a man who was easily enthralled by a slick makeover and cheesy pickup lines. "How long were they married?" She only knew the part of his history that he'd revealed in his magazine column...which wasn't a lot.

He began walking again. "They were married a little over thirteen years before her death."

"I'm sorry." She squeezed his arm. "Then Queen Mildred of Shire-topia is your stepmother?"

"Could we please move on to a more pleasant topic?" he said tensely.

"One more question."

"And that is?"

"I know you said we have no spark, but did you feel *any* instant emotion for me upon first impression?" She would use his answer in next Monday's show as a follow-up to her one on the importance of second glances. The show that had started this whole fiasco.

"Instant irritability," he said. "When I first listened to you bash me as a columnist."

"That's fair since I felt instant prickliness toward you when I read your January column. But how about when you first saw an image of me?" He was, after all, one of the many men who'd swiped past her profile in under one second.

"Honestly, the first time I saw your image, I was flipping through candidates on the same dating app you were on as part of a work project. You didn't fit the profile required for the column, so I rejected you."

Oh. He hadn't dismissed her as not right for him, but as not right for an assignment. Interesting. "I don't recall your doing a column on the dating app?"

"That's because Frankie vetoed the idea when I pitched it to her."

They stopped at a crosswalk and waited for the light to turn. "What makes Scott Landshire tick?" Perhaps if she better understood him, she'd be better able to know when he was lying.

"Word to the wise: men do not like a woman who psychoanalyzes them." His tone was light but with a hint of caution. "I would hazard to guess that's one of the reasons so many men zipped past your profile image. You were holding that damn cup that shouted, 'I'm analyzing your ass.'"

Fair enough. "Hazard of the trade," she said, lightly. "Tell me, are you still irritated by me?"

He looked down at her. "Like you, my irritation has turned to intrigue."

"What about me intrigues you?"

He gave her a devilish smile that did things to her stomach. "For starters, those pants you're wearing."

"Like, who designed them?" she asked. The light changed, and they moved with the other pedestrians.

"More like, what are you wearing beneath them?"

She frowned, recognizing his response for what it was...his need to reinforce his rake status. And as any good psychologist would do, she blocked the maneuver. Honesty was founded in vulnerability. "Since you've taken this conversation to a personal level, have you given any further consideration regarding my prediction about your…um, gentleman's equipment?" Now might be a good time to put his mind at rest and explain her analysis of the dream.

Scott surprised her by coming to a complete stop—causing rude comments from those who now had to go around them—and gave her a look. One not laced with horror but instead humor. "You mean my penis?" he said, causing a few startled pedestrians to look their way.

She grinned. There was that humor again. She really liked a guy with a sense of one. "I do."

Scott winked at her and continued to walk. "How does a woman as educated as you buy into the idea that repeating a nightmare before breakfast can make it come true? It's like believing in the Tooth Fairy, but less fun and more terrifying."

"The short answer is every proper romantic comedy heroine needs a flaw. That's mine."

"And the long answer?"

"I'm observant. Always have been, according to Mother. As such, I noticed patterns. For instance, any time Father left for an overnight trip, Mother would dress up and go out with friends. Or if they fought in the morning, Mother would buy a new expensive bauble and show it to Father as soon as he came home. Anyway, once I mentioned to Mother that I had a dream that one day Father was going to leave and never come home. The very next day, he did just that."

"You're a pattern seeker," Scott said. "I can respect that. But Doc, you do realize that correlation doesn't always mean causation, right?"

Lux glanced up at him. "Since when did you start using psychology terms? 'Correlation doesn't always mean causation'—that's straight out of my professional playbook."

A twinkle of mischief lit his brown eyes. "Ever since you tore into my first column on *RAKEish*, I've been tuning in to your show. A guy can't help but learn a thing or two from that...even if the subject matter can be, well, a bit dry at times," he finished.

Lux burst out laughing. "Dry? I'll have you know I strive for the perfect balance of informative and engaging."

"Oh, it's engaging, all right," Scott said. "Especially when I'm trying to figure out how not to become the subject of your next episode's cautionary tale."

Lux shook her head, a smile still playing on her lips. "Well, I'm both flattered and surprised. I didn't peg you as the type to indulge in psychological discussions, especially those that don't directly revolve around the art of being a rake."

Scott patted her hands, which were still utilizing his arm for balance. "Let's just say, you've opened my eyes to a whole new perspective. And who knows? Maybe one day I'll surprise you by not being such a rake after all."

Strangely, the thought of him doing just that pleased her. The only clear reason for her to care was the one that stood out plainly. "If you did that, you would have single-handedly proven my topic from this week's Monday's Musings—the importance of giving others second glances."

Scott suddenly slowed his pace and came to a stop. "We're here." He gestured toward a dimly lit establishment.

Lux's gaze followed his gesture, landing on a faded sign that read 'Velvet Vice.' Trepidation rippled through her and sweat formed on her nose. The outside had the whole *vice* vibe going on with its barred windows and security flanking either side of the door.

If Frankie had sent her here to practice her pickup line, Lux had no doubt it was a bar infamous for its clientele—a haven for the city's most charming and notorious bad boy bachelors. The kind of place where hearts were won and lost in a single evening.

The kind of place where someone like Luxury Stone would make a fool of herself.

Her earlier confidence wavered. Was she really going to go through with this?

Scott leaned in closer and wiped the sweat from her nose. "Remember, I'll be here the whole time. We'll communicate with texts." His voice was a soft but firm anchor in the night. "You're not alone in this."

Lux exhaled hard and mustered the same boldness that had carried her through the days following her first viral skirt-in-the-underwear faux pas. "Okay," she replied, her voice steady despite the butterflies in her stomach. "Let's do this."

"Walk in and head straight to the bar. Have a seat and order a drink. Not water."

"Why not water?"

"It's not flirty."

"Then what?"

"A glass of wine will do."

"Fine."

"Don't try to pick up any man until after I've entered and you know where I'm sitting. It will be somewhere within earshot."

"Why earshot?"

"In case you need help."

She blinked. "Why would I need help?"

"Because while we've talked about your picking up a man in a bar, we've not discussed your skill level at turning one down…especially an entitled one not used to the words 'not interested.'"

"Somehow, I don't think there will be any rakes kicking up a fuss over my not fancying one of them."

"Then you don't understand the power of leather pants on your body," he said.

She rolled her eyes and stepped toward the entrance of the establishment. As the door swung open, laughter and the clink of glasses spilled out. She stepped into a world where seduction and sincerity were likely as blurred as the drunken vision of the patrons.

Lux nodded at the bouncer who stood just inside the door. She glanced around to get her bearings as she showed the burly man her identification. The bar's atmosphere was an intoxicating blend of smooth jazz and subdued conversations. Even so, it did little to steady her jittery anticipation. Tonight was about practicing her pick-up lines—a simple task in theory but daunting.

As she carefully made her way to the bar, her attempt at a graceful entrance was slightly marred by an untimely stumble over someone's misplaced foot. She recovered with a quick, embarrassed smile, hoping the dim lighting hid her blush. Lux found an empty stool at the bar—and awkwardly clambered onto it, trying to look nonchalant and pretty sure she only partially succeeded.

Settling in, she took a deep breath and surveyed her surroundings, quickly realizing she was a novice among experts. Every man in the room oozed composed confidence. And the women wore sophistication like she wore sweats on the weekend.

When a man slid onto the seat next to her, Lux startled so hard, she all but fell off her bar stool. Luckily, his back was to her. Thankful to be so thoroughly ignored, Lux prepared herself for a silent, unnoticed evening.

But then, to her surprise, he turned and spoke to the mixologist behind the counter.

Lux's heart skipped a beat. This was her opportunity to step into the spotlight, to try out the pickup line she'd been practicing.

He was about to become the first test subject in Lux's stumbling journey into the art of seduction. One that was meant to land her the heart of a rake but surely wouldn't. The sooner that could be proven, the sooner she could get back to the life she preferred.

Gathering her courage, Lux cleared her throat to get his attention. "Hello." This was it—her moment to test one of the lines that Scott had suggested in a column back in March. One he swore worked, but she highly doubted it.

"Do you have a quarter I could borrow for the tampon machine in the ladies room?" she blurted a bit too loudly. The man looked taken aback, his smooth facade momentarily faltering.

That's when she realized what she'd said. She'd just blurted the line she'd used in a nightmare she'd had once. A nightmare that...now that she thought about it, she'd repeated to her best friend before breakfast a few years back.

"Excuse me?" He raised an eyebrow.

Lux pressed on, her cheeks burning. "Sorry. I meant to say, 'do you have a quarter I could borrow for the condom machine in the lady's room?'"

There was a brief, excruciating silence. Then, he burst into laughter, not the charmed chuckle Lux had hoped for, but a full-on guffaw that drew the attention of nearby patrons. "That's good! I mean, it's terrible, but it's good," he managed to say between fits of laughter.

Lux wanted to disappear into the floorboards. Her attempt at seduction had turned into a comedy sketch. She forced a laugh, trying to salvage some dignity.

The man, still chuckling, gave her a friendly pat on the knee. "I'm sorry, I didn't mean to laugh. It's just...that was unexpectedly hilarious. You're not really trying to pick me up, are you? Was this some type of dare? Did you lose a bet?"

Lux mustered a smile, acknowledging the absurdity of her attempt. "No dare. Just me trying for the first time to use a pickup line."

The man nodded, amusement still dancing in his eyes. "Keep at it. Maybe leave out the part about a tampon next time."

As he stood and walked away with his Old Fashioned, Lux let out a sigh of relief mixed with embarrassment. She was just reminding herself to wait for Scott to enter the establishment before trying this again, when she felt a tap on her shoulder.

Turning around, she came face-to-face with her nemesis, who had an unmistakable twinkle in his eyes. It dawned on her in that moment—he had been there the whole time, a silent observer to her catastrophe.

Scott's grin was both sympathetic and slightly teasing. "Well, that was...something," he said, trying to stifle his chuckle. "I must say, I've never heard that particular line used on a man."

"Did you hear...all of it?"

"Every painful word," Scott confirmed, his tone light but encouraging.

"Hell's fudging bells," she muttered, eliciting a chuckle from him, which did nothing to ease her embarrassment.

"But hey, it's all part of the learning process, right?" he said. "And for what it's worth, I think you showed a lot of courage pushing through despite the beginning blunder. Not everyone can recover on their feet so quickly."

Lux managed a small, wry smile, appreciating Scott's attempt to lighten the mood. "Thanks, I guess. Next time, I'll stick to hello. Or maybe just a friendly wave from afar."

Scott's laughter was warm and infectious, and Lux found herself laughing along, the remnants of her embarrassment melting away.

"You know," Scott said, his eyes twinkling, "there's something quite charming about a woman who can laugh at herself."

Lux raised her brows. Did it mean anything that they both found that an attractive quality in a person? "Endearing or not, let's not forget this is a winner takes all challenge. One of us will be leaving Manhattan when this is all over. And at this rate, I'm really liking my odds."

Scott leaned in, his expression one of mock seriousness mixed with a hint of playful challenge. "Oh, I wouldn't count me out just yet. We've only just begun, and trust me, I've got more than a few tricks in my arsenal. This game is far from over."

"Tricks? As in plans to cheat?" she snapped, all humor dissipating.

"I swear on Mum's grave, I'd never resort to cheating to win a bet. Scoundrels cheat. Rakes win fairly."

Relief flickered inside Lux. She believed him. Which meant he and Frankie weren't in cahoots. Which meant she was going to win their bet. All the tricks in the world wouldn't get her to the point a rake found her datable, let alone lovable. "If you say so," she said cheekily. "But if you ask me, Frankie knew you never stood a chance. She took one look at me and decided I was her ticket to get rid of you."

Scott's eyes glimmered with mischief. "Frankie adores me. And though your pickup line flopped, there's a certain charm in your awkwardness that I plan on exploiting from now on."

"How, pray tell, can you exploit that in your favor?"

"There are certain men who will find flirting fumbles...enchanting."

"Just as there are some women who sees a good fixer-upper man, such as yourself, and think to themselves, 'Ah, a new project.'"

"Like you?" he asked.

"I prefer my men move-in ready."

"Men?" His voice held a note of something she couldn't quite define.

If the thought weren't so ridiculous, she would label it jealousy.

"Have you had several?" he finished.

"Why Prince Landshire, I'm shocked," she teased. "Are you asking me for my number?"

"What?" he asked.

"It's not polite to ask a woman how many move-in ready men they've said yes to."

"Humor me anyway."

"Are we talking about ones that were truly move-in ready—no cleverly disguised wiring issues—or just the grand total? Because, sadly, the first is a far more exclusive club."

"By all means, tell me the move-in ready number?" Scott replied, his voice lowering, laced with a hint of desire.

Her number would be peanuts compared to his. A number so painfully low, he'd feel sorry for her. "I do not orgasm and tell," she responded. "To do so would be unladylike."

He closed the distance between them, his eyes intensely fixed on hers. "That response is too enchanting to go unrewarded." He leaned in. "May I kiss you?"

"I think you may," she said, befuddled by the gentlemanly request. Surely, rakes did not go around requesting permission to kiss a woman.

He leaned in and captured her lips in a kiss that was far from brief or playful. One that was definitely rakish.

So rakish it ignited a fire that seemed to consume them both. When he finally pulled back, she was left breathless, her mind reeling.

"Doc, should you ever need a man who is wired correctly in all the right places, I'm at your service."

Lux, still spinning from the kiss, somehow managed a coherent thought which should have led to a coherent response. But didn't. "I just may take you up on that eventually."

"I await the day."

She started to reply, but he held up a finger. "There's no rush. For now, I'm going to leave without you, which will leave every man in here curious as to why you didn't go with me. Then, in three minutes, you should leave and there will be a black sedan waiting to take you home."

"Got it."

He pushed her hair off her face. "And Doc, don't let anyone else charm you on your way out. If they didn't flock to your side the moment you arrived, they don't deserve you."

With those sweet words, Scott sauntered away, leaving Lux standing there wondering what sex with the Prince of Shiretopia would be like.

Dare she call his bluff?

CHAPTER 10

SCOTT SAT AT HIS desk, fixated on the previous night with Doc. He'd kissed her twice now, and both times he'd had to force himself to stop. Kissing her had not been a part of the assignment, so he had only himself to blame.

A gentle knock on his office door pulled him back to the present. He glanced up. Ms. Birdie stood there, her presence as commanding as it was unexpected. "Twice in one week. To what do I owe the pleasure this time?" Scott rose to greet her.

"I've stopped by to invite Luxury and you to a lovely event I'm hosting tomorrow evening." She handed him an invitation. "I understand your last flirtation lesson will occur tonight, and then she'll be thrown into the dating segment of Frankie's mad plan."

"Which means I won't be at liberty to bring her to your party." He opened the invitation and scanned the contents:

The Flirtation Gala

A Night Where the Art of Conversation and Unspoken Words Intersect

Date: Friday, May 24th

Time: 9:00 p.m. to 1:00 a.m.

Location: Revealed upon RSVP

"Not to worry. She will receive her own invitation. This one was solely for you," Ms. Birdie explained.

"Is Frankie aware of your event? She's given me an agenda, and a Flirtation Gala is not on there. According to Dragon Lady, I'm to set Doc up on a blind date tomorrow evening...unless she surprises us and lands a date tonight during her lesson."

"Frankie knows of my invitation...and has signed off."

"I thought you weren't in a position to question her decisions for the first year of her employment at *Naked Runway*."

"Information was brought to my attention which made it necessary for me to get involved."

Scott groaned. "Don't tell me. She had the whole thing somehow rigged?"

"The party will help me achieve both my goals."

Her goal for him was that he'd win the arrangement. "You haven't hired someone to pretend insta-love for her? I won't stand for that. I don't cheat."

"I should box your ears for suggesting I would."

"My apologies."

"For your information, I've invited a number of men whom I believe will provide Luxury with the perfect opportunity to find herself a rakish gentleman—that she'll like—whose heart is free to be stolen over the remaining days of your arrangement."

"What's so special about these men that Doc will be attracted to them?"

"They're genuine yet socially cautious, intelligent but a bit shy, and kind-hearted while being just a tad reserved," Ms. Birdie replied, her eyes twinkling.

He groaned. "They're beige?"

Ms. Birdie marched across the carpet and stopped in front of his desk and wagged a finger at him. "Do not put words in my mouth, young man. The men I've invited are not everyday beige."

"Aren't they?"

"Just because they're the exact opposite of macho doesn't make them boring. They all possess successful careers, are good looking, and are well bred. Terms I'd use to describe you, as well."

"What you didn't say was they are risk takers, ladies' men, and damn good at pleasuring a woman."

"As I told Frankie when I dropped off her invitation," Ms. Birdie said, showing no signs of being perturbed by his comment. If anything, her eyes were twinkling. "They are rakes in the rough."

Realization struck him. "You're coaching them. They're part of your latest fairy godmother project. The gentleman you've invited are men who wish to become rake-like. They are part of the program you asked me to consider spearheading." That had been the second thing she wanted to discuss with him when he'd met her for coffee. She'd asked him to take over the program.

"Not that it's any of your business since you declined my offer, but they are. And much like our dear Luxury—who was a vixen in the rough until your Glam Team got ahold of her—they are rakes in the rough. But once I've helped them strengthen their confidence, they will shed their outer shell of cinnamon roll heroes and become full-fledged rakes...with hearts. I think the young crowd call them alpha-roll heroes."

Scott groaned. "You're either a rake or you're not."

Ms. Birdie gave him an amused look. "If you can teach Lux how to be a vixen, I can teach gentleman how to become rakes."

That was the second time she'd referred to Doc as a vixen. He hadn't liked it the first time, and he didn't like it now. Vixens were fine for fun and games, but that wasn't Doc. She wasn't a fluff girl. She had much more substance than that. His goal was to teach her how to capture the attention of a man so she could then let him see her substance. His goal was not to take away what made her special.

Then again, none of this was about what he wanted. Because if it were, he would have dragged her to the nearest hotel room and told her last night to shut the fuck up and take his dick in her mouth like a good little girl. She wouldn't be able to joke about his penis falling off once she developed an appreciation for it. "Why not just let her chase a real rake? Where is the fun in catching the heart of a wannabe?"

"Our Luxury is a woman who wants to be loved for her brain by a man who will love her when her beauty fades and her body wrinkles…thus the type of man I've invited to my gala."

Doc had been busy hiding her beauty in the hopes of gaining forever love. Interesting. Now it made sense why she'd used the blandest picture ever for her profile picture on the dating app. "She doesn't believe true love can happen with a man like me." He said the words more to himself than to Ms. Birdie, but she gave him a speculative look as if she'd picked up on something in his voice and misinterpreted it as telling.

"If I do my job right," Ms. Birdie said before he could set her straight, "Lux will get the best of both types…Good Guy blended with Bad Boy. And he will get Girl Next Door blended with Vixen. It will be a win-win for both of them."

That sounded nice. A guy who fell in love with that combination of woman would be lucky indeed. Too bad he didn't have enough of the good guy part to be a perfect match for a woman like Doc. Not to mention the damn curse. It prevented him from giving his heart to any woman. "Sounds like you've got it all figured out."

"The best part is no one has to end up with a broken heart at the end of Frankie's 'How to Win a Rake in Eight Days' campaign."

Scott sat with the knowledge Doc's heart might soon belong to another. To one of the men who would be at Ms. Birdie's gala. Men who were, for all intents and purposes, his opposite. They were the kind who'd never suggest incorporating kink in the bedroom.

They were the kind of man who could make Doc happy.

Or could they?

More than likely, yes. After all, she'd all but admitted last night she'd never been fucked by a real man. A fake rake would probably seem like a thrill ride to her.

Hell, he'd be doing her a favor if he took her to bed and gave her a taste of what she'd be missing if she settled on a wannabe. Then again, that lesson could work both ways. He could discover what he'd be missing by not being good enough for Doc.

"Well. Don't just sit there scowling at me," Ms. Birdie demanded with a smirk. "Say something useful."

"It makes me happy to know that when she loses the challenge, she'll have at least found love with someone she can love back." The words rolled off his tongue like he told them to, but his brain gagged at the sincerity he had managed to infuse into his tone. Why his brain hated the idea, he couldn't pin down.

"I knew you'd understand once you got over your ego," Ms. Birdie said, reaching across the desk and patting his hand.

Ego? Was that what was hurting right now? "If one of them falls in love with her," he muttered more to himself than to Ms. Birdie, "Isabella can spin him as a rake in sheep's clothing on NR's online accounts before anyone can say he's not a rake."

Ms. Birdie studied him. "That's exactly what Frankie said once she realized I wouldn't allow her to cheat."

Scott snorted. That was what made Ms. Birdie a force to be reckoned with. While she had a heart of gold—spending her own fortune to make wishes come true—she was also a ruthless businessperson. Her attention to detail topnotch.

"And Frankie agreed to play by the rules?" He couldn't afford to lose this competition on a technicality. Too much was riding on it for him and for others. Doc's worst-case scenario was having to find a new job. His was ten times worse.

"I'm her boss." Ms. Birdie glanced around his office. "Is that a penis in a bottle?"

Scott glanced at the glass penis sitting atop the bookshelf in the corner of his office. A gag gift that had been on display on his desk when he'd arrived Tuesday morning. A note had been attached to the tiny statue. *Break in case of emergency.*

Before he could respond, his intercom beeped. "What?"

"Mr. Landshire, I'm sorry to bother you, but your father is on line three. He says it's urgent."

He glanced at Ms. Birdie. "Do you mind?" Urgent for Father could be nothing more than needing to know the answer to a crossword puzzle clue, but still, it could also be something awful.

Ms. Birdie smiled. "I have a party to organize. I'll see you tomorrow evening."

He picked up the phone and waited for Ms. Birdie to shut his door before he replied to Char. "Put him through."

His phone rang. "Your Majesty, to what do I owe the pleasure of a phone call from you in the middle of the day?"

"There is no pleasure to be had in this call," the King of Shiretopia blustered. "In fact, it pains me greatly to have been placed in a position where this call could not be avoided."

Scott thrummed the fingers of his free hand on his desk. He knew this tone of voice. It was usually reserved for when Mildred insisted Father discipline Scott for a misdeed that Father did not find as loathsome as his second wife did. "I'm sorry to hear that, Father. What business is at hand that has you so uncharacteristically disgruntled?"

"It's a private matter that I do not wish to broach over the phone. As such, I will be in New York, New York on Saturday to discuss it with you."

Scott grinned at the way Father insisted on referring to Manhattan as New York, New York. "Father, I'm in the middle of a big assignment with the magazine. I'm afraid this weekend is not an option. Perhaps early June would be a better time for you to visit."

"Change your plans," Father ordered. "This cannot wait. Hell, it may not wait until Saturday. We will talk more when I arrive. Good day."

Before Scott could offer a rebuttal, the phone went dead. Unease had him picking up his cell and calling his best friend, Mark, who still lived in Shiretopia. It went straight to voicemail. "Bloody hell," Scott muttered. He disconnected and called Mark's soon-to-be fiancée, Rose. It went straight to voicemail. He hung up and texted them both.

Father is coming to town. Are there any new developments I should be made aware of before he lands?—Scott

The three of them were walking a tightrope. One wrong move could spell disaster and become a bigger scandal even than the time Father had thumbed his nose at his fate and instead eloped with Mum. Rose was Mark's future bride, all right...if all went according to plan.

If not, she was Scott's bride-to be, via an arranged marriage.

He really needed things to go according to plan.

CHAPTER 11

"Quite the choice Frankie had for the location of your third lesson in seduction," Scott said, glancing around The Gilded Lily as he pulled out a chair for Doc. He'd been surprised when he'd discovered Dragon Lady had chosen the location. The atmosphere didn't lend itself to instructing a person on romance. It was more geared toward falling in love with the one you're dining with.

"I feel like I've stepped into another world," Doc whispered, taking a seat. "Every person's laugh sounds prep school perfect."

He understood why Doc felt intimidated. The small restaurant was a fortress of wealth. The people who dined here were the type who owned things like banks or small countries. If one listened carefully, they could hear the clink of money being made over the clatter of silverware. The diamonds worn on the fingers of the ladies present could fund Ms. Birdie's fairy godmother habit for a year.

"Oh," Doc said, looking startled by his sliding into the seat next to her rather than the expected one across the table.

"Being this close is crucial." He spoke in a hushed tone. "I wouldn't want all my strategies to become public knowledge."

"I call bullshit." She gave him a bland look. "They're already public knowledge. You've written about them in your columns."

"A man never shares all of his secrets."

"Interesting...or at least, I hope the secret strategies are better than the ones you've shared," she teased.

He liked that their hostility toward one another had turned into something else. Something comfortable. He watched Doc as she took in the lavish surroundings.

"I feel like a fish out of water," she confessed when she turned back to him, her brows puckered.

"That's part of the lesson." He resisted an urge to smooth her brow with his fingers. "Rakes are naturally drawn to a woman who can hold her own in opulent settings—someone adept at navigating the worlds of both old money elitists and new money innovators. Last night, you hung out with the new money crowd. Tonight is the old money. Try to enjoy the experience."

Doc burst into an unexpected, hearty laugh. A laugh louder and more uninhibited than anything Scott had heard from her before. One more out of place than someone wearing white at a royal funeral.

Scott loved it. Her unguarded moment, so starkly contrasting with the poised environment of the restaurant, was refreshing in his world. He raised a brow and waited for her to explain.

"Enjoy?" Doc managed to say between chuckles. "That's like my gynecologist telling me to strap in and relax."

Her explanation caused Scott to laugh. After a moment he shook his head, grinning. "You're something else, you know that?"

A smirk played at the corners of her lips. "I aim to please," she replied, the words wrapped in the same velvety tone as her laughter. She took another look around the restaurant. "I can't help but wonder what diabolical reason Frankie had for insisting tonight's lesson took place at a snob-fest like this."

He leaned back. Snob-fest. Another new saying for him to add to the list of America's unusual idioms. "It has been my experience," he began, "that anytime Frankie gives a diabolical order—"

A server stopped at their table, cutting his reply short. "Is everything to your satisfaction?" he asked with a practiced smile.

Scott nodded.

"Excellent," he said. "May I take your drink orders?"

Normally, Scott would order a bottle of their best Cabernet Sauvignon, but that would defeat part of tonight's lesson, so instead he glanced at Doc. "What would you like to drink?" The drink a woman ordered told a man a lot about her personality. The right one was a pickup line all in itself, and after last night's fiasco, it was obvious to Scott that Doc would be far more successful if the man approached her instead of the other way around.

She glanced at the drink menu and then blinked up at him as if caught in her undergarments. "You go first."

"I'll have a dry martini, Hendrix, in and out with the vermouth, stirred, not shaken, three olives." He smiled at Doc. "And for the lady, she will have...?" He waited, giving her the space to choose for herself.

"I love olives," Doc said, her tongue briefly darting out to wet her lips. "I'll have the same but make mine dirty."

Scott felt a jolt of surprise. Had it been his imagination or had the reserved psychologist just put a suggestive spin on the word *dirty*? Clearing his throat, he quickly regained his composure. "Please bring us an assortment of your appetizers as well," he told the server. "We have work to do before we're ready to order dinner."

"As you wish." The server departed their table, his nose in the air.

"So, what's on the agenda for tonight's lesson?" Doc inquired, her fingers grazing his arm.

The awareness the casual touch sent through him momentarily stalled Scott's response. His mind wandered back to last night's kiss—a moment that had lingered in his thoughts, keeping him awake and restless well into the early hours. Regaining his focus, he said, "I think we'll start with the importance of your drink order when trying to capture the attention of a man."

"Yes. Yes. I know," she said, ruefully. "I'm not allowed to order water. Although I think the rule asinine."

Scott leaned in, enjoying his role as seduction coach. Something Ms. Birdie had approached him to teach the group of men who'd be at tomorrow night's gala. Men she'd set her fairy godmother sights upon.

Men who—according to the dear busybody—desired to possess more rakish qualities.

He assumed she'd found another for the job. Was their coach any good? Would every one of them have the ability to capture Doc's attention tomorrow night at the Flirtation Gala? Would tonight truly be his and Doc's last evening together with him acting the part of teacher and her the naughty student? The possibility didn't settle well.

He ordered himself to stop thinking about how his and Doc's relationship would end. "One of the easiest ways to capture the attention of a man in a bar is by ordering a drink that intrigues him. Just like leather pants, it's a silent pickup line."

"How is it a pickup line?" Doc asked.

"Men will form an opinion about you based on your drink of choice. Something intriguing can be a perfect conversation starter."

"In other words, a rake will come running if I loudly order a screaming orgasm?" The corners of Lux's lips twitched with amusement.

Scott chuckled, appreciating her boldness. "You do that, and every rake in the room will think you're confident in your sexuality and looking to hook up. On the other hand, it will scare off the nice guys."

"And a Bloody Mary?" Doc asked, her eyes gleaming with interest. "How would you interpret that order?"

Scott mulled over the drink's name. "I'd be intrigued and on alert."

"Alert?" Her curiosity was evident.

"It says you're comfortable with edginess, maybe even a bit of danger," he said.

"How did your brain go there?" Doc asked, fascination written all over her face.

He shrugged. "The mention of blood."

She nodded thoughtfully. "As a psychology professor, I find this entire exchange compelling."

"I thought you might." It pleased him that she'd engaged for real in this conversation.

"What kind of man will a frozen strawberry daiquiri net me?"

Scott pinched the bridge of his nose. "That order will catch the eye of the professor you're secretly hoping to snag someday. The one who wears elbow-patched sweaters, corduroy pants, brown shoes, and enjoys a pipe and the Sunday crossword puzzle in the New York Times."

Doc's mouth dropped open. "How in the hell do you know the type of guy I long for?"

Because after Ms. Birdie had left his office, he'd gone in and read Doc's dating profile. Just as Ms. Birdie had hinted at, Doc's ideal man was the antithesis of everything Scott embodied. "I did a bit of homework," he admitted. "I went through your profile on the dating app. You were quite specific about the type of guy you're looking for, which, incidentally, limited your options. Guys who didn't fit the bill, like me, dismissed you."

Her perfectly groomed brows shot up. "Men like you?"

He leaned back slightly. "I'm a rake with honor. I don't pursue nice girls whose hearts are yearning to be loved."

Her response came swiftly. "My heart is most certainly not *yearning* to be loved. I believe a woman can be perfectly happy without a man.

In fact, I believe they are most likely to be happy without one, because men are fickle. They love you today, and ten years down the road, they chase after a prettier bauble."

Scott felt a twinge of something unexpected at her words—anger...for her. "It's not every day you meet someone who dreams of the white picket fence yet views relationships like the most seasoned rake."

"Who taught you to be a rake with honor?"

The question caught him in the heart. "Before Mum passed away, she sat me down for a serious talk. Not the typical sex talk, but about how to treat a woman with respect and integrity."

"I bet it went nothing like my mother's version of the 'how to treat a man' talk," Doc said dryly.

"No?" He'd never met her mother, but instinctively did not like her.

"Not unless your mother advised that the way to a man's heart, especially for a plain girl like me, was through his balls. Her exact words were, 'Keep them empty, and he'll stay around longer. Not forever, but longer.'"

"Your mother called you plain? Was she blind?"

"Multiple times, and no, she wasn't."

Scott had to unlock his clenched jaw to respond. "Your mother sounds...like Frankie. A person with horrible people skills."

"She's not great." Doc hesitated before adding, "To her credit, though, my father cheated on her and broke her ability to trust a man. Since then, she's made it her mission to date only men who are at least a decade older than her, and then she leaves them before they have grown tired of her."

Doc's response hung in the air, and Scott found himself momentarily lost in thought, as the weight of her words settled over him. "Bloody hell. That's rough," he finally said. "I take it she never remarried?"

"That would seem logical, but no one has ever described Mother as logical. Her solution is to marry a man for five years and then divorce him," Doc explained.

As they spoke, the server arrived, balancing a tray of artfully arranged finger foods and their drinks.

Once they were alone again, Scott raised his glass and initiated a toast. "To unlikely connections. Ours."

"To unlikely connections," Doc echoed, her glass clinking gently against his. She took a tentative sip, and immediately her face contorted in disgust, and she coughed.

Scott quickly patted her on the back and handed her a napkin. "Did it go down the wrong pipe?"

Doc's expression was one of pure horror. "This tastes like rubbing alcohol. How do people drink these things?"

Scott couldn't help but laugh, drawing disapproving glances from nearby tables. Doc, oblivious to the stares, frantically rubbed her tongue with the napkin, trying to rid herself of the gin's sharp taste.

Their moment of levity was abruptly interrupted as Frankie appeared at their table, her expression a blend of shock and disapproval. "What on earth is going on here?" she asked, her eyes darting between Doc's frantic napkin rubbing and Scott's barely contained amusement. "You two are representing *Naked Runway* and this behavior is not acceptable."

"To be fair, Doc is representing Columbia University," Scott corrected.

The withering glower on Frankie's face told him exactly what she thought of that.

Why did he have the feeling she wasn't here to wish Lux good luck with her upcoming dates, but instead because she was working an angle to get around Ms. Birdie's *no cheating* rule?

CHAPTER 12

As Lux desperately tried to rid her mouth of the martini's horrid taste, she looked up at Frankie Peterson. Her demeanor was one of calculated interest, a person carrying a camera trailing behind her.

"Quite the performance," Frankie remarked dryly, her gaze sharp as she observed Lux and Scott.

"Frankie," Lux managed to say, hastily discarding the napkin and straightening up. Beside her, Scott's demeanor changed instantly, the remnants of his laughter giving way to a more guarded expression.

"To what do we owe the pleasure?" Scott asked his boss.

"I came to see firsthand how our little experiment is unfolding. And it seems I've arrived at a most...interesting moment."

The photographer, a silent observer until now, raised his camera, subtly capturing the scene at the table.

"Frankie, we're just—" Lux started, but Frankie held up a hand to stop her.

"Woman-to-woman, Lux, I'm going to give you a free piece of advice. Do with it what you may."

"I'm listening," Lux said as the photographer continued to snap shots.

"My dear, as you muddle your way through this challenge, don't make the mistake of falling for a rake. I mean, it's one thing for you to prove Scott correct by winning a rake's heart, but quite another for you to give a rake yours. Trust me when I say they are not relationship material."

"I completely agree," Lux said emphatically. "And I can assure you, I won't." How in the hell had Frankie concluded she was at risk of losing her heart?

"I've seen many bright young women lose their way, charmed by the likes of him." Frankie nodded toward Scott. "Just remember what's at stake. This is a challenge, not a romance novel. Keep your eyes on the prize you're after, not the player who presents as a worthy loser's trophy."

Lux could feel tension coming off Scott and was surprised he wasn't responding until she glanced around and noticed other patrons looking at them. "Got it. Thanks."

"And Scott," Frankie said. "I never received a read receipt from you on the text I sent earlier. Be a dear and read it."

"I'll do that before morning comes."

"Now," Frankie ordered.

Scott frowned and pulled out his phone. Read it. Showed no reaction other than a slight tightening of his lips. "Got it," he said to Frankie.

"Excellent," Frankie said, giving a slight nod. "Very well." Her tone shifted back to one of cool detachment. "Carry on then while I observe."

With a swift, commanding presence, Frankie moved to a nearby table that offered an unobstructed view of Lux and Scott.

Lux exchanged a quick, knowing glance with Scott, a silent communication passing between them. "I know Frankie warned us that she had eyes everywhere, but I never imagined she'd personally be one of those pairs of eyes."

"Don't let her presence throw you off." Scott signaled to the server with a discreet gesture.

"Yes, sir?" the server inquired, approaching their table.

Scott handed him Lux's barely touched drink. "The lady would prefer a chocolate martini, instead."

Lux couldn't help but smile. "I do have a soft spot for chocolate martinis. How can they be so delightful, yet a dirty martini taste so vile?"

Scott leaned back, a twinkle in his eye. "It's much like dating. Some people seem like the perfect catch, but once you get to know them, you realize they're nothing more than a facade. Always look beneath the surface before committing to any potential relationship."

Lux wrinkled her nose, a little taken aback by his suggestion. "Are you implying what I think you are?" Was he proposing two individuals should have sex *before* getting serious? But of course he was. He was a rake. A rake who'd already offered to teach her a sexual thing or two.

"Have sex. Yes," Scott replied. "Or, if that scrambles your good-girl sensibilities, you could simply watch them dance. Someone who knows how to move, who can really dance—they're usually worth taking home."

Her cheeks warmed with a blush. She blamed her body's reaction on the lingering effects of last night's kiss and Scott's offer. An offer that left her wanting to temporarily ditch her good-girl status and her good-guy standards. "Do you jump straight to sex, or wait and see how they dance?"

Scott leaned back, casual yet candid. "When I meet an intriguing woman, I invite her to my bed. If there are no sparks, there's no need to waste time dating."

"And women actually say yes to this approach?" Lux asked in what she knew he heard as a prudish tone, but she couldn't help it. Never in her life had she engaged in what could quite possibly be nothing more than a one-night stand.

"I'm a rake, Lux. Women expect me to skip societal formalities." Scott gave her a smirk. "It's part of the fun."

"You're making my hypothetical professor seem more and more appealing by the minute," Lux said, mostly meaning it.

Through her peripheral vision, she noticed Frankie leave without her photographer. Had she found them too mind-numbing to spend another moment observing?

"People with too much in common often end up bored," Scott said, drawing her attention back to him. "In my experience, sex is the glue of a good relationship."

"People who have nothing in common can quickly become disenchanted with each other," she countered. "Shared interests are the real glue in a good relationship. I can't imagine marrying someone who's my complete opposite."

"Interesting," Scott said as he leaned in. "I'd never marry a woman who was just like myself." His husky whisper sent hot liquid down her spine.

Their words hung between them like an old-fashioned Western standoff. Common Interests versus Opposites Attract. She was probably the most unlike-him person he'd ever shared an intimate conversation with. Did that make her—in his eyes—his perfect mate?

The server whisked by, depositing her chocolate martini with an uppity flair, and a glance at Lux that felt very much like a complete sentence. One that said, "You're absolutely not his perfect mate."

"This looks fabulous," Lux said, ignoring the server, banishing her silly thoughts, and instead placing all her focus on the sight of her new drink.

Scott nodded to the server. "We'll signal when we're ready to order dinner."

Lux picked up the drink and wrapped her lips around the martini's chocolatey edge, the cool glass contrasting with the warmth still lingering along her spine. As the rich, smooth chocolate cascaded down her throat, she let out a contented sigh, the sound mingling with the click of ice. "Delicious," she purred.

"Always stick to drinks you know when flirting in a bar," Scott said, falling back into his coaching mode, but not before Lux caught the briefest flicker of desire in his eyes. "Save the experimenting for home or with friends." His gaze lingered just a second too long on her lips before he hastily reached for a napkin, dabbing at a non-existent spill by his glass.

The corners of her mouth twitched upward. "Or with dating coaches who will smoothly come to your rescue."

He cleared his throat, visibly steeling himself. "Ready for another of tonight's lessons?"

"Give it to me," Lux said, before savoring another sip of her martini.

A flicker of dismay crossed his features before he swallowed hard. "Doc, piece of advice," he began, his tone grave. "Never say 'give it to me' to a man unless you're in the market for...a different kind of proposition." His gaze darted away, as if to ensure no one was listening in, and then back.

Heat filled her cheeks. What was it about this guy that made her blurt innuendoes? "You've got to admit, it's not as bad as the time I inadvertently invited you to go down on me."

He groaned. "You're killing me, Doc."

It was her turn to swallow hard. *Don't play with fire* was a saying for a reason. Those who did invariably got burned. She had no desire to be singed by a rake. "How about those lessons you promised me?"

He nodded, as if agreeing their conversation needed a new path. "First, stay away from the crowd. It's simpler for a man to make a move if you're alone or with just one friend."

She took another sip of her drink. "Why only one?"

"Men usually meet a friend at a bar for drinks, not a crowd," he explained.

"What if a guy approaches that I'm not interested in?" Lux asked.

"Be clear but kind. Rudeness can turn off other potential suitors who might be watching."

"That's a no brainer." Lux watched Frankie's photographer leave.

"You'd be surprised," Scott countered, his tone suggesting a wealth of experience. "Many women miss this and lose out on other opportunities."

"I usually go out in groups. It feels safer," Lux admitted, her mind drifting. What was Frankie's end game with those photographs? Would they be used in the next issue of the magazine? And more importantly, who'd hurt Frankie that she'd given Lux such a stern warning not to fall for a rake? Was that mystery person the reason behind Frankie's prickliness?

"If you're in a crowd, try standing a bit apart from them. This allows a guy to approach without the intimidation of a group's worth of eyes on him."

"That makes sense," she said, setting aside her psychoanalysis of Frankie. "What else?"

"Try to make eye contact. Not staring, just a flirtatious glance. If he looks back, it's an invitation."

She reached for a tapa, considering Scott's words. "Got it. Travel in pairs, eye contact. Next?"

"If it works, he'll come over with a pickup line."

The mention of pickup lines had her squirming. Her attempt last night had to have been the worst one ever. A morsel Scott would someday entertain his friends with. "And if he just says hello?"

"Then you say hello and wait." Scott's tone suggested there was an art to even this simple interaction.

In her profession, the ability to wait until a client spoke was practically a job requirement. "Got it. Sexy hello followed by psychologist dead air."

He frowned. "Do you have a sexy hello?"

She nodded.

"Let me hear it."

She fluttered her lashes and gave it her best shot. "Hello," she said, low and throaty with a hint of a growl.

A brief pause hung in the air as he adjusted his tie. "Stick with a normal hello and then wait. Trust me, he will move into his pickup line. It might not be smooth, but he'll have something planned."

Lux took another sip of her martini, mulling over the dismissal of her seductive hello. It hadn't been that bad. Hell, she'd practiced it several times today. "What's up next on your coaching agenda?"

"The importance of touch. It's a crucial part of flirting."

"I'm not sure I follow," she whispered, awareness rippling through her.

Scott's gaze turned smoldering as he leaned in, his thumb ghosting over her lip with deliberate slowness. "You had a little chocolate there," he whispered, the simple words charged with an undercurrent of something more.

"Oh." Her cheeks flushed with a warmth that spread far beyond her skin, even as she dabbed at her mouth, though he had already swept the sweetness away. "Thanks." What was it about his touch that made her quiver, stirring a yearning even when her mind screamed *abort*?

"A touch indicates interest," he said, his tone clinical, a gentle reminder that this was instruction, not initiation. "It's a way to gauge the situation. If a touch lingers too long or feels off, always trust your gut."

She exhaled a featherlight breath. "And if I'm interested?"

"While women often respond to the brushing of their hair away from their face, men react positively to a touch on the arm or knee, especially when seated."

"But how do I justify touching him?" Lux pondered, quite certain she'd never boldly graze a man's leg.

"No pretense necessary," Scott explained. "Fold it seamlessly into your interaction. But be cautious, touching a man's knee can send a certain signal."

"Like what?"

"Like you want to get out of there and hook up."

Lux blinked. Was he teasing her, testing her gullibility? "How do they leap to that conclusion?"

"We're simple creatures," Scott said, an amused smile curving his lips.

Lux chuckled. He was dead serious. "That much is obvious." The idea that a simple touch could be so misinterpreted was almost comical, and yet, the intensity behind Scott's gaze was undeniable. If she weren't careful, the night would tip into dangerously deep waters. It was time to steer back to the shallows. "What lesson did you skip to tell me about touch?"

Scott's eyebrows rose in silent acknowledgment, a slight tilt to his head as if he, too, recognized the precarious edge they'd been skirting. He leaned back, creating a space that felt suddenly vast. "The art of small talk. It's crucial. Master it, and it can be as effective as good looks in getting a date."

She stiffened, the implication snagging her pride like a thorn. Had she been a natural beauty, she bet he would have skipped this lesson. "That's good to know, because once our sessions are over, I plan on reverting to my old self."

Scott gave her a warm, reassuring smile. "You know, Doc, there's something compelling about a person who is comfortable in their own skin. It's not the look, but the confidence that truly captivates."

"Those are pretty words, but I fear reality hasn't proven you right...yet."

Scott dropped his chin and raised a brow, his demeanor earnest. "That's because, up until now, you haven't had a full arsenal of flirting tools at your disposal. With these new techniques, you might be surprised at how many men ask to buy you a drink, whether you're decked out in makeup, or just flaunting a swipe of lip gloss. Take my friend, Rose, for instance. She might not be the first one you notice when you walk into a bar, but she can captivate anyone she chooses, simply because she's mastered the art of flirting."

"Even you?" Lux probed, intrigued by the mention of a woman in his life.

Scott's eyes narrowed slightly, a faint crease forming between his brows as if he was deciphering a cryptic message. "Even me what?"

"Would she be able to catch your attention? Or do you only go for traditionally beautiful women?"

Scott's smile faltered, just for a moment. "I'm not only interested in beautiful woman."

"Prove it," Lux challenged, half-joking, half-serious.

"How?" Scott asked, a spark of interest in his eyes.

"Show me a photo of someone you dated this year who isn't traditionally beautiful."

Scott's pause was a beat too long. "Our ideas of beauty might differ."

"Because I'm a plain Jane, and my standards are lower?"

He ran a hand through his hair, a silent admission of discomfort.

"Forget it," Lux cut in before he could formulate a reply. "I wasn't looking for flattery." The last thing she wanted was a pity compliment. "Tell me about this friend of yours who's a great flirt despite not fitting the classic beauty mold. How long were you two together?"

"We didn't date. She's a friend from back in Shiretopia," Scott clarified.

"A friend?" She knew very little of his prior life.

"Yes, a friend. Nothing more. Nothing less," he said, with an air of finality that didn't quite reach his eyes.

Lux's stomach dropped. "What you're saying is that despite your assurances—when faced with the chance to pursue someone who wasn't a classic beauty—you chose to stick her in the friend zone?"

"Her appearance had nothing to do with that decision," Scott said, his jaw tightening.

"Then why?" Lux pressed.

"I can't discuss it."

Lux wasn't ready to obey the silent order to change the conversation. "Can you at least tell me her secret? How she manages to enchant any man she sets her sights on?"

Scott smiled. "She calls it playing the subtly alluring card."

"Why subtle?"

"She believes there's no need to overdo it for anyone's attention," Scott said. "And it works for her."

Lux leaned toward him, eager to hear more. "I need to learn how to pull off this low-key thing, because it sounds way more doable than all of this." She did jazz hands around her face.

"It's a matter of being interesting enough to arouse their curiosity while leaving them wanting to know more," Scott said.

"Kind of like how you've kept your followers guessing about why you left Shiretopia."

Scott smirked. "Exactly. When a guy hits on you in a bar, leave him guessing if you're a one-night stand kind of woman. Queer or straight. Smart or dumb. Vanilla sex or if you're the kind of girl who knows what S. T. F. U. A. T. M. C. L. A. G. L. G. stands for. It's all about the intrigue."

Lux blinked and quickly glanced away before he could read her face. According to his lesson in mystery, he did not need to know that she knew what all those letters stood for.

Once she felt composed, she asked. "And when am I allowed to put all these questions to rest?"

Scott's eyes darkened slightly. "Once he's invested in you. When you're actually dating."

"And until then I'm to blather on about inane topics?"

"Until then, you are to wow him with your witty dialogue, which is the next lesson on the agenda for this evening."

"And if witty banter isn't my strong suit, then what?"

Scott's hand gently cupped her cheek, his touch sending a flutter through her. "If words aren't your forte, then being exceptional in...other areas can be just as captivating."

Lux felt a rush of emotions at Scott's touch, a gesture that was both unexpected and unsettling and sending mixed signals to her lady parts. She slapped away his hand. "You want conversation, I'll give it to you." Her mind raced for something intriguing to say.

"I'm waiting."

"Did you know Lake Superior is the perfect place to dump a body?"

Scott looked charmed. "And why is that?"

"Because the bacteria that causes bodies to float doesn't survive in Lake Superior's cold-ass waters."

He laughed, a genuine sound that made Lux's heart flutter. "Morbid, but excellent. You've managed to entertain and show depth simultaneously."

She nodded, feeling a mix of accomplishment and anticipation. "What's next?"

"Tomorrow night, we go out. You'll put all this to the test while I observe," Scott said, a hint of challenge in his voice.

"And where will we meet?"

"We've been invited to a Flirtation Gala. Did you not receive the invitation?"

She shook her head. "I did not."

"I'll send you the details. We will arrive separately and will not interact. It will be your opportunity to apply what I've taught you—to set up dates with rakes for the remaining days."

"And if I fail to get a date?" The prospect of actually courting a rake sent a shiver of dread through her. "What then?"

"Then I will step in and arrange one for you."

The sudden realization that their sessions—and their connection—might soon end doused her mood like cold water. The idea should have been a relief, yet it left an inexplicable hollow inside her. Frankie's caution echoed in her mind, a bell tolling a warning.

"I can hardly wait to stumble through this and finally be free from our delightful little charade." She had meant it to sound indifferent, casual, but the words were a shield, hastily erected to guard against an unexpected ache.

Scott's reaction was subtle—the slightest stiffening of his posture, the barest dimming of his eyes. It was clear that her barbed words had found their mark. His own walls, usually so invisible, rose visibly between them. "Now that we're done with your lessons for the evening, shall we order dinner, or would you prefer to call it a night?" His cool, detached voice mirrored her feigned disinterest.

The air around them grew thick.

"I'm sorry. What I said was rude." The apology spilled out, genuine and raw. She prided herself on kindness, and the bitter taste of her own harshness was a jarring reminder of that value. "I don't want to call it a night. Not yet."

He raised an eyebrow. "Then dinner?"

Lux's pulse quickened with a sudden, daring impulse. "I have a better idea."

The hurt in his eyes gave way to cautious intrigue. "And what might that be?"

Without breaking eye contact, Lux let her hand drift to his knee. "Let's get out of here." Thankfully, her voice came out steady...betraying none of the inner turmoil that set her pulse hammering.

But his lips pressed into a thin line, a silent rebuff that had her hand retracting as if burned.

She opened her mouth, intent on taking it back. "I'm—"

"Doc, I have plans for later this evening," he cut in, voice even, but Lux caught the briefest flicker of something more behind his eyes.

Her mind scrambled, floundering for any lifeline in the wake of her blunder. What on earth had possessed her to make such an audacious move? This wasn't a date. It was a coaching session, nothing more. They weren't bonding. He wasn't here because he wanted to be. "My bad," she choked out, the words like gravel.

He ran a hand over his face—a gesture of weariness or frustration, perhaps both. "I'll see you tomorrow night at the Flirtation Gala."

Grasping at the threads of her composure, she forced a lightness she didn't feel into her voice. "Who knows? Maybe the next guy I dare touch will actually appreciate the gesture, instead of having better plans." Her smile was forced, but it would have to do.

CHAPTER 13

THE FLIRTATION GALA TOOK place at a pop-up bar in lower Manhattan. According to the social media buzz surrounding it, the money raised would go to feeding the homeless. Per Ms. Birdie's request, Scott had arrived early. Doc would come later. He'd been told the Glam Team was busy transforming her into Cinderella for the evening.

He'd wanted to text her this morning and explain last night, but his nondisclosure agreement with *Naked Runway* prevented him from doing so. And Frankie's damn text last night had been clear. Be seen out on the town with a woman—any woman—other than Doc.

This so that when Frankie leaked the photos of him and Doc having a cozy dinner, it would be juxtaposed against him out on the town two hours later with twin models. All to remind *Naked Runway* readers that Scott Landshire didn't just play the part of a rake... He was a rake.

"You're awfully quiet," Ms. Birdie, who stood next to him, said. Tonight, she wore an elegant formal gown. "Is there something on your mind?"

There were a lot of somethings on his mind, not the least of them his response to Doc's hand on his knee. It had been immediate and jolting and different. It had awakened something in him he couldn't define. Not desire—he'd already admitted to himself he desired Doc. Whatever it had awakened had left him on edge all day. Not that he would burden Ms. Birdie with his emotional discombobulation. "I'm scouting the men in attendance and wondering which, if any of them, will grab the attention of Doc."

"My money is on the gentleman in the green corduroy jacket over at the bar."

Scott tensed as he glanced in that direction. The man in question leaned against the wooden frame, surveying the room with a bored expression. And while his attire was better suited for a gathering in the country, the rest of him had a more sophisticated air. "He's one of your projects, isn't he?" Scott asked.

Ms. Birdie laid a hand on his arm. "He is. My star pupil."

"And you believe he's the perfect man for Doc?"

"Unless you have someone else in mind—like perhaps yourself—I do."

"Doc and I are oil and water."

"Only because you are under a most unfortunate curse. If that were to be eliminated, my keen matchmaking senses tell me you would be perfect for Lux," she mused.

"Curse or not, I'm wrong for her. She's made that abundantly clear the past few days."

"I see. That's a shame, but I respect a woman's right to follow her common sense instead of her heart." She nodded as if convincing herself of what she'd just said. "Now I'm doubly glad to be hosting tonight's event."

"Doubly?"

"Not only will Lux have the chance to try out your methods—a requirement of your challenge—but it will also give her the opportunity to connect with some gentlemen who could quite possibly meet her common-sense criteria."

"Like green corduroy?"

She nodded. "I believe he is primed to fall for her charms quicker than you can say rakish, and more importantly, if you're truly not on her radar, I believe there's a fine chance she will fall for him as well."

The thought gave him heartburn. "What is it about him that you believe will capture her common-sense-ruled heart?"

"Let's just say, he's well read, a romantic, and, unlike you who had a very busy evening last night, is ready to settle down with just one woman."

"Last night was orchestrated by Frankie."

"Was it, now?" Ms. Birdie said, a faint frown marring her brow. "Perhaps that's just as well."

"Just as well?" He ground his back teeth, biting back a storm of words.

"I believe your stunt last night will have Lux all bristly, which will result in her going all in on her mission to find the right man. Once she learns Mr. Corduroy's parents have recently celebrated their thirtieth wedding anniversary and have demonstrated to him what a happy marriage looks like, and that that is something he wants for himself, she'll give him serious consideration as a future husband."

"I take it you coached him to get those pieces of information out there?" Scott would like to think Doc would take one look at the man and turn the other direction, but his gut told him he was wrong. The man represented a cozy Sunday afternoon. Exactly the right type of man for her.

"Indeed."

"He doesn't look the sort to rush into a relationship. I thought you were stacking the odds in my favor to win our challenge. Have you changed your mind? Have you gone all fairy godmother on Lux and decided to leave me to fend for myself?"

Ms. Birdie patted his cheek. "Stop fretting. I've adjusted my plan in lieu of your certainty Lux wants nothing to do with you, but my goal for you to win is very much alive."

He shifted his stance. "Are you sure you're not spreading yourself too thin? Perhaps you should hand Doc off to another of your associates."

"I am perfectly capable of multi-tasking," Ms. Birdie said, shaking a finger at him. "I'll have you know, I've never had a failure in my fairy godmother endeavors, and I don't plan on starting with two of my top-ten favorite subjects ever. When the dust has settled on your How to Win a Rake in Eight challenge, you will have won, and Lux's consolation prize will be the prince of her heart."

Scott scrubbed a hand down his jawline. "A prince who wears patches on the sleeves of his jacket instead of a crown on his head is a sorry excuse of a loser's prize if you ask me."

"Then it's a good thing I didn't ask you. Now, enough with your massive ego. I must go say hi to our Luxury."

Our. He'd be lying if he said he didn't like the sound of that. "I'll come with you." He turned in the direction Ms. Birdie glanced, saw Doc, and stopped breathing. Never had he seen a more beautiful woman in his life...ever. Next to her were Ziggy and Isabella.

"Nonsense," Ms. Birdie said. "You're here as a single man. She's here as a single woman. The only time the two of you will interact will be if your numbers align in an activity."

"Numbers?" he asked.

"You'll see." With that cryptic reply, Ms. Birdie floated off in the direction of her newest guest.

Scott forced his gaze off Doc and headed to the bar. If he was to survive the night, he needed a stiff drink and a good spot to survey his competition. Yes, competition. Suddenly every man in the room had the potential of taking Doc from him, and fuck if he would let that happen...yet.

"I'm going to marry that woman," said a man coming to a stop next to Scott.

Scott turned to see who'd spoken. Fucking Mr. Corduroy.

"And which woman would that be?" Scott asked.

"The beauty in the pink, wearing the tiara," Mr. Corduroy replied. "The moment she walked through the door, I felt my heart leave my chest."

Scott managed a laugh and not a growl. "Slow down. I don't think even love at first sight works that fast." Did it work that fast?

The guy, his gaze still on Doc, smiled. "It does in my family."

"Ladies and gentlemen," Ms. Birdie said, a microphone in her hand. "It is time to commence with the flirtation part of this gala. I'd like to assure each of you that everyone present has been carefully vetted. What does that mean? It means that you're all considered wonderful candidates for dating. That being said, not everyone is adept at making an initial great impression. Thus, I'd like for all of you to be open to giving one another a second glance after the event is over. To assist in this, each man has five cards. On the front, they've been instructed to place their first name and contact information. On the back, they were to list their favorite movie, favorite holiday, favorite date night venue, and their favorite saying. They've been instructed to hand out all five cards by the end of the gala. Then they will await your call if you're interested after this evening.

"Ladies, I'd like to remind you to exercise kindness when a gentleman hands you a card, and if they don't hand you one, it doesn't necessarily mean they're not interested. It may mean they're nervous and they forgot, that they plan to approach you later, or they're afraid you're out of their league.

"Now for the rules of the Flirtation Gala. First names only. Show grace to one another as you have fun practicing your flirtation game. And remember everyone is not everyone's cup of tea and that is okay.

"Men, if you will take a seat in a red chair, the ladies will come and take a seat in a green chair." She pointed toward two long rows of chairs facing one another. In between each set of chairs was a short screen to block the view of those who sat beside them. "There are no assigned seats. Once everyone is in place, I will explain the rules of Speed Flirting."

As if they were in a race, individuals scurried to claim a chair. Scott did not. He wasn't in the mood to speed flirt. Instead, he watched as Doc took a seat across from a man who looked as nervous as Doc had the night she'd tried out a pickup line on a stranger. He'd be in good hands with Doc. She'd treat him gently even if he had no game.

Scott made his way over and stood where Doc couldn't see him, but he could hear the conversations. Frankie, who had a conflict and couldn't attend the Gala, had given him strict instructions to keep an eye on Doc and make sure she didn't fall for some idiot they couldn't spin as a rake to the public. But to also make sure Doc didn't blow the whole thing off and not try to land a rake using Scott's techniques.

"Now that everyone is in place, here are the rules of speed flirting. This event is very similar to speed dating, but instead of getting to know each other, you will spend one minute engaged in flirty conversation before moving to the next person. Gentlemen, you will begin the conversation by offering up your best pickup line. And begin."

CHAPTER 14

L UX GLANCED AT THE man sitting across from her. Was he a rake? He had all the hallmarks of one—a man cut from the same cloth as Scott.

Last night, after their encounter, he'd left to twirl twins around a dance floor, while she had been left to untangle her feelings alone. The sting of that leg touch, so boldly offered and coolly declined, lingered. The chemistry she had imagined had been a one-sided affair.

Scott Landshire represented excitement, high energy, and sexual tension. That type of guy wasn't attracted to safety nets. Why would he be? Safety nets caught people. He didn't want to be caught.

And yet, there she'd been, caught up in a daydream where the infamous Rake of Manhattan might choose a forever love with her. In her musings, she had allowed herself to envision a life of glamorous events, passionate nights, and a love that would never dim. That she could give her heart to him and have faith he'd never hand it back battered and bruised. That it would be safe to have a man like him look at her like the sun rose and set with her. That she could trust he would never get tired of her.

But that wishful thinking had died a painful death when she'd seen the photo of him with the twins. Tonight, she would throw herself whole-heartedly into the spirit of the Flirtation Gala. Not because she suddenly believed Scott's training would help her land a rake, but because it was time to reel in her heart before it spiraled out of control and became permanently enraptured with the myth of being the one who tamed the Rake of Manhattan. Where was he? If she had to participate, he should have to as well.

Lux's gaze drifted and landed on Ms. Birdie. Standing there in a luxurious, gold-tone gown that shimmered like liquid wealth, holding a golden microphone, she appeared both mysterious and powerful.

What had Ms. Birdie's end game been when she'd sent Lux to speak to Frankie? And Lux was certain Ms. Birdie had one. She didn't do anything without a plan. But to know her end game would require knowing where her loyalty lay. Was she more concerned with landing the best possible candidate for her alma mater, or a company she'd owned?

"Men, your job is to woo the lady across from you with your best pickup line," Ms. Birdie said. "And go."

The guy sitting opposite Lux gave her a nervous smile. "Hello, beautiful. Here's my card before I blank out and don't give you one."

"Thank you." Lux took the card and slipped it in her purse and waited for him to offer his best pickup line, just like Scott had taught her.

"Umm. If I said you had a beautiful body, would you hold it against me?" he said.

Lux bit her tongue to keep from laughing out loud at the line she recognized from a song of years gone by. She cocked her head and thought about her response. "No, but I would allow you to buy me a drink later."

He laughed. "Hi. I'm Tim, and it's been a long time since I've spouted off a pickup line. I'm recently divorced and just getting back into the dating scene after a decade out of it."

What tiny bit of interest she had in him died. While she knew it wasn't fair to dismiss a man simply because of a failed marriage, she just couldn't help herself. "I'm sorry about the divorce." Should she give him his card back? Explain why?

He shrugged. "We got married too young. Once we settled into our mature personalities, we realized we had nothing in common."

Was that what had happened to her parents? Had they gotten married too young?

"Time," Ms. Birdie said. "Ladies, please move one seat to your right. If you're on the end, move back up to the front of the line."

Lux stood and sat at the next seat. The guy sitting across from her looked old enough to be her father, but the amount of jewelry he wore told her he was loaded and looking for a young partner. She immediately didn't like him.

"Men, begin."

The guy wiggled his brows. "I'm a billionaire in need of a companion when I visit Manhattan. Someone willing to be a kept woman. Are you interested in knowing more? If so, I'll give you a card."

Lux blinked and then scowled. "Are you for real?"

He laughed. "No. I've just always wanted to say that and see how a woman would react. I have to say, the one before you jumped at the offer. I couldn't hand her a card fast enough."

"If I were you, I'd try something different. The kind of woman you're going to land with that is only going to be interested in your money." As she dispensed her wisdom, Lux couldn't help but remember Scott's counsel on her unintentional innuendoes, and the memory brought a smile. A smile the guy across from her must have taken as encouragement because he sat up a little straighter, a peacock preening.

"Exactly," he said, moving his arm in such a way that his Rolex watch became visible.

Lux scowled.

"Time's up. Move one seat over," Ms. Birdie announced.

Rolex was followed by several unremarkable men, neither good nor bad. Their pickup lines were: 'Would you like a back rub.' 'I'm no organ donor, but I'd be happy to give you my heart.' 'What's your name? Or can I call you mine?'

They were followed by an idiot whose idea of a line was, 'Want to blow this popsicle joint? This party sucks.' To which Lux scowled.

"Change partners," Ms. Birdie said.

Still scowling at Mr. Popsicle, Lux moved one spot and found herself sitting across from a gentleman with a charming smile who wore a green corduroy jacket. Her frown immediately morphed into a happy grin. This guy was her male mirror. That was if she'd been allowed to come to the gala wearing something out of her own closet.

"Begin," Ms. Birdie said.

Lux tensed. Please let him be—

"Forgive me for what I'm about to say," he said with a nervous hitch to his voice. "It's going to sound corny and cheesy and—"

She couldn't stand the suspense, not to mention precious seconds were flying by. "Just say it," Lux encouraged.

He gave her a sheepish grin. "Do you believe in love at first sight?"

Hell's fudging bells. She didn't. Love at first sight was all about loving someone's looks, not their personality. "Only if the man is blind."

He nodded as if he completely understood her response. He handed her a card. "Allow me to take you out and prove to you that insta-love isn't a bad thing."

"Insta-love?" His use of a term used to describe a popular romance trope caused her to pause. "Are you by chance a reader?" She tucked his card away.

He blushed. "Guilty. My grammy loves her romance novels. When she became ill last year and could no longer read, I started reading them to her."

Lux placed her hand over her heart. "That is the loveliest thing I've heard in a long—"

"Time," Ms. Birdie announced.

Lux didn't want to move. She wanted to stay right where she was and learn more about the man across from her. A guy who read to his grammy was not a rake. Not a serial flirt. "I hope to see you again tonight." With that, she stood and started to move to the next seat but realized they hadn't exchanged names. She was about to ask him when another woman sat in her vacated seat.

She turned to her next partner and blinked. Scott was her next speed date, and he was glaring. When had he joined in on the fun and games? Whose seat had he taken? The last she'd seen of him, he'd been behind her...no doubt analyzing her game so he could tell her what she was doing wrong. Had she already screwed up? Had he sat to give her pointers?

"Please tell me you didn't believe his I-read-to-my-grammy line," he said.

"That is none of your business," she snapped.

"Men, begin," Ms. Birdie instructed.

Scott said nothing.

"You're here," Lux prompted. "You might as well flirt with me. Keep your edge sharpened."

When he still said nothing, she sighed. "Fine. I'll go. Tell me, Scott, have you ever voluntarily gone out with an ordinary woman? One not beautiful but instead smart and funny and awkward?"

"I'm a rake," he said flatly. "What do you think is the answer to that question?"

His response hurt in an irrational way. It wasn't like she cared. Not much, anyway. "At least you're honest."

He sighed. "Why are you looking at me like I just insulted you? You must know you're the most beautiful woman here tonight. Hell, you're the most beautiful woman I've ever sat across a table from. Take the compliment."

She rolled her eyes. If ever a rake had said a rakish thing, it was that. She'd bet her career that was his favorite pickup line. "I may look a little different on the outside, but the inside me is still the same. A woman who hasn't been able to keep a guy interested past date one."

He opened his mouth as if to say something and then closed it. When he opened it again, she knew he'd chosen something different to say by the way his jaw tightened and the light in his eyes dimmed ever so slightly. "When you look like you do, your body does the flirting for you. Guys don't care what comes out of your mouth."

"I don't want my body to do the flirting, or my face for that matter. I want my conversation to do the flirting."

"Why?" he asked, rubbing a hand down his chiseled jaw.

She got a whiff of his aftershave. Something woodsy and rugged. It was different from what he'd been wearing this week. Was this what he wore on dates? Or did he change out his aftershave the way he changed out women? "Because I want a man who will love me when I'm old and wrinkled. One who fell in love with the superficial will not. One who falls in love with my intellect hopefully will."

His expression turned thunderous. "Then you'll have to wait until you're old and wrinkled before falling in love, because trust me, the new you is—"

"Time," Ms. Birdie said. "And that ends this portion of tonight's events. Our next flirtation activity will begin shortly.

"The new me is what?" Lux asked.

"It will prevent you from finding the unicorn capable of separating your beauty from the rest of the package."

"Hell's fudging bells." She stood.

"Unless he knew you as plain Jane first. Like—"

"Hey, there you are," Mr. Insta-Love said, coming to a stop next to her. "May I buy you a drink?"

Lux bit her bottom lip. According to Scott, Mr. Insta-Love's view of her was now tainted. She'd never know if he could love plain her. Then again, just because Scott said something didn't make it gospel. "I promised another I'd have a drink with him. But later, for sure."

Mr. Insta-Love smiled. "Of course. I'm looking forward to getting to know you better as the night moves forward."

Watching him walk away, Lux sighed. "He's really quite nice...isn't he?" she said to Scott, who had listened to the whole exchange instead of moving on like a gentleman.

"Boring was what I was thinking."

She raised her brows. "Which I'm sure is what you were thinking last night when I propositioned you. But luckily, your boring might just be my Mr. Right."

"You're wrong, you know," he said. "About me. You're wrong."

She moved a little closer, not wanting to be overheard. "I don't think so. Actions speak a lot louder than words, and your actions have deafened me."

"Whatever you think they said, you're mistaken."

"I doubt that."

He swore softly. "Just remember, Doc, you're obligated to give it your all to try to land a rake using the methods I've taught you."

"Then get the hell away from me, so I can."

"Ladies and gentlemen. It's time for part two of the flirtation gala. Men, you've offered the ladies your best pickup line—now it's time to show off your dance moves. When the music starts, make your way to the floor and grab a dance partner. Each time the music changes, pick a new partner."

Lux glanced around for Insta-Love. She refused to write him off just because Scott had put doubt in her head. Knowing him, that was one of his rakish moves to defeat the competition. Right as she laid eyes on Mr. Insta-Love, a woman walked up to him and said something that made him smile.

"May I have this dance," said a gentleman stepping in front of Lux. A guy who looked a tad like a younger version of Jason Momoa.

"You may." Lux placed her palm in his, a bit dazzled by his movie star looks.

The music started, a Latin song, and her dance partner twirled her onto the floor, causing her to laugh in surprise.

Then he pulled her into his chest. "Do you know how to cha-cha?" he asked, even as he spun her out.

Before she could reply, he spun her back in and started moving his feet and his hips. "Just follow my lead."

She did her best to keep up and found herself wondering if Scott was right. Did great dancers make great lovers?

The music changed, and she felt a tap on her shoulder. Turning, she saw a smiling Mr. Insta-Love. "My turn." He pulled her into his arms.

She waited for excitement to zip through her and was disappointed when it didn't. "I didn't catch your first name."

The music turned to a slow song, and her partner moved her around the floor like a man comfortable on the dance floor. "It's John. And yours?"

"Lux." *Fuck Scott and his head games.* This guy wasn't a dud. Just like she wasn't a dud.

"I'm sorry if I startled you earlier with my insta-love question," John said. "It's just that my parents fell in love the first night they met, and they just celebrated their thirtieth wedding anniversary, so it's on my mind."

Lux stumbled and stepped on his toes. "Sorry," she murmured.

"Don't be," he said with a kind smile. "Mistakes happen."

"My parents didn't make it to their fifth."

"I count myself lucky to have had such great role models." He pulled her a little tighter. "They are as in love today as they were the day they got married."

She stepped back enough to look into his eyes. "Then age hasn't dimmed your father's love of your mother?"

"Oh, God no. In his eyes, she's as beautiful today as she was in her twenties. You should see the way they still flirt with one another."

"Was she a beauty in her twenties?"

"She was a model," John said. "So I'd say the answer is yes."

"Oh." That threw water on Lux's theory. "I wonder if she ever worried about him losing interest when she no longer looked like a model."

John chuckled. "It was dad who worried she would someday find him not handsome enough. Especially once his hairline receded."

Interesting. Lux had never considered men suffering from the same sort of insecurity as her. She would never stop loving a man just because he had aged. To do so would be the shallowest of shallows. A narcissist of sorts. A person only interested in what made them top dog in a situation.

"While I believe in love at first sight," John said, "I also believe in taking the time to verify there's a connection after your heart's settled down and your brain has had a chance to get involved in the decision-making process."

"You've given me something to think about. To be honest with you, I've always viewed insta-love as nothing more than insta-lust."

John blushed. "I look forward to proving to you that when I say I fell for you instantly, it wasn't just because you're beautiful."

Before she could form a reply, the music changed, and a strong hand landed on her shoulder. She knew who her new dance partner was before she turned. "You," she said to Scott.

"Me," he replied.

The music was a pop song, but he didn't even pretend to try to follow the beat. Instead, he pulled her tightly against him and just swayed.

"You two looked quite chummy," he growled against her ear.

"Probably because we were," she shot back. "And if this is your idea of dancing, no wonder you turned down my offer last night. You don't want me to discover you suck at sex."

He brought a hand between them and lifted her chin, forcing their gazes to meet. What he saw in hers must have distracted him, because he stopped dancing, and slid his hand over the curve of her jaw before allowing it to rest at her nape. "I don't suck at sex. But please, don't take my word for it. Let's get out of here, and I'll prove it."

Her knees turned to jelly and her brain to mush. Yes. This is what she wanted. One night in his arms. One night to remember as she went about living her life. But to say yes after the way he'd humiliated her last night would be pathetic. She raised her hand and cupped his strong jawline. "I can't. As you reminded me earlier, I'm here to do one thing and one thing only...practice my flirting until I land myself a rake."

With those words, she pulled out of his arms and walked away, not looking back and not stopping until she found Mr. Insta-love, who now stood next to Ms. Birdie, chatting as if they knew each other quite well.

CHAPTER 15

S COTT INTENDED TO LET Doc walk away, to vanish into the crowd with Mr. Corduroy. After last night's blunder, he knew he'd earned the cold shoulder, and she certainly deserved a shot at joy, even if it was with a guy who had the allure of a dishrag. But as she moved toward Mr. Corduroy, that insufferable purveyor of insta-love, a raw, seething something clawed at Scott's insides.

It was a feeling that gnawed at him, dark and voracious, one he couldn't shake off. The acrid tang of it suggested jealousy, but that couldn't be—because a man cursed to never know love couldn't possibly know the first thing about jealousy, could he? Yet, what else could twist his gut like this?

He was moving before he could slap a label on the emotion, striding toward them with purpose. He reached for Doc's arm just as she paused by Ms. Birdie, his fingers closing a touch too firm, a silent declaration of his presence.

Doc's reaction was swift, her arm snapping away from his grip, her eyes shooting daggers colder than any ice. "Excuse me." Her voice was arctic, and it should have cut him to the core—should have, but it didn't.

"Sorry to interrupt, but Frankie needs to see us," he lied smoothly, the deception rolling off his tongue like second nature. Well, it wasn't an outright lie; Frankie had texted, just not for tonight.

Doc's suspicion was palpable, even as she apologized to Corduroy. Scott watched as the guy's attempt at charm elicited a smile from Doc, a smile that had no right to stir anything in Scott yet did. It fanned the flames of that unfamiliar, gnawing feeling as he watched another man touch her.

"We need to get going," he interjected, his impatience not entirely feigned. The longer she lingered with Corduroy, the more the unfamiliar sensation grew, tainting his mood.

Doc ignored Scott and her gaze locked with Corduroy. It was as if Scott had faded into the background.

"No one makes Frankie wait," he said with a touch more urgency, steering her away, the need to separate her from Corduroy burning through him like wildfire.

Once they stepped outside, Doc made her indignation clear, wrenching her arm free from his hold. "What is wrong with you? I liked him." The tension that sizzled in the air between them was electric, almost alive.

A gentleman would regret his actions, but regret was a stranger to Scott. "I saved you from a mistake with Corduroy."

"Mistake?" she echoed, disbelief etched into each syllable.

"You deserve better," he insisted, and it was true. She did. But why it mattered so much to him, he couldn't fathom.

"And you think you're better?" she challenged, her eyes ablaze with a fire that he recognized all too well—it was the same fire that ignited whenever they sparred.

"Fuck, no," he said, the curse sharp and raw. "But if you're hell-bent on throwing yourself at someone who'll never make you burn the way you do with me, then let me at least show you what you'll be missing." It was a low blow, even for him, and yet he couldn't help but lay all his cards on the table. Because if she was going to choose someone, anyone, it sure as hell wasn't going to be Corduroy. Not if he had anything to say about it.

Her mouth formed a perfect O. "Frankie doesn't want to see us tonight, does she?"

He could only offer a rueful shake of his head. "Monday is soon enough for her."

She drew back her hand, clearly aiming to slap him, but he was quicker, capturing her wrist and pinning her gently against the brick wall. "You'll understand later," he murmured, locking her gaze with an intensity that belied his casual tone. And in that moment, he vowed silently to himself that he'd spare no expense to see her in emeralds, the color that would make her eyes pop—a lavish indulgence, but then, what was the point of wealth if not for grand gestures?

Her response was a hiss. "There won't be any thanks coming from me."

Despite her struggle, he held firm, not willing to let her escape just yet. Instead, he pressed against her, allowing her to feel his desire. A move as bold as the one she'd offered last night, yet driven by more than just lust. "Are you certain of that?"

Doc's eye roll was a thing of beauty, even in defiance. "While I'm happy for you, I really am, that my nightmare hasn't yet come to pass, your chance of showing off your skills with that...thing"—she paused and glanced down between them—"you have proudly pressed into my belly is long gone."

Her fiery response hung between them, and he couldn't help but marvel at her spunk even while bristling at her mention of that damn dream. Doc would keep the lucky bastard who eventually married her on his toes. A guy that could never be him. He shoved that thought aside and placed his lips against her ear. "What if I told you why I had to decline last night, and why tonight is different?"

"I know why you said no—I saw you with the twins."

"But what you don't know..." He paused, ensuring he had her full attention. "Frankie orchestrated that whole scene. She sent me to that club with a clear directive to be snapped looking like I was up for more than just drinks."

"Why would she demand such a thing from you, and why would you comply?" There was a note of bewilderment in her voice, mingled with a hint of something softer.

He leaned closer, his voice dropping to a whisper. "Frankie has invested heavily in the rake persona she's crafted for me. She's not about to let her investment go without a fight. She planned those photos, our cozy little scene at the restaurant, and then juxtaposed it with those taken later with the twins to reinforce that narrative." Some day he might regret breaking his NDA, but tonight wouldn't be it.

"That's a nice tale." Skepticism laced Doc's words.

He responded not with words but with a kiss planted softly on the tender skin of her neck, savoring the involuntary shiver he drew from her. "The only person I envisioned in my bed last night was you."

His confession resulted in her pushing against his chest, her strength surprising him into taking a step back.

"You should have said that last night," Doc snapped, "instead of leaving me to believe that I'd made an utter fool of myself."

"I couldn't, because I'm tied up in an NDA with *Naked Runway*."

"Yet here you are revealing it when it's convenient for you." The skepticism was back in full force.

Damn. She made a valid point. "Convenient is the last thing it is from my perspective."

Her eyes searched his, as if hunting for sincerity. When they dimmed, he knew what she'd found—nothing but the echoes of a rakish prince more adept at crafting headlines than holding onto relationships, a truth that sat heavier on his heart than any crown on his head.

"And what perspective is that?" she finally asked.

He took a breath, his mission unwavering. "One of a guy who audaciously believes the woman in front of him deserves a scandalous night with a rake before she settles for a man who thinks corduroy is black-tie appropriate."

"That would be an error in judgment—one I narrowly escaped last night," she said with resolution.

The gentleman in him wanted to back off, to respect her stance. But the rake? The rake wanted to push, to persuade. "And what if I were to confess that seeing you with others tonight made me uneasy? In a way I've never experienced before?"

Her nose crinkled adorably. "Are you trying to tell me you were jealous?"

He traced a line down her cheek, a rogue curl yielding to his touch as he tucked it behind her ear. "What I mean is you stir feelings in me that are entirely new."

Her snort was dismissive. "Probably because I'm the only woman who hasn't fallen for your rakish charm."

"I seem to recall you announcing your plan to give me a second glance."

"Not you. Your column," she countered. "And I have been."

"I've given you, the person, a second glance, Doc, and I am enthralled with my discovery. Perhaps, if you did the same with me, as a person, not a column, you'd have a similar experience." The accent he usually kept polished and subtle now twined through his plea, an unintended, yet earnest reveal of his vulnerability.

"Reevaluating you doesn't necessitate us sleeping together."

"But it could?" He was ready to back off, to hail her a cab if she rebuffed him again. "Oh, by the way. These are for you." He pulled out his five cards from the Flirtation Gala and handed them to her.

"You kept them all?" she murmured, not glancing at the back of them.

He leaned in, hoping his smile was as disarming as he intended. "I saved them all for you. Even wrote my favorite saying on the back just like Ms. Birdie instructed."

One-by-one she flipped them over and read:

"First looks are often deceiving…"

"…but second glances can reveal secrets…"

"In every jest, there is truth…"

"Turn over a card, as you might a new leaf, and let's write a midnight story that starts with 'What if?'"

She stopped reading and shook her head as if she were having a conversation with herself, and she didn't like the answer herself had just given her.

"You should listen to that inner voice you're trying hard to ignore," he prompted.

Her gaze met his, amusement and challenge mingling there. "If we're doing this, I'm expecting the full rake experience. Don't give me the sanitized version."

The groan that escaped him was half frustration, half anticipation. "Can you be more specific?"

"I want something...different. Uncharted territories, not the well-trodden path," she said, her voice a mix of curiosity and determination.

He had to ask, even as he braced for her answer. "As in dirty talk, Doc, or are we venturing into kinkier domains? BDSM?"

Her cheeks flamed. "Are you into BDSM?"

His laughter was light, trying to ease the tension. "Dirty talk it is. Anything else?"

When she licked her lips, it was as if she'd struck a match, igniting something fierce within him. "Just a heads-up," she warned, pointing her finger in playful admonition. "Don't catch feelings. This is just a detour on my road to self-discovery. It's not a journey to love, but I'm betting it ends with a climax."

He couldn't resist the jibe, his confidence peaking. "I guarantee multiple climaxes," he corrected, signaling for a taxi with a flourish. Her teasing had been a spark, but his promise? That was a blazing commitment.

CHAPTER 16

Lux's nerves buzzed with a cocktail of anxiety and excitement as the elevator ascended to Scott's floor. To ease the growing tension, she cast around for casual conversation. "How did you end up living in Chelsea?" she asked, surprised to find his world orbiting so close to hers.

The elevator dinged at his floor, but it wasn't until the doors glided open that he answered, taking her hand as they stepped out. "This was my mother's place. It came to me after she passed."

"How old were you then?" she asked softly.

"Twelve," he said with a simplicity that belied the depth of such a loss.

They moved down a hall that was pleasantly scented, a stark contrast to her own building's aroma. "I often take for granted that I still have my mom, even with our constant button-pushing. I should re-member that the next time she drives me crazy."

"I'd give anything for one more piece of Mum's advice." Scott's voice was tinged with a rare wistfulness as he unlocked the door.

Inside, Lux's eyes swept the space. "It's beautiful," she said, though the word 'cozy' echoed silently in her thoughts. Rakes, she assumed, wouldn't appreciate such a homely compliment.

"I've kept most of it as she left it," he admitted. "I should update it, but parting with her choices is something I haven't managed yet."

Lux traced her fingertips over the furniture, her touch gentle as she searched for a connection to his past. "Why did she have a place here, in the States?"

"She was American. Dad gave her this apartment when they married. They wanted a foothold in both countries. It became her haven; now it's mine."

"Dual citizenship then?" Lux asked, joining him at the window with its expansive view.

He sighed, the sound laden with bureaucratic frustration. "It should be that way, but my birth certificate is a mess. I'm fighting to fix it. Until then, I'm here on a visa."

"That explains Frankie," Lux mused aloud, piecing together the constraints of his situation.

"My stepmother was my first lesson in tolerating the intolera-ble," Scott said, a shadow crossing his features.

"Was she cruel to you?"

Scott shook his head. "Not cruel, just...resentful of the son of her rival."

Lux let out a low whistle. "Sounds scandalous."

"You could say that." A smirk played at the corner of Scott's mouth.

"So your mom married a man cursed to never love her. That must have been a sad arrangement."

"Not at all. Mom loved Dad and he adored her. Their story, though far from traditional or royally sanctioned, was one of laughter and shared passions."

"Will you follow in your father's footsteps and someday get married despite your curse?" Lux pressed, her curiosity piqued. "Or will your tombstone declare: 'A rakish bachelor until the very end?'"

"That's a story for another time," he reiterated with a gentle firmness that nudged her from her historical inquiries back to the moment. "Right now, there's something more immediate I need to know."

She locked eyes with him, her pulse quickening at the gravity in his gaze. "And what's that?"

"As we move forward, are there any lines I should be conscious of not crossing?" His voice was low and serious, underscoring the importance of her comfort and consent.

Lux hesitated, her tone wavering between caution and curiosity. "Like what, exactly? I'm not sure..."

"If you feel uncertain or want to stop, just say so. A safe word is important."

Her laugh was nervous, a release of pent-up tension. "That's rather...cinematic, isn't it?"

"I'm equipped with handcuffs, blindfolds, and yes, even open to providing spankings...if that intrigues you."

The offer seemed to straddle the line between proposition and provocation. She couldn't tell if he was earnest or coaxing her out of her shell. And yet, the thought of yielding, even if just a whisper, to the rake's desires sent a thrill through her.

Taking a steadying breath, she nodded. "My safe word—or rather, phrase—is..." Her voice faltered as if the gravity of the moment was suddenly too real.

He leaned in, encouraging. "Go on."

She mustered her resolve. "Hell's fudging bells," she declared, the phrase that had always signified chaos now repurposed as her anchor.

His laughter was genuine, a rich sound that filled the room. "Perfect," he said, and with that single word, he acknowledged not just her choice of safe phrase but the unique blend of strength and vulnerability she brought to the brink of their adventure.

Lux couldn't suppress the grin that spread across her face, buoyed by the richness of his approval. What had seemed like an absolute disaster the night before was now shaping into an encounter charged with promise.

Scott reached out to her, a silent beckoning. "Let's begin with the basics. Follow my lead, and never forget—you're in the driver's seat. Anything feels wrong, you just use that safe phrase."

Her fingers entwined with his, and she felt a wave of audacity wash over her. "I think you'll appreciate the choice I made for my underwear tonight."

His brow creased slightly. "So you considered the possibility of leaving with someone after the gala?"

"Absolutely," she lied. "Just because you rejected me yesterday didn't mean I was out of the game. What with my new look and all your flirtation coaching, I'm no longer a nothing to every man I meet."

"You've never been a 'nothing' to me," he said solemnly. "Always a 'something.'"

She slipped off her heels and set her purse aside. "Did you ever imagine me as your sordid little secret for one night?" The prospect of being in Scott Landshire's embrace, surrendering to the kind of passion that until now had been confined to the pages of her well-thumbed novels, sent a thrill through her. The woman she'd become under his tutelage didn't care if the doorman, the elegant woman from the elevator, or the entirety of Chelsea was privy to her indiscretion—though practicality nudged her to hope it wouldn't reach the ears of those who could sway her professional future.

But the rest of the city...sure, let them know.

"Not until just recently," Scott said, his nostrils flaring. "But once it lodged in my brain, I admit I've been unable to wait for us to go from being enemies to dirty-filthy lovers."

"Oh," she squeaked. The way he said those last three words in a gravelly voice turned her on like she'd never been turned on in her life. "Me, too." Would he expect her to talk dirty to him? She tried to recall some of her recent reads where sex had happened. What had the women said during those sex scenes? Of course, her brain couldn't recall.

He smiled, as if he knew her struggle. "Tomorrow, we'll go back to being adversaries hell-bent on beating the other in a winner-takes-all challenge."

"Exactly," she said, shaking away the worry. Tonight wasn't about impressing him with her dirty-talk skills. It was about him impressing her.

Scott swung open the door and stepped into his bedroom. "Luxury, this is my domain. When you're in here, I'm in charge. Do you understand?"

Lux's breath hitched, but before she could reply, he pulled her into his arms and covered her mouth with his, causing the anticipation that had been building inside of her for the last twenty-four hours to explode like Fourth of July fireworks.

"Open your mouth," he ordered against her lips, pulling her against him.

She did, and his tongue met hers in a heated dance of lust. "Holy wow," she murmured, feeling him grow hard against her. "Is that all you?"

He chuckled and took a step back.

She took the reprieve to quickly catalog the room. A king-size bed luxuriously done in dark grays; windows with a view of his neighborhood. A fat-bottomed lamp sitting on an end table, giving off a golden glow.

She inhaled to calm her racing heart. The air was thick with the scent of him, a mix of cologne and something undeniably male.

"I'm going to take you to places you've never thought to dream of, Doc," Scott said. "I'm going to make you forget every polite, gentle touch you've ever known."

His words caused her sex to clench and her panties to grow damp.

"You like that idea, don't you?" He reached out, trailing his fingers along her jawline, a touch that was soft yet promised more. "You want to feel what it's like to surrender completely to a man."

Lux's breaths were now coming in short gasps, her mind reeling. "Yes," she managed to whisper, her voice betraying the arousal that his words evoked.

Scott's hand moved from her jaw to her hair, gripping it just enough to tilt her head back. "Look at me," he commanded. "I want to see your eyes when I take you, when I make you mine."

Lux met his gaze. "I'm yours, Scott. Show me what I've been missing."

With a growl that was both primal and achingly sensual, Scott once again pulled her close, his mouth finding hers in a kiss that was nothing short of devouring.

Lux melted into him, her body aflame with need, her thoughts consumed by the promise of the bad girl sex she had requested.

The bedroom, with its subtle luxury and shadows, was about to become their world—a world where Lux would discover a new side of pleasure, guided by Scott's years of experience.

Lux's lips curved into a coy smile as she pulled slightly away from Scott, the heat of their kiss still lingering between them. "I'll admit, I didn't think it would be, but I'm not mad it's you who gets to take my new panties off me tonight," she teased, her voice a playful whisper.

Scott raised an eyebrow, his interest visibly piqued. "Is that so?" he asked. "Let's see if I'm not mad."

Expectancy hung in the air as he slowly lifted the hem of her dress, his fingers grazing her skin with a touch that was both gentle and suggestive. Lux's heart raced, the excitement of revealing her carefully chosen lingerie adding to the thrill of the moment.

But when Scott finally unveiled her new unmentionables, he burst into laughter, a deep, rich sound that filled the room.

"What?" she demanded, yanking her skirt out of his hand and smoothing the fabric back over her exposed body.

"Doc, this is your idea of sexy underwear?" Amusement danced in his eyes.

Heat crept into her cheeks. "It's... Yes."

"They're cotton," Scott said.

"So." What was wrong with a cotton thong? Too late, she recalled Isabella telling her that the cotton lingerie that had been added to her wardrobe were for day wear. The silk for night.

Scott leaned in, his lips brushing against her ear. "Oh, Doc," he whispered, his voice a mixture of humor and desire. "With every moment I spend with you, my idea of the perfect woman gets rewritten."

She tried to be upset, but instead heard herself laugh. "What? Did you just add: must wear silk underwear to your definition?"

"On the contrary. Cotton panties are now my new favorite thing."

His smooth words—words she believed—sent a new wave of heat coursing through her, washing away any embarrassment. She had him turned on. A thrill of confidence swept through her. Her journey into the world of bad girl sex was going to satisfy his cravings as much as it did her own. "If that's the case," she purred, "why am I still wearing mine?"

"Because when I take them off, I plan on enjoying every fucking moment."

"Oh." Lux melted into him, letting go and surrendering to Scott's overpowering charisma as his lips crashed down on hers.

When he pulled away, she whispered, "This is even better than the fantasy."

"Share with me the fantasy," Scott whispered, his breath a tender brush against her skin as he turned her around and slowly began undoing each of the buttons that ran down her back.

"We were at a bar. I was perched on a bar stool; you were lounging at a table. Our eyes met, a moment of electric connection, then I shyly looked away."

"And then what?" Scott asked, brushing his lips against exposed skin.

She giggled, the brush of his lips tickling. "I ordered a Screaming Orgasm, just to catch your attention. When I glanced back, I caught you still watching me, a hint of intrigue in your eyes." It was easier to weave her fantasy with him behind her, where he couldn't see if she blushed as she made stuff up. "I shifted, uncrossed my legs, and slowly recrossed them, allowing you to see up my skirt. To know I wore a black cotton thong beneath."

He groaned, sounding quite appreciative. "And then what?"

"You rose from your table and approached me with the confidence of a man who'd never heard a woman say no."

"You've told me no." He bit her shoulder as he pushed her dress over it, allowing the material to pool at her feet.

"Without a word, you offered your hand, a silent invitation to an adventure," she said, as he slowly turned her around so that she faced him wearing nothing but CAKES and a thong.

"And then what" he growled, reaching out to free her nipples.

She swallowed. "We left the bar and took the elevator to the top floor...to the penthouse. While riding the elevator, you pushed me against the wall, slipped your hand up my dress, and my clit rode your thumb." The last phrase came out sounding awkward. Had she said it wrong? No matter. He didn't seem to notice. "But before I found my release, the door opened, and you swept me up in your arms and brought me here...to your hotel room. Did I mention we don't even know each other's name?"

Scott gently cupped her face, his thumbs caressing her cheeks. "Then let's make your fantasy a reality," he said, his voice deep and seductive. "Alone in the room I stripped you of everything but your panties, pushed you against the door, and took your mouth in a kiss that didn't pretend to be nice." His mouth crashed down on hers. The kiss hard and delicious. Then he pulled back. "My hand found your wet pussy, and I pinched your clit through your cotton panties causing you to whimper and push against my hand."

When his hand did what his lips said, she moaned.

"Take your panties off," he ordered.

"But I'm a good girl," Lux said, not sure if his command was part of the fantasy or not.

"Not tonight, Doc. Tonight, you're a real bad girl. Now, take off your panties."

He cupped her sex, and she moaned. "Yes, sir." She wiggled out of them and handed them to him. "Now what?"

"Unzip my pants and pull out my cock." He held her panties to his nose and inhaled.

She fumbled with his belt but did as he said. The anticipation of what would happen next was unbearable, a sweet torment. Lux's eyes fluttered closed as she felt the full length of him in her palm. "Much bigger than in my fantasy."

He groaned, and his lips crashed down on hers, moving with a purpose that sent waves of heat coursing through her body. Lux leaned into the kiss, her hands finding their way to his chest, feeling the unsteady beat of his heart under her fingertips.

Scott deepened the kiss, his tongue tracing her lips before delving inside, exploring her mouth with a fervor that mirrored her own growing passion. The kiss was a dance, a perfect synchronization of desire and response, as if they were two parts of a whole that had finally found their match.

Lux's world narrowed down to the sensation of Scott's lips on hers, the taste of him, the feel of his body so close. The room, the outside world, her own doubts—all of it faded into insignificance in the wake of the overwhelming sensation of being kissed by him.

When they finally broke apart, breathless and flushed, Lux looked up into Scott's eyes, and saw in them a reflection of her own desire and excitement. "It's your fantasy now," she said. "What happens next?"

He walked over to the bed, grabbed a pillow, and brought it back to where she stood. He dropped it on the floor.

"I don't under—"

"Shut up, kneel on the floor, and take my cock in your mouth like a good little girl," he ordered.

His demand shattered her every thought of how this night would play out and replaced it with an image of reality. A dirty, filthy reality she was absolutely into. Had been since the first time she'd read a book where a variation of that order had been given by the dark hero. Ask any smut reader what the acronym S.U.G.D.O.Y.K.A.S.M.D.L.A.G. L.G. stands for, and they'll tell you: 'Shut up, get down on your knees, and suck my dick like a good little girl.'

Lux dropped to her knees. "As you wish, Your Highness." She took a moment to familiarize herself with his cock. As cocks went, it wasn't one to be ignored. Sure, she'd read about ones this big, but she'd never experienced one up close and in person. So...much...cock. She grazed her palm around it, and he hissed. "Do you like that?" she murmured.

He leaned forward and placed his hands on her shoulders, bringing his cock that much closer.

She leaned forward and put the tip of him in her mouth, teasing him with her tongue. His hands tightened on her shoulders. "I think you like that," she whispered against him, adding impishly, "I already grieve the day it falls off."

He fisted one hand in her hair. "I'd like it even better if you'd stop talking and took all of me into that dirty little mouth of yours."

The knowledge she could drive him crazy made her lightheaded. Licking her lips, she slowly slid them down his length, inch by magnificent inch—pausing at one point because...well, it was a lot of cock to swallow. Once her throat grew accustomed to something touching the back of it, she began sliding his cock in and out, all while stroking him with her hand. The pressure of his fingers in her hair let her know when she did something particularly well...like take all of him. And when she blew on him. And when she licked the length of him.

Suddenly, his hands were on her arms, and he was pulling her up and kissing her.

"But I haven't made you come yet," she complained.

"Fuck my mouth with your tongue," Scott said against her lips.

She obeyed, causing him to groan.

The lust between them sizzled the air with the heat it conducted. She'd never known it was possible to want a man so badly as she did in this moment.

"What do you want, Doc?" he asked against her lips, his voice a gravelly whisper.

The question dazed her. Never before had a man asked her that question, and for it to be a rake of all men... Tomorrow, next year, on her death bed, she'd have to reformulate her definition of a rake, because a man who asks you what you want couldn't be irredeemable. "I want—" She started to say *to be made love to*. But that wasn't dirty. That was vanilla. "You to fuck me."

Those words coming from her lips simultaneously took her breath and empowered her. Why not tell a man exactly what you want to feel good?

Scott's lips curled, and he made quick work of undressing and retrieving a condom from his billfold.

She smiled. "Always prepared."

"I'd be a fool not to be prepared for this moment."

"And what moment is that?"

"One of life's pivot points."

She blinked, and not because he suddenly had her in his arms and was carrying her to his bed. "Yours or mine?"

He dropped her in the middle of the massive mattress. "Mine."

"Like—"

Her question faltered when he straddled her and settled his buttocks on her hips, his erection large and proud. "You were asking?" He leaned down and placed a kiss in the curve of her neck.

"What kind of pivot point?" she gasped out as his lips traveled down to her breasts.

"The kind that changes everything."

He circled her nipple with his tongue and either her eyes closed involuntarily, or Manhattan had a momentary power outage.

"You think it will be that good, do you?" she murmured.

He raised up on his elbows, his beautiful eyes smoldering with heat. "The moment you first took me to task over one of my articles, I knew if the day ever came that I had the pleasure of pleasuring you, my world would be forever tilted toward the sun." He slid down her body and landed tiny kisses on the inside of her thigh.

"Wait. You thought about this way back then?" The mere idea caused her to swoon. But then her brain reminded her of the game at hand. "Or are we still role-playing?"

He didn't reply.

"Never mind. Dumb question." His pivot reply had been nothing more than the perfect thing for her fantasy man to say. Nothing more.

"You're thinking too much," he said, moving his kisses upward.

"Or I'm not thinking enough." She let go of the bedding and tried to think. To remind herself this was a one-night thing. "We're just a couple of adults, having a dirty one-night-of-role-playing stand."

"The only role I'm playing is that of a man lusting for a really, really bad girl." His tongue emphasized each really by licking her clit.

She put her hands in his hair. "Oh baby," she moaned. "I'm not just bad. I'm naughty."

Her confession was rewarded with long languid licks, and sharp flicking licks, and licks that unglued her ability to do anything but writhe in hot, wet pleasure.

"Being naughty is so much fun," she panted out. "I've never come being tongued."

He sat up and settled his penis against her opening. "Naughty girls aren't allowed to come until they've been punished." With those words, he slid inside of her.

The air whooshed out of her lungs. "Holy mother of happiness, I'm so glad that thing hasn't broken yet."

He gave a half grunt, half chuckle. "I'm serious. Punishment first, then I'll give you a holy-mother-of-happiness orgasm like none you've ever had. Do you understand?"

Yes, please. She pushed and wiggled against him. "I'm feeling so punished right now. Please, punish me more."

"Not this kind of punishment," he said, slowly thrusting.

"Then what kind?" she asked.

"The kind that leaves a red mark on your ass before you're allowed to come."

Her body shouted *yes, please!* But her brain wasn't on board. He was, in the light of day, the enemy. "Nope."

"Yes." He continued thrusting at such a delightful angle she was pretty sure she was going to come before their argument resolved itself.

"What if I come anyway?" she managed to ask.

He stopped moving. "I'm in charge. You will only come when I say you can come. Do you understand?"

She moaned. And considered her options. Play by the rules, use her safe word, or have an orgasm and not let him know. She decided on the last option. "Fine." Only he must have known her decision because he chose that moment to pull out.

He sat up. "Lay across my lap."

She swallowed hard. "Are you serious?"

"Look at my erection. Do I look like a man who wanted to interrupt sex to punish a very naughty girl?"

Now that she knew what punishment entailed, she bit down on the urge to make another joke. "No—"

He stuck a finger inside her and then ran his wet digit over her clit. "Nor do you feel like a woman who wants to argue instead of taking her punishment so we can resume our night of pleasure."

She huffed, sat up, and lowered herself over his lap. But only because he'd made a valid point.

His hand palmed her ass, and she squeaked.

"I haven't done anything yet," he said.

"If you let me skip the punishment," she bargained. "I'll play the part of your naughty Cinderella that you whisked away from the ball and let you come in my mouth." Thank God he couldn't see her face. Just saying those words made her feel...on fire.

He jerked. "Doc, as tempting as that is, I want to come in that tight little pussy of yours."

Before she could respond, he spanked her ass, and she cried out. "Fuck."

"Do you want to use your safe word?" he asked.

Once the initial shock wore off, she realized something. If she'd been turned on before, she was really, really turned on now. Who knew getting spanked could feel so damn sexy? "That wasn't very nice," she said in a pouty voice. "I wasn't done bargaining."

He spanked her again.

She groaned.

He spanked harder.

Her sex quivered in delight. "Now I feel the need to be extra naughty just to prove a point," she said, practically begging for the spankings to continue.

The next spank startled her with how hard it landed.

"Ouch." She scrambled off his lap and glared at him. "That one hurt."

"Jesus Christ, Lux," he said, pushing her back onto the bed. "You can't say something like that to a rake and expect him to respond like a prince." His mouth came down on hers in a hot, demanding kiss, while his hard cock slid inside of her, causing her to gasp.

Her last thought before she came the first time, but definitely not the last time, was that he'd called her Lux. Not Doc.

He was as rattled as she was.

CHAPTER 17

L UX, HER EYES STILL heavy with sleep and her body languid from the remnants of last night's lessons in filthy sex that had gone on for hours, stretched cautiously in the plush bed, noting the areas of her body that were not their normal perky selves.

Outside of the obvious area which hadn't seen any action in a very long time, her butt hurt, her leg muscles were sore, and her skin tingled from so much nipping, and nibbling, and the scraping of five o'clock shadow burn.

All-in-all, it was a night that could only be described as pivotal. Just as Scott had predicted. Pivotal in that it shredded the judgy love curtains she'd been hiding behind for years, leaving her with glimpses of other, viable ways to look at relationships.

Case in point, while she didn't fully buy into love at first sight, she was now facing the definite plausibility of love at first orgasm. A thought that both terrified her and... Well, no, that was it. Terrified for the win.

Reminding herself she was in charge of her thoughts and had the power to switch them to a new channel, she inhaled a deep breath of bravery. Exhaling her fear, she rolled over and reached for Scott. He'd get a kick out of her musings. After all, wanting to talk about last night would be a natural progression from their uninhibited exploration. A way to bring them back to some semblance of balance.

Her breath whooshed out. The other side of the bed was deserted. She patted the spot where Scott should be and found the sheets cool to the touch. Disappointment hit her in the stomach. "I hope you've gone to fetch me some coffee," she said, putting an optimistic spin on his desertion. Scott, the consummate charmer, could very well do something like that.

Then again, last night—perfect as it was—had been about fulfilling a fantasy. Her fantasy. A dirty-filthy-one-night-stand fantasy.

What would a rake do after delivering such a night? She threw her arm over her eyes to block out the harsh light of day as the answer came to her.

He'd slip away while she slept, avoiding any sentimental goodbyes or confessions. Being the heartbreaker he was, he would have learned that lesson over the years.

Knowing what she'd find before she ever searched for it, she leaned up on her elbows and made herself look.

There it was. The dreaded note left behind on the bedside table.

Maybe he really did go out for coffee, said the part of her brain still clinging to a sliver of hope that morning orgasms were in her vagina's future. She grabbed the note and flopped backward on his pillow to read it.

Mysterious Beauty,

Our shared night was a thrilling escape from the ordinary. A memory I will cherish.

Dawn calls me away. May fate smile upon us again.

The Man from the Bar

She twitched her nose to hold back tears and stared up at the ceiling. This was for the best. His being gone was a good thing. It allowed her to better process the hot mess of emotions currently clogging her throat without his witnessing any tears that might escape in the process. Bonus of all bonuses, his being gone prevented her from making a premature announcement of *I think I'm falling in love with you.*

Hell's fudging bells. That wasn't just some hysterical thought. As sure as she was a cognitive-based psychologist, Dr. Luxury Stone truly was on the precipice of falling head over heels for a rake. How was it possible she'd gotten to this point?

The answer was simple. She'd let her walls down and allowed herself to become vulnerable. She knew better. Her loins had been girded, and she'd permitted them to be ungirded by a makeover and a smooth-talking rake.

The question was had he left to neatly wrap up their fantasy, or had he left because that was his go-to move? In no part of her brain did she wonder if he'd left because he needed to work out his own thoughts of love for her. The guy was conveniently cursed not to have that emotion.

Where could she find herself a witch to curse her own heart? Because a heart cursed to never know love surely had the better deal in this scenario.

Seeking a distraction, she turned on the TV, manically flipping channels as her eyes filled with tears and her lungs filled with sobs.

That was until an image of the country of Shiretopia popped up on the screen and then panned to a news reporter who was live at an airport.

"In an unexpected turn of events at JFK this morning," the news reporter said, "The King and Queen of Shiretopia, who were rumored to be arriving on a private jet this morning, were notably absent. Instead, witnesses report that an unidentified woman exited the aircraft and made a concerted effort to hide her face."

The camera panned to a brunette, posed at the top of the stairs, scanning the crowd before waving at someone out of frame. Then it zoomed in, revealing a man standing outside the hanger, beaming back at her.

Not just any man. The Prince of Shiretopia. Lux's dirty, filthy lover of last night.

The woman ran straight into Scott's open arms, causing Lux to flinch. When he lifted the beauty and twirled her in a joyous embrace, Lux bit down on her tongue to keep from whimpering.

Lux's mind raced as she tried to piece together the unfolding narrative that had her reacting so irrationally. Scott wasn't the love of her life. Hell, he wasn't even the flavor of the month. He was just a man she'd had sex with in the midst of a winner-take-all challenge.

She refocused on the couple and tried to analyze the situation dispassionately.

The way they were looking at each other made it obvious—the two had a deep connection. One that stood in stark contrast to whatever moment in time Lux had shared with him.

"Speculation is swirling that she's the woman rumored to be betrothed to Prince Landshire," the reporter said. "Has Lady Rose come to once and for all tame the rake of Shiretopia?"

Lux stilled. *Rumored to be betrothed?* Since when?

Her phone buzzed, and she snatched it up, hoping it was Scott even while knowing it wouldn't be. He was still onscreen, intimately conversing with the woman. But maybe it was a text someone had sent on his behalf telling her not to believe what she was seeing. Telling her it was another publicity stunt.

It was a text from Ms. Birdie, inviting her for coffee.

"Coffee!" Lux snorted. She couldn't think about that at a time like this. Right now, she had a mystery to unravel. She glanced back at the television. Scott had his arm around the woman, and they were walking away from the camera.

"This just in," the reporter said, coming back on screen. "The Queen of Shiretopia has confirmed that the mystery woman is indeed Scott's betrothed. She was sent to America by orders of the king to tell the runaway prince the wedding date has been set, and it is time for him to come home."

Lux tossed the phone and again flopped back on the bed. "Mystery solved. Scott was engaged and never bothered to mention it." She closed her eyes, told her heart to stop belly aching like a damn teenage drama queen, her mind to stop spinning like a yoyo, and her body to hop off the damn merry-go-round she'd been riding on with her hands in the air like some type of damn daredevil ever since meeting Scott in person.

It was time to focus on what was important. Her career. She picked up her phone and reread the message from Ms. Birdie. There were two possible reasons for her to want to see Lux. One would be to discover if Lux had lined up a date with John—or, as Scott liked to call him, Corduroy. Last night's speed date who believed in insta-love and read to his grammy.

Two would be because she had news about the interview. That reason made more sense than the first. Had the committee made an early decision? Had there been something on social media last night that had swayed them before the challenge between Lux and Scott had ended? Before they knew if *Naked Runway* would go through with their threat to sue?

She opened up Instagram and searched #TeamRakeVSTeamDoc. Then she scrolled through the long, long, long list of posts.

One post, on Secrets of the City's account, caught Lux's attention. Secrets of the City posted on a variety of topics, anything from crimes not being reported, to secret marriages, to scandals within relationships. It was an image of Scott slipping into an elevator with twins.

She zoomed in on the image to get a better view of the ladies and saw far more than she wanted to see. The picture had been snapped in the lobby of this building. She recognized the door attendant. Which meant Scott had not only left the bar with them the night before last, but he'd also brought them home with him.

Scott had lied to her.

"I can't believe I fell for the whole publicity stunt story he spun." How many other women had he given that excuse to when he'd been caught red-handed cheating on them? Not that he'd lied to Lux because he was cheating on her. It's not like they were an item. They'd been a one-night stand in the making.

Which left her with only one logical explanation for the lie.

He had lied for no other reason than to further his chances of getting lucky...with her...all while being freaking engaged. Had the last nine months been his semester abroad? His time to sow his last wild seed before settling into his duties back home? Had his bride-to-be been given the same privilege? Lux damn well hope she had been hopping from bed to bed the way Scott had since coming to America.

Would last night be Scott's last hurrah before becoming a one-woman man? Was Lux his last sordid hookup? Had he known she would be? Had he chosen her to be his last? He must have, because he'd known to go to the airport this morning.

She didn't know if she should be flattered or pissed.

On the one hand, she was the woman 3,214 men had swiped past without a second glance, and here she'd gotten the Prince of Shiretopia so hot and bothered he'd chosen her vagina for his last supper...so to speak. That definitely suggested she should be flattered.

On the other hand, thanks to him, her catalog of sexual positions tried and achieved had greatly expanded. Wait...no, that would also go in the flattered column.

On the other, other hand, she knew—as sure as she knew life wasn't fair to plain Janes—she'd given Scott a piece of her heart. *Hell's fudging bells.*

She sat with that truth, letting it churn and bubble until sadness fermented deep within her belly, leaving a bitter aftertaste to her and Scott's heated encounter.

CHAPTER 18

THREE HOURS LATER, Lux stepped into The Whimsical Brew. The café's cozy warmth immediately enveloped her, a welcome respite from her chilly thoughts.

Thoughts she couldn't shake no matter how hard she tried to put them in clinical perspective.

She had dodged a bullet with Scott. Giving her heart to such a man would have been a recipe for disaster. Hell, he hadn't even bothered to send her a text.

Probably because he was too busy doing all the sightseeing things with his betrothed.

It was time for Lux to focus on the rest of her life, which meant she needed to finish the challenge. The way she saw it, she had three cards from three different gentlemen from last night's gala and three nights left to either prove Scott's methods would not land her a rake, or admit she was wrong.

Her plan was to go on a date with each of the men...starting with Corduroy. She'd call him as soon as her meeting with Ms. Birdie was over.

The familiar scent of espresso cinnamon tickled her nose, causing her to sneeze. She removed a tissue from her purse, blew her nose, and scanned the crowded room, pausing to notice the little quirks that made the cafe unique—the eclectic mix of vintage and modern decor, the mismatched but charming armchairs.

Her gaze finally landed on Ms. Birdie, who greeted her with a generic wave and a poker face. A shiver of unease swept through Lux. What was with the blank expression? Was Ms. Birdie upset Lux had left last night before the gala ended?

Pushing past her trepidation, she smiled and wove her way through the maze of tables, the chunky heels she'd chosen to wear with the sensible dress clicking ominously against the wooden floor.

Today had been her first walk of shame. That had been empowering in an uncomfortable way...especially on the subway. She was a strong advocate that women should never feel bad about spending an impromptu night at a guy's place. The philosophy in theory was lovely; in practice, it meant broadcasting your decision the next morning to anyone with any common sense.

She'd tried to disguise her walk as much as possible by borrowing a pair of gray sweats and a soft T-shirt from Scott's wardrobe, but there had been no getting around the necessity to wear her stilettos with the ensemble.

One simply did not wear hooker heels with sweats unless one had just left their lover's lair.

"Hello, Ms. Birdie," Lux greeted.

Ms. Birdie stood, an aura of elegance surrounding her. "Please, have a seat. Time is short."

Lux's heart skipped a beat. "I was surprised to get your text." Lux sat down, carefully placing her purse next to her using a bag magnet—germs were everywhere in Manhattan.

Ms. Birdie pushed a steaming cup toward her. "I hope you don't mind. I ordered you today's special—a caramel-infused latte with a hint of cinnamon. They're known for it."

Lux wrapped her hands around the warm fat cup, its fragrant aroma momentarily distracting her from her tension. "Then you've been here before?" She tried to sound casual. "It's quite inviting."

"This cafe and I have seen many a season come and go together," Ms. Birdie replied, her eyes briefly flitting around the room with a wistful look that spoke of memories and secrets.

Lux gave the room another glance, her gaze landing on a vintage poster on the wall. It was adorned with intricate, old-fashioned lettering that read *Spirits, Secrets, and Spells*. She rubbed her arms, a sudden draft bringing goosebumps to the surface. She glanced around. There were no open windows or doors. *Weird.*

"That poster...I feel like I've seen it, or something like it," Lux mused aloud. "Perhaps in another life." Once her brain caught up with what her mouth had just said, her cheeks heated. Unlike her belief in her nightmares coming true when spoken before breakfast, she'd made it a practice in life not to reveal her beliefs regarding reincarnation to casual acquaintances. It was one of the few things she and Mother agreed upon.

Ms. Birdie's eyes twinkled with a hint of mischief. "It's advertising a business that is just down the street. You might have walked past it without even knowing."

Lux chuckled. "That explains the chilling feeling of déjà vu. Have you ever frequented Spirits, Secrets, and Spells?"

Ms. Birdie, with a practiced grace, patted her red lips with a napkin, her jewelry clinking softly. "On many occasions. It specializes in the extraordinary and the arcane. Two realms I occasionally have a need for."

"I'm trying to imagine a single situation in which you would need the arcane," Lux said. The thought of Ms. Birdie, with her air of high society, delving into the world of the obscure was both intriguing and amusing.

"You'd be surprised how often those in my circle find themselves seeking peculiar solutions for unique problems," Ms. Birdie said, her smile hinting at knowledge not everyone was privy to.

"Such as?" Lux asked, leaning forward.

Ms. Birdie's expression turned cryptic, a hint of reluctance in her eyes. "That's a lengthy discussion for another day." Her tone was now more tart than sweet. Definitely not one that invited further nibbles of nosiness. "Shall we get down to the business of why I invited you here?"

Unease replaced Lux's curiosity. "I assume it has something to do either with the gala or with the interview committee."

Ms. Birdie leaned in, creating an intimate space between them amidst the bustling cafe. "Darling, when I sent you on this journey to prove you were right and Scott was wrong, I did so with the best intentions."

"But?" Lux asked when the woman stopped there. "There is a but coming, correct?"

"But," Ms. Birdie said, shadows of regrets in her eyes, "you know what they say about good intentions."

"The road to hell is paved with them," Lux finished glumly. "You asked me here to inform me I will not be given the position at Columbia regardless of how mine and Scott's challenge ends. My reputation is too tattered."

Ms. Birdie nodded, reaching across the table enveloping Lux's hands with her own. "Don't look so defeated. I haven't abandoned you. I've a new plan. An improved one."

Lux sighed, exhaustion making her shoulders heavy. An exhaustion that had nothing to do with how little sleep she'd gotten last night but everything to do with the emotional rollercoaster she'd been riding without a seatbelt. "I'm listening."

Ms. Birdie withdrew her hands and sat back, her posture regal. "It starts with breaking the curse that prevents Scott from falling in love."

Lux gave a half-assed derisive snort. She simply didn't have the energy to pull off a convincing one. "Why would I care about his curse if my winning will net me nothing?" What would she do next year? Where would she teach? Without permission or warning, a tear slid down her cheek. She quickly wiped it away.

"Darling, this is not the time to cry over wayward plans." Ms. Birdie paused and offered Lux a sympathetic glance. "It's the time to look at a new set of blueprints."

Lux frowned. Easy for her to say. Her life wasn't circling the drain. "I should have never gone to Frankie. This is all…"

"My fault," Ms. Birdie finished when Lux didn't.

Lux blew her nose. She wasn't a fan of the blame game. She was an adult, and no one had forced her to do anything. "I crossed a professional and on-air line. I have no one to hold accountable but myself."

"Blame is a fruitless endeavor," Ms. Birdie said, her eyes soft with empathy. "Right now, we need to focus on finding the best outcome for both you and Scott given the current news."

"And that would be for Scott to win so he has the option of keeping his position at *Naked Runway* should he decide to abdicate from Shiretopia." It wasn't until she spoke the words out loud that she even realized a pathetic part of her hoped that was his plan. That he would stay and choose her over his country and his duties. *Stupid. Stupid. Stupid.*

Ms. Birdie gave her a startled look but nodded.

"I see," Lux said. The Rake of Manhattan was absolutely not the right man for her. End of story.

Well...it wouldn't be the end of the story. No, Lux had no doubt she would someday be a footnote in some PhD's thesis. A thesis titled: Penis Gate. That time a professor blew up her career by publicly predicting the demise of a man's penis.

Ms. Birdie's gaze locked with Lux's. "I promise if you help me help him, I will find a solution for you that will surpass your dream of landing the tenure-track position at Columbia."

Lux offered a wistful smile. She liked Ms. Birdie. "I suppose I've nothing left to lose."

"Then you'll help break the curse?" Ms. Birdie asked.

Lux nodded as she allowed her analytical mind to kick into gear. "If it's a psychological curse, I could refer him to a therapist." And of course it was psychological. While this morning she'd entertained the idea of it being real, common sense said otherwise. Then again, common sense said her spoken nightmares before breakfast wouldn't come true either, yet they had up until her broken penis prediction. Neither it nor the analyzed version had panned out. "A good one could help him work through whatever's blocking him from accepting love."

Ms. Birdie chuckled softly. "Oh, my dear, it's far from psychological. His great, great and possibly another great grandfather managed to infuriate a wicked witch, resulting in a curse on him and all his first-born descendants."

Lux raised her eyebrows. Ms. Birdie was turning out to be far more intriguing and way less conventional than Lux had initially assumed.

"You genuinely believe in his curse? You don't think it's a fanciful tale Scott concocted to use as a pickup line in a bar?"

Ms. Birdie's grin broadened, showing off lovely laugh lines. "A wealthy, handsome prince like Scott doesn't need fanciful tales to garner attention. But really, how effective do you think a line like *I can't fall in love* would be in a bar?"

Lux leaned back. "There is a certain type of woman who's drawn to a man claiming his heart is irreparably broken. This type of woman is compelled to try to mend a man. Just as there is a type of woman who will fall all over themselves to prop up the man who complains his wife does nothing but tear him down."

"Interesting insight," Ms. Birdie mused. "But I can assure you, this curse isn't a figment of Scott's imagination."

Lux tapped her chin as she thought, her training at high alert. "But could a curse be an imaginative creation of the ancestor who supposedly first incurred the witch's wrath? His get-out-of-a-relationship-free card? And upon his death, the myth was passed down through the generations. And now Scott has simply accepted it as truth?"

Ms. Birdie leaned in closer, her expression somber. "He did not fabricate it, Lux. I have reasons to be certain."

"How can you be so sure?"

"That's where things get a bit tricky." Ms. Birdie's gaze shifted to a nearby table that had just become occupied. "It's getting rather crowded," she said in a voice barely above a whisper. "Shall we take a walk? Some fresh air might do us good for this part of the conversation."

"Where to?" Lux pushed back from the table and gathered her purse.

"You'll see," Ms. Birdie replied.

Once they were walking along the bustling streets, Ms. Birdie spoke. "Tell me, Lux, do you believe in the supernatural?"

This felt like a trick question. Hadn't they just been discussing the validity of a curse? "I don't disbelieve, but I can't say I'm a firm believer either. Why do you ask?"

"Because what I'm about to share will require an openness to the unseen, the unexplainable."

Why the hell not? "I'm listening."

Ms. Birdie took a deep breath, and Lux gave her a sideways look. What was so bizarre it required a steadying breath?

"A couple of years ago," Ms. Birdie said, "a dear friend of mine passed away. After her death, I was unexpectedly invited to meet with a young woman named Molly Thorn. Molly possesses...certain skills that are quite unique."

"Like what?" There were a lot of special skills that could fall into the unique category. Brain surgeon, professional ball player, encyclopedic knowledge of soap opera expert.

Ms. Birdie pulled her to the side and whispered, "She has a way of communicating with the dead."

Lux laughed before she could stop herself. "You met a medium?" She tried hard not to double down with a pudgy-judgy look—which should be easy considering what she did for a living—but must have failed if Ms. Birdie's pinched lips were anything to go by.

"She's not exactly a medium in the traditional sense, but for simplicity's sake, let's just call her that." Ms. Birdie waited for a couple to pass them before continuing. "I bring her up because when I discovered Scott's curse, I couldn't help but wonder if Molly Thorn could reach the witch responsible and negotiate an antidote."

"Negotiate with a witch's spirit?" Lux's tone failed to hide her incredulity.

"Yes, barter, if you will," Ms. Birdie continued.

"Was the bartering successful?" This was starting to sound like one of those paranormal romantic comedies Lux adored.

"As it turned out," Ms. Birdie said, sighing, "that particular wicked witch had already turned to dust, making contact with her impossible."

Was this the onset of a late-life crisis for Ms. Birdie?

"At least you tried," Lux said.

"Fortunately, Molly has quite the network in the second veil," Ms. Birdie added.

Lux had two options. She could steer the conversation away from the bizarre path they were traveling, or she could go all in and embrace the topic. She ignored the vanilla option and chose the fun one. "The second veil? Is that some kind of ghostly VIP lounge?" After just one short week with Scott, it appeared her taste in a lot of things had changed.

"According to Molly, it's a realm where spirits with unfinished business congregate," Ms. Birdie explained.

Then again, it would be negligent on Lux's part to avoid signs of a problem, just because she'd gotten a taste for what it was like to live your life not thinking beyond the moment.

"Ms. Birdie, are you sure you're feeling okay?" Lux asked in her Dr. Stone voice, half-expecting the woman to start talking about befriending Beetlejuice next.

"Yes, dear, I'm perfectly fine," Ms. Birdie assured her, a hint of exasperation in her voice. "I know it sounds outlandish. Maybe one day, I'll introduce you to Molly. Seeing is believing, after all."

"That would be...enlightening." And a hoot. Lux hoped Ms. Birdie followed through with that offer.

"Moving on," Ms. Birdie continued. "Molly sought out anyone related to the wicked witch who might know about the curse on the Landshire first-borns."

"And?"

"Well...not to bore you with the details," Ms. Birdie said. "She unearthed a rather helpful detail about all curses."

"Do tell," Lux encouraged.

"The antidote to any curse must always be hidden within ten miles of the newest of the cursed individuals."

"That is very thoughtful of whomever came up with the laws governing those who cast curses. It's like evil with customer service." How much money had Ms. Birdie paid Molly Thorn for this information?

"And the antidote must be hidden in plain sight," Ms. Birdie added.

Lux bit her tongue until the desire to laugh had passed. "This Molly Thorn is full of fascinating tidbits. I bet she's the life of every soiree."

Ms. Birdie smiled wryly. "The wicked witch who cast the spell on the Landshires used a loophole in the rules and broke the antidote into two sections. The Landshires discovered the first half. In short, it states the curse can only be broken by a certain deed performed by a woman who loves the youngest among them. Which, in our case, is Scott."

Lux's eyes widened in mock horror. "Don't tell me—that deed is oral sex. Am I right?" *Hell's fudging bells. Did I just say that out loud to this pillar of society? What is wrong with me?*

Ms. Birdie's lips tightened, her expression one of mild reproach.

"Sorry. That was crude," Lux quickly apologized. "What exactly is the nature of this deed?"

"The specifics remain a mystery," Ms. Birdie said. "That part of the antidote hasn't been discovered. But it's somewhere here in Manhattan within ten miles of Scott's residence."

"That's all you've got to go on?" Lux asked, not bothering to hide her skepticism in her tone or face.

"Not all," Ms. Birdie replied, tartly. "Molly received a cryptic hint from a good witch who is currently living in the second veil."

"Of course it was cryptic," Lux said. Cryptic was another word for vague.

"Cryptic," Ms. Birdie said, with sharply raised eyebrows, "because she's bound by a witch's code of conduct which frowns upon one witch interfering with another's handiwork."

"What was the hint from the good witch?"

"'*Peculiar is as peculiar does, she's hidden the answer just because. Seek within, where enchantment dwells, a place where secrets and magic swells.*'"

"That's it? That's the helpful clue?" Lux asked. "It sounds like a riddle from a children's book."

Ms. Birdie pointed to the quaint shop they stood in front of. "According to Molly, the answer is through those doors. But, as I've stated, only a woman truly in love with Scott can uncover the antidote. To all others, it will remain hidden. Which is why, despite my giving it a go, I was unable to locate the antidote." Her gaze lingered on Lux meaningfully.

Lux self-consciously touched her face. "What? Do I have whipped cream on my nose or something?"

After showering, other than a touch of mascara and lip gloss, Lux had not reapplied her makeup. Today, more than ever, she needed to feel like the woman she'd been before meeting Scott Landshire in person. The woman with a good head on her shoulders and a wall around her heart.

"Your face is fine," Ms. Birdie said. "It's your heart I'm looking into."

"You can see my heart?" At this point, Lux wasn't dismissing anything.

"Not exactly. But knowing Scott as I do, women can't help but fall for him. I suspect this has happened to you. And I suspect the sensible side of you is now searching for a way to prevent those feelings from growing stronger," Ms. Birdie said gently.

"What makes you think I don't want to love Scott?" Lux asked, a hint of defensiveness in her voice. "He's not a bad guy."

Ms. Birdie looked at her speculatively. "You mentioned in your dating profile that you're seeking a grounded man, someone who stays committed even when the initial charm fades," Ms. Birdie said. "Scott, with his history and charm, doesn't currently fit that description. That's not to say he won't eventually do the work to change. The question is, are you willing to risk your heart on that eventuality?"

Lux's thoughts drifted to her mother—a cautionary tale of love gone wrong. The idea of falling for someone like Scott—charismatic but potentially fleeting—was terrifying. Better to guard her heart now than face life-altering heartbreak later. "You're right. I may have given a section of my heart to Scott, but I can't—I won't—let those feelings take over my whole heart. It's too risky."

"Then you're the ideal person to break the curse," Ms. Birdie said, a trace of relief in her voice. "Going into that shop will empower you to protect your heart."

Lux furrowed her brow. "You truly believe the curse is real?"

"I know it's real," Ms. Birdie said without a second of hesitation.

Lux nodded. "I trust you. And if you say it's real, I believe you. That being said, how does my not wanting to love him make me the ideal someone to break the curse?"

"The contents of the spell were documented in the journal of the rake who triggered this curse. In one of my conversations with Scott, he recited to me the curse. It goes like this:

"'This curse I cast upon thee can be broken by a loving heart deed.

But she who unknots his loveless heart will never win his forever hea rt.'"

The weight of the revelation hit Lux like a ton of proverbial bricks. The curse was a cruel twist of fate, a heart-wrenching irony that a woman in love could break the spell yet never claim the love she liberated. "That's...incredibly sadistic," Lux muttered.

"Wicked witches are known for their merciless curses," Ms. Birdie nodded sadly. "You both will walk away from this with a heart that is forever bruised."

"Not both," Lux muttered. "Scott doesn't love me. I'm not sure he even likes me. Prince Landshire will walk away from this with his precious job and an unscathed heart—and apparently a betrothed waiting for him back in Landshire once he's sown all his wild seeds here in the States."

Ms. Birdie studied her. "First, the betrothed is the result of an arranged marriage. One Scott does not plan on fulfilling. That's why he left Shiretopia. He refuses to marry a woman he doesn't love."

"They sure looked like they were in love for the camera this morning," Lux said grumpily, even as she wanted to believe what Ms. Birdie said. Wanted to believe Scott wasn't a man who could sleep with other women while planning to marry another. Then again, he was a rake.

"Looks can be deceiving. Lux darling, I'm willing to bet Scott loves you. His heart just doesn't know it yet."

Lux scoffed. "Agree to disagree."

"Darling, how could he not? You're perfection for him." Ms. Birdie said, giving her a sad smile.

"I don't know about that."

"I do, and what I need to know from you is...does being told he's going to love you back as soon as the curse has been lifted—assuming it's not you who breaks the curse—make you want to change your mind? Or do you still want to ruin all chances of you and he ever being together—all in the hopes of your eventually finding a man who more aligns with your views of the perfect man?"

On the surface, the thought made her want to cry. But beneath the murky waters, all her reasons for not pursuing love with a rake, with Scott, were solid. When it came down to it, she wasn't a gambler. There was no such thing as a sure bet, let alone a bet where the odds favored a rake capable of forever love. Her best course of action was to find the antidote, give it to Scott, and remove any probability of the two of them having their happy ever after.

"Why do you believe the antidote is in this shop?"

Ms. Birdie gave her a sad smile as if she were a mother allowing her child to make a wrong decision so she could learn from her mistakes. "I've frequented this shop for years. After speaking with Molly on the matter, the vintage poster—the one you pointed out this morning—appeared next to my regular spot. Coincidence? Perhaps. Most likely, it was the Universe nudging me toward the answer to the riddle given to Molly by the Good Witch."

Believing in the curse was one thing. Wrapping her head around this Molly woman was proving to be harder. Everything sounded too convenient. "Molly gives you a hint, and then a mysterious poster shows up. That, to me, feels very much like a setup."

Ms. Birdie patted Lux on the cheek. "Molly Thorn doesn't need staged theatrics to prove her worth."

Before Lux could reply, Ms. Birdie pulled out her phone and made a call. "Carl, I'm ready."

"Aren't you coming into the shop with me?" Lux asked, a twinge of dismay in her voice. "How will I know if I find the antidote?"

"My dear," Ms. Birdie said. "Only you will know when you find it."

"Because I love him?" Lux asked.

Ms. Birdie nodded. "Now, I've done what I can do to help remove the curse from Scott and save you from falling for the wrong man. And, speaking of the wrong man, here." She handed Lux several cards. "These are John's remaining four cards. He wanted you to have all five. He very much wants to see you again."

"I'm not sure I want to see him," Lux said.

"The decision is yours, but let me just point out, he checks off all your boxes for the perfect mate. If those are no longer your requirements for the perfect match, I beg you to take a moment and consider what your new requirements are. It would pain me greatly were you to break the curse only to later discover Scott checks off all your new boxes."

"Oh, fudge no. In no universe will the Rake of Manhattan ever be that man," Lux said, wondering why her words didn't ring with more conviction.

"From your lips to your fairy godmother's ears," Ms. Birdie said.

"What?" Lux asked.

A sleek black limousine pulled up. "Nothing. Just the babblings of an old woman." Ms. Birdie stepped toward the car, then paused to give Lux a final look. "Remember, Lux, sometimes the most unexpected paths lead to the greatest treasures. Give John a call."

Curses, ghosts, and fairy godmothers...oh my. Lux's world might be in disarray, but nothing about it shouted boring.

Lux watched the limousine disappear into the bustling street and then turned toward the door of Spirits, Secrets, and Spells. But she didn't put her hand on the doorknob. Not yet. She needed to think first.

The last time she had followed Ms. Birdie's advice, it had led to unexpected complications. And this time, there was more at stake than a job.

Her heart was at stake.

A heart counting on her to protect it from being broken.

A heart counting on her to hold out for the perfect man to love.

CHAPTER 19

L ux stood outside the quirky store, her brain and heart in major conflict. While her brain kept playing the image of Scott at the airport with his betrothed in his arms, her heart kept shouting, 'But what if?'

So much had happened in so little time, and it had all begun when she had spoken about the importance of giving others a second glance. When she'd asked Manhattanites to stop judging on first impressions. When she'd promised to give the Prince of Shiretopia, and his column *RAKEish*, a second glance.

In the process, she'd discovered he wasn't all bad and his advice wasn't all wrong.

Bonus, she'd unveiled first-hand that he knew his way around a woman's body.

Of course, that last bit hadn't happened until after she'd changed her outer layer to better match his image. That's when they'd begun to click. That was knowledge she couldn't un-know.

She'd also discovered more about the curse. While Scott's mother had chosen to marry a man not in love with her, Lux wasn't cut from the same cloth. There was no way she'd say, "I do," to a man who wasn't madly in love with his bride. That would be ill-advised.

Not that love guaranteed happiness, but it gave a couple a fighting chance.

How much of a fighting chance was up to the two individuals. If they had done their homework and knew what they wanted in a life partner other than love, the chance was decent. If they hadn't, their chance of a happy forever was slim.

Curses and Ms. Birdie's statement that Scott had no intention of going through with the arranged marriage that awaited him back home—and let's not forget her prediction Scott would love Lux once the spell was miraculously broken by anyone other than her—aside, Lux had done her future husband homework, and Scott possessed none of her important requirements.

He wasn't reliable. He wasn't a homebody. He wasn't a lover of jigsaw puzzles. He wasn't a romantic—a romantic wouldn't have left the bed of one woman to hurry into the arms of another. AKA—he wasn't a one-woman man.

And yet, she'd somehow found herself on the precipice of loving him. And by precipice she meant one foot had fully stepped over the edge.

Which was why she stood outside of Spirits, Secrets, and Spells with every intention of entering. If she found the antidote to the curse and gifted it to Scott, according to Ms. Birdie, it would eliminate any chance of an entanglement between Lux and Scott because the curse had spelled out as much. It had gone something along the lines of: *The one who loved him and broke the curse would never be loved by him.*

She grabbed the old-fashioned knob, twisted, and tugged open the door. A melodic chime welcomed her. As she stepped across the threshold, she noticed the late morning sunlight streaming through the store's stained-glass storefront window. The rays cast kaleidoscopic patterns on plaques that hung from the ceiling directing shoppers to different areas of the store and illuminated dust particles that swirled like tiny, enchanted fairies in the air.

"Good morning. Welcome to Spirits, Secrets, and Spells," an elderly shopkeeper greeted, his voice a soothing melody that seemed to dance with the magical dust motes. "How may I assist you today?"

"Just browsing." Lux twitched her nose, which itched from the subtle scent of aged parchment and exotic herbs in the air.

The shopkeeper nodded, his long, silvery beard catching a glint of the sunlight. A black cat, sleek and graceful, leaped onto his shoulder, her green eyes shimmering like emeralds as she stared at Lux.

"This is Ms. Princess," the shopkeeper said, gently stroking the cat. "The two of you share the same unique eye color. She feels you are part of her clan."

"It would be an honor to be a part of her family," Lux said in good humor, watching, fascinated, as Ms. Princess jumped off his shoulder and onto the counter. Her movements were fluid, almost choreographed, while she edged closer toward Lux.

"Aren't you just as pretty as last night's sunset?" Lux cooed, scratching the feline behind the ears.

The cat purred loudly, then with a graceful leap bounded away, leading Lux's gaze to an area labeled *Spells*. When the cat paused mid-stride and glanced back at Lux as if to say, "Why aren't you following me?"

Lux did just that. "Coming."

"Watch your step as she shows you around," the shopkeeper said.

Each step Lux took seemed to echo with a soft heartbeat, as if the wooden floor beneath her feet lived. A sensation that bordered on eerie...or magical, depending on your mindset.

The cat jumped and landed on a heavily laden table, nearly toppling an ornate box off a pile of haphazardly stacked books.

It then turned toward Lux and mewed.

"Oh. You want me to pick that up?" Lux said, as if conversing with a cat was the most natural thing in the world.

The cat nudged the box with her head.

Lux picked it up and discovered it had a knob on its backside; realizing it was a music box, she wound it and then opened the lid. A haunting melody filled the room. One she didn't recognize, but the shopkeeper must have because he started humming along, his voice rich with nostalgia and unspoken stories.

Inside the box, under a cockeyed faux bottom, Lux discovered a folded showbill. She pulled it out and opened it. Her heart stopped beating as her brain spun in circles.

The showbill was from a Shiretopian performance. No way could this be a coincidence.

Lux flipped over the aged paper, almost expecting to see that a Landshire had performed in the musical, only to discover a recipe had been scrawled there. A recipe for love knots.

Love knots.

Interesting. The curse had spoken of the one who unknots his loveless heart.

"Is this the antidote?" she asked Ms. Princess, who sat licking her paws as if well-pleased with herself.

When the cat didn't reply—because of course she didn't—Lux took a picture of the recipe and tucked the showbill back into its secret compartment. Now what was she supposed to do? She replayed the curse.

'This curse I cast upon thee can be broken by a loving heart deed.

But she who unknots his loveless heart will never win his forever heart.'

Would the loving heart deed be accomplished by simply giving Scott the recipe? Or did it require her baking cookies for him?

To be on the safe side, she'd do both. And then Scott would read the recipe, eat a cookie, and boom...the curse would be broken, and his heart would be free to love anyone but her.

"Which is what I want," she said to the cat, which was busy giving Lux judgmental eyes.

When Ms. Princess continued with her look of reproach, Lux added, "Not that I expect you to understand, but for the good of my long-term happiness, I need all temptations of Scott to be removed from my life choices."

Ms. Princess continued to judge.

Sighing, Lux took a step toward the door, only to stop in her tracks when the cat meowed quite loudly. Lux turned and glanced at the animal, who still stood next to the box. "What?"

The cat meowed again.

"She wants you to buy the trinket box," the shopkeeper said. "Within it lies the answer to what you search."

"How does she know I'm searching for anything in particular?" Lux asked, her suspicions on full alert.

The shopkeeper shrugged. "Ms. Princess long ago went through her nine lives. She's now living in the second veil, where's she's been assigned the job of helping those like you."

"Like me?"

"That is all I'm allowed to know, but I trust you know the rest, or you would have never attracted her attention. She's quite finicky about whom she associates with."

"And how do you know she's a ghost?"

"I've seen her walk through walls. The question you're really asking is how I know Ms. Princess has a job in the second veil. I received that information from a medium who stopped in one afternoon not too long ago. A lovely woman. I believe she said her name was Molly."

Ms. Princess purred and pawed the box.

"Oh," Lux allowed her fingers to brush over the musical trinket box as she pondered his words. If she was willing to dispend her doubt as to the validity of curses, why not ghost cats with careers? Doing so could not hurt, other than diminishing her bank account. Not doing so could mean the difference between success and failure. "It is lovely." She could always give it to Scott as a wedding gift. Her way of proving to him that, even though a part of her loved him and that's why she could break his curse, she had no plans to wilt away from a broken heart once he was out of her life.

The cat nudged her hand with a paw as if trying to help her make the decision.

"It's the least I can do since you got me this far," she said to Ms. Princess.

Lux gathered the box and brought it to the counter. "I didn't recognize the song it played. Do you know its name?"

"I'm afraid not. The words just came to me," the shopkeeper informed her, his eyes reflecting a depth of unspoken knowledge. "When that happens, it's usually a sign of a shift in the universe."

A chill went through Lux...because of course one did.

Her purse pinged, causing both her and the cat to jump. Lux pulled out her phone and saw a new meme in which she'd been tagged. It was of a prince and a princess getting married. Instead of a crown on the princess's head, there was a frog with Lux's face imposed on it. The hashtag read: #Alwaysthefrog-nevertheprincess

"Rude," she muttered.

Four hours later, Lux stood in her kitchen, a fresh batch of love knots ready to be delivered. She'd burnt the first three batches. Not giving herself time to think about it, she sent Scott a text.

Can we meet? I have a gift for you. —Lux

Three hours later, he replied. Three freaking hours. In that time frame, she added another item to her list of things her perfect man would possess. Timeliness. He'd show up to things on time. He'd respond to texts on time. He'd say I love you at the correct time. Not too quickly. Not too late.

Meet me at the comedy club on Wooster at 9:00 p.m. —Scott

For a hot second, she thought about ignoring his response, because it dawned on her, in the eyes of all of Manhattan, she was now the other woman in this scenario. He was betrothed. Then again, she'd be doing that woman a favor if the love knots broke the curse.

A woman Lux had no doubt was already in love with him. How could she not be? The Rake of Manhattan was too charismatic not to give him the key to at least a piece of your heart.

CHAPTER 20

S COTT, SITTING ACROSS FROM Rose in the dim ambiance of Matt's Speakeasy Supper Club—where one had to belong to get a table—swirled his whiskey absentmindedly, his mind a tumult of thoughts.

Upon orders of the King of Shiretopia, Scott had been forced to flee his warm bed this morning, where Doc had laid languid and gorgeous and fuckable, to meet the royal jet. He'd done so only because Scott had been led to believe Father would be arriving.

That had been twelve hours ago.

Luckily, the cameras had been on Rose and not him, when he had realized he'd been duped. Father had sent Scott's intended bride to bring him home. A beautiful woman whose warm and generous heart belonged to another—Scott's best friend.

Once Rose had run into his arms and whispered in his ear to please play along, he'd done just that. No questions asked. He trusted her that much. Unfortunately, the paparazzi had followed them all day as they'd done the sightseeing thing for Rose—who'd never been out of Shiretopia—giving them no choice but to stay in character. Just like Frankie had spies everywhere, so would the King of Shiretopia.

Moles or not, Scott couldn't risk a plan that had been painstakingly laid out over the course of several years, just to pump Rose for quick answers. So, they'd played the long game. Twelve hours of pretending to be in love and thrilled to see one another.

But now, sitting in a private club, he and Rose were alone.

"We should be safe here," Scott said, glancing around the familiar room one more time. "Tell me what's happened."

Rose took his hands in hers. A move a lover would make. As the future queen of Shiretopia, she'd obviously learned over the years how to mask the true content of a conversation. "The Queen knows about me and Mark," she whispered. "And she's furious."

Scott's insides fisted. This was the worst news possible. The three of them could handle Father, but not his stepmother. Mildred was a force of ruthless calculation. "What has she done?"

"She's had Mark arrested. He'll be released once you return and marry me."

The news hit Scott like a gut punch. His threats of abdicating from the crown if Father did not release Scott from his duty to marry Rose had failed.

Anger rolled around in him, a storm on the verge of exploding.

"You're frowning." She laughed. "If we're being watched, that is telling."

Scott forced a smile as he moved to the other side of the booth so they could sit next to one another. He turned to face her, blocking anyone's view of his expression. "I can't believe Father would allow Mildred to go to such lengths. If word gets out, the optics will be bad."

Rose looped her hands around his neck and kissed him lightly on the lips. "He's been convinced by the Queen that the curse will punish you the way it punished him if you are allowed to find an avenue around it the way he did with your mum. She's persuaded the King that forcing you to follow through with an arranged marriage is the only way to protect you from future pain."

Scott let out a soft bitter laugh. "A curse that dictates the path of our hearts is medieval. Father was on to something when he tried to beat it by marrying Mum. A woman who made him feel different than all others he'd been with. A woman his gut told him would be his true love if not for the curse. He should encourage me to do the same. Although Father never knew the full emotion of love with Mum, they made it work. She accepted that flaw in him and loved him anyway. He should want me to find someone who makes me feel different. Someone who sees my flaws and shrugs because my unflawed parts are enough."

He thought of Doc, her fiery spirit, and how she challenged him to be a better man. A woman that his brain had been whispering, *she could be the one.*

"I agree, but you didn't see his face or hear his tone when he sent me to bring you home," Rose said softly. "There will be no leniency."

"I refuse to cave," Scott bit out while trying to not look like he wanted to commit murder. "We'll find another way. I realize Father is trying to protect me from future pain, but by doing so, he's sentencing you and Mark to broken hearts."

The server brought them their drinks and took their orders before either one of them said another word.

Scott raised his glass. In Shiretopia, it was bad luck not to toast. "To beating the patriarchy."

Rose bit her bottom lip. "I won't play Russian Roulette with the life of the man I love. We will do whatever it takes to free him." She clinked glasses with him.

"The life of the man we both love. He's my best friend," Scott responded. "Please tell me you have a plan that doesn't involve our ending up facing one another at an altar."

Rose leaned in and spoke softly. "Mother believes if we were to find the antidote that breaks the curse, it would make our marriage unnecessary, because the King would then—and only then—allow his first-born son the chance to find the love of his heart."

The burden of his family's legacy, and the curse's chains, weighed him down like an anchor. If an antidote was going to be found, it would have happened by now. "How does your mother know of our plan?" Scott asked. Was that how Mildred had found out? Had Rose's mother gone to the Queen?

"I needed someone to talk to, and she's always been my most trusted confidant outside of Mark."

"The antidote to the curse is nowhere to be found. The best detectives have searched for it and come up empty. I even shared the details of the curse with a friend who has unique sources not available to the rest of us, in the hopes that if anyone could come through, it would be her."

"And could she?"

He shook his head. "The last we spoke, no."

"Then you must come home with me," Rose said.

"And do what?" he asked.

"We'll get married but not consummate the marriage. This will allow our vows to be dissolved when the day comes that the antidote is discovered."

"And if it's not discovered in our lifetime?"

"I choose to manifest its discovery. I believe the antidote will be discovered before we're forced to say I do."

"Manifest?" That sounded like something Doc would believe in.

"If curses can happen, manifestations can happen," Rose said confidently.

His phone vibrated. He'd had it on do not disturb all day and didn't recall taking it off. He took it out and read the message.

I have something to give you. A wedding gift. Can we meet?—Lux

Fuck. Of course she'd been following today's media circus. She knew about Rose.

He reread the message and noticed it had been sent hours ago. He could only wonder what Doc been thinking or even imagining at being ignored for so long. He should have told Doc he was betrothed. Explained the situation. Without that information, she'd probably spent the day believing he'd known all along he'd be getting the hell out of their bed this morning long before she awoke and reuniting with the woman he supposedly wanted to marry.

He glanced at Rose. When it came down to it, he'd never allow his best friend to stay in prison. And right now, it looked very much like it had come down to it. "There's something I need to take care of before I return to Shiretopia."

Rose let out a soft sigh. "Then you will come back with me? You won't allow Mark to stay in prison? You'll give up your freedom for his?"

"We're the Three Musketeers. We protect one another. Of course I will," Scott said. Which meant he'd also give up Doc...for now. But not forever.

"And Scott?"

"Yes?"

"Mark has to remain our secret. Queen Mildred made it quite clear she'd banish him to a black cell where he'd never see light again if any hint of a rumor surfaced regarding our love. Please, promise me you'll tell no one...at least not until he's released, and we have a path forward."

"There's one person I need to tell—"

Rose's face went white as she shook her head. "It's not safe. Promise me you won't."

Scott's heart ached so much at the idea of what Rose was asking of him. A heart that couldn't love, shouldn't ache. Scott had no doubt Lux was his one. The one he was meant to love.

CHAPTER 21

A T TEN AFTER NINE, Lux stood outside the bustling comedy club, the neon sign casting a colorful glow on the busy street. She'd dressed carefully for the occasion—a pair of Judy Blue Jeans hugging her figure, a crisp white blouse that whispered of fresh starts, and black Chelsea boots, grounding her. Her hair was once again restrained in a ponytail—a symbol of the control she yearned to exert over her chaotic emotions.

Her face, though, told a different story. She hadn't stripped back to the bare essentials with her makeup. If she was to walk away from Scott, she wanted her departure to signify the confidence with which she chose to leave. Which meant she held her head high and her dignity intact. An image for her brain to replay to her heart when it tried to confuse Lux with thoughts of having walked away from the best thing in her life.

"Where in the hell are you?" she muttered, her phone offering no solace. His multi-hour delayed response to her first text, now coupled with his tardiness, gnawed at her. It would serve him right if she shucked the showbill with the antidote recipe written on it, along with the freshly baked cookies in the trash and left. Then again, giving them to him was more for her than for him. They were her one-way ticket to never having Scott return her love.

With a resolve that belied her turmoil, Lux pushed open the club's door, bracing herself against the wave of recognition that would follow. In the #TeamDoc vs #TeamPrince drama, she was the current favorite, though the internet's memes continued to paint a less flattering tale.

Pausing first to square her shoulders and lift her chin—an armor against the scrutiny—she marched toward the bar. Halfway to her destination, she found her path thwarted by a towering drag queen, wearing a tiara that rivaled the club's neon for brilliance.

She attempted to sidestep, but the patron's exuberant squeal stopped her.

"Dr. Lux Stone, in the flesh!" With a flamboyant flare, a hand flopped in front of her, sparking memories of the day she'd met Ziggy.

"Umm. Hello," she stammered.

"Eddy's the name, but you, doll face, may call me Eddy," he declared. "He, him."

Lux, confused by the privilege, nodded her thanks. "It's nice to meet you, Eddy."

"The pleasure is mine to wallow in," Eddy cooed. "Your show lights up my Mondays better than a disco ball at a drag queen bingo night."

"Thank you." Lux glanced around. There were both smirks and smiles aimed her direction from the onlookers listening to the exchange.

"You and your sass are all the rage with the Manhattan Knitters," Eddy said, unperturbed by the attention he drew. "We love to hate on that devilishly charming Scott Landshire."

"The Manhattan Knitters?" Lux asked, ignoring the mention of Scott.

Eddy turned and pointed to a table in the back corner where three ladies sat, all wearing tiaras that matched Eddy's. They greeted her with enthusiastic waves that seemed oddly charming amidst the comedy club's cacophony.

"It's always a pleasure to meet my listeners," Lux replied, her words feeling strangely hollow as she waved at the Manhattan Knitters.

"Is he here with you?" Eddy asked, his voice booming with curiosity.

"Who?" she asked.

"The Prince. The Rake. The deliciously handsome man you're schooling on the finer points of relationships. Just between you and all of Manhattan," he continued in a conspiratorial whisper, "we're rooting for you to win the challenge."

"Oh. You know about that."

"Honey, it's all Manhattanites are talking about. Which of you will stay in the limelight. Which of you will go."

Lux swallowed hard. It would be her who faded away. "We're hoping it doesn't come to either of us giving up what we love." She'd meant to say that to herself but must have said it out loud because Eddy gasped and slapped a hand over his mouth.

"I insist you come sit at our table and spill all the juicy details on the rake," Eddy ordered. "He's, like, our favorite character to dissect."

Feeling a mix of amusement and curiosity, Lux nodded. "I suppose I can join you for a bit while I wait for him." If Scott didn't want to be the topic of tonight's conversation, he should have shown up on time. The least he could have done by now was send her a text.

Eddy beamed and ushered her to the table, where his friends greeted her with cheers and excited whispers, immediately making room for her.

While Lux ordered a glass of wine, they shared stories and opinions with such passion she found herself almost glad Scott had stood her up. Within no time, she'd vowed to learn to knit and then fill out a questionnaire to join their exclusive club. They promised to give her serious consideration.

"Honey, let's talk hypnosis," Eddy said to Lux during a lull in the conversation.

The others at the table broke into giggles.

"What about it?" Lux asked.

"It's the one thing you've given Scott grief over that I simply cannot condone. I, myself, find the mind-bending practice to be quite delightful."

"Oh," Lux said. "I do as well…when used wisely." Perhaps if her heart hurt too much after she did what must be done this evening, she could turn to hypnosis to forget.

"But you see, your definition of wisely and mine are at odds," Eddy said.

"How so?" Lux asked.

Eddy ran his pink feather boa over his shoulders like he was about to start a strip tease dance. "I'm one of the subjects that was hypnotized on the evening of February 14th that prompted Scott's column that women might benefit from hypnosis to turn their shy ways into guy ways."

Lux frowned. "You were hypnotized into having on demand orgasms?" Her imagination couldn't even picture him up on stage doing what Scott had described in his column. "And you're not livid?"

"Oh, doll face," Eddy said. "I will take orgasms on demand twice a day every day." He flicked his hand through the air as he spoke, drawing her attention to his bracelets and rings and pink nail polish. "I knew what I was getting into when I went on that stage. No one exploits Eddy. Not anymore, anyway."

"Is it true, then," Lux said, still trying to wrap her brain around what Eddy was saying. "You had orgasms…in front of the audience!"

He dropped his knitting and leaned toward her. "Honey, if I didn't want to be talked about, I wouldn't wear white before the first day of spring." He placed his hand over his mouth while fluttering his crazy long, pink eyelashes. "Or dress drag. Or volunteer at an after-midnight comedy club to be hypnotized."

"Enough about Eddy," said Abby, one of the club's founding members and owner of a nearby yarn store. "Lux, for your sake, we're all hoping like hell you are as allergic to commitment as Prince Landshire is. We'd just hate to see you get hurt."

"Umm. Hello," Eddy said. "We were talking about Eddy—"

"Don't mind him," Wendy, the president of the Manhattan Knitter's club, said. She sported a low ponytail, ragged sweatshirt, and jeans. "His boa has been in a tinsel tangle ever since his off-Broadway production was cancelled and replaced with a naughty version of Cinderella as a nod to Prince Landshire moving to America and choosing Manhattan as his new home, thus our fondness of flaying the man."

"How awful," Lux said to Eddy, forcing herself to contemplate how hard it would be to learn to knit and absolutely not allowing herself to recall Scott's comment about adoring his Naughty Cinderella who wanted to swallow.

"Trust us, he has plenty of other irons in the fire," said Annie, the only non-founding member of the club. If Lux recalled correctly, she was a lawyer.

"You know, Lux, you make me wish I was in college just so I could take your Psychology of Your Twenties class," Abigail said in a thick southern drawl. "God bless my hometown, but it did not prepare me for the intricacies of meshing adulthood with knitting needles that double as secret weapons and cozy mystery novels that turn out to be more real than I ever imagined."

The others gasped at her, and she looked sheepish. "Pardon my blathering. That was overshare. Ignore me."

Lux frowned. "Do you stumble upon dead people often?"

"More times than I can count on one hand anymore," Abigail said with a straight face.

Lux, who'd been expecting an *I'm joking* response, gasped. "Really."

"Oh, sugar pie," she exclaimed, her voice tinged with a mix of shock and amusement and syrup. "I have just revealed more than the bosses allow."

"I'd say," said Eddy. "Not that I'm ever again going to rat you out. I learned my lesson last time."

Abigail giggled. "Pay him no mind. He thinks just because he had a chat with some of my people, he's suddenly on their hit list. I mean, it's not like they have a hit list or anything."

As if Abigail's people had been conjured and were here to place Lux on a hit list, someone touched Lux's shoulder, causing her to yelp. Turning, she breathed a sigh of relief to discover it was Scott and not a hitman. His presence was as commanding as it was belated.

"Scott, you made it," Lux said breathlessly, her heart still pounding from the fright.

"I'm sorry I'm late," he said.

"Darling, you're beyond fashionably tardy," Wendy said, her voice cutting through the conversation. "You're rudely behind schedule, and our Luxury deserves better. Especially from a man who's been two-timing her all day long."

Lux felt every pair of eyes at the table urging her to demand the respect she was due.

"You're right. She does," Scott said with a grimace. "Doc, I've procured a table for two over there." He pointed to the opposite side of the room. "If you'll just give me a chance, I'll explain everything."

Lux stood. "Thank you all so much for keeping me company this evening," she said to the Manhattan Knitters, before tucking her hand in the fold of Scott's arm and allowing him to guide her away, the warmth of his touch a bittersweet contrast to the rehearsed coldness of her impending speech. "Where's your friend?" she asked, only to be interrupted by a waiter.

While Scott ordered a bottle of wine, Lux casually memorized him—the tilt of his head, the promise of his smile, the depth of his gaze. These were details she could tuck away deep in the sanctuary of her heart. Remnants of a love not meant to be.

CHAPTER 22

SCOTT GATHERED HIS THOUGHTS as he poured the wine, while Doc sat across the table, studying him like he was a bug pinned to a board as part of a science project. "I take it you've been watching the news today," he said, handing her a glass. "And you're aware of the latest rumors that I am party to an arranged-marriage contract back in Shiretopia."

"Are arranged marriages really a thing?" she asked stiffly.

"They are in Shiretopia." He could only imagine how little she thought of him at this point. He'd done exactly what she was afraid all men eventually do...leave a woman for another. She must view him as a complete shit, believing he'd slept with her last night while willingly betrothed to a woman back home whom he'd planned on meeting at the airport this morning. "I owe you an apology for not telling you about her."

She snorted. "You owe me nothing. We're not an item. We had a one-night stand. Nothing more. If you owe anyone an apology, it is your bride-to-be."

"You're wrong. We have an understanding."

Doc narrowed her eyes. "An open relationship?"

He swallowed. "Doc, return to Shiretopia with me, and I'll explain everything." The request was unplanned and selfish. Yet, he allowed it to hang between them.

Doc's laugh, when it came, was short and harsh. "Why would I do that?"

"Isn't that obvious?"

"Not in the fucking least."

He opened his mouth to explain, but no words spilled out. Hell, he wasn't sure what the answer was.

"Forget it," Doc said. "Your why doesn't matter, because I have no desire to attend your nuptials to an open marriage." She did air quotes around the last two words. "And then allow you to set me up as your tart on the side."

The pain in her voice gutted him, and he reached out, hovering his hands over hers, waiting for a sign it was okay to touch her. "I want you to return to Shiretopia with me because last night wasn't just a moment—it was meaningful."

She pulled her hands back and picked up her glass. "How can that possibly be when your heart doesn't work?"

"Because long story short, last night, you cracked something inside of me."

She gave him a what-the-fuck look. "I'm going to need the long story," she snapped. "The short version makes zero sense. Unless you're telling me I cracked your penis and it has fallen off. That would make total sense and let me just be the first to say...I told you so."

He groaned. "Damn it, Doc. My cock is fine. What I'm trying to say—and failing at miserably—is that even though I'm not capable of love, if I could, you're the person I'd want to give my heart to."

"That's pretty and all, and just might make some women swoon at your feet, but your heart doesn't work, so your words mean jack."

"Not jack. Last night, being with you caused a crack in my heart which allowed my soul to slip out."

"I'm to believe rakes have souls?"

"Of course we have souls. And you have a soul. And I believe our souls have mated, and that's why I feel what I'm feeling toward you. Just like what happened when Father courted Mum."

She glanced down at her wine. "And how many times have your ancestors used that particular line on women over the years?" While her words were blasé, the thickness of her voice told him she wasn't as unmoved by his words as she'd like for him to believe.

"I deserve your skepticism, but it's true. It's like every minute I've spent with you has chipped away at the curse holding my heart hostage and last night, you cracked it." He reached out, placed his hand under her chin and raised it so he could see into her eyes. They were stormy with emotions as she stared mutely at him. When a tear fell down her cheek, he wiped it away. "You've disrupted my status quo, and I'm not mad about that."

She sniffed. "Let's say I believe you, which I don't, but if I did, you still haven't said why you want me to return to Shiretopia with you."

"My hope is if I bring you home and tell Father you're my I'll-give-up-everything-for-her person, he'll not force me to go through with the arranged marriage."

She sniffed again. "But if the king says no, you won't actually give up everything for me. Correct?"

He reluctantly shook his head thinking of his friend sitting in prison. An explanation sat on the tip of his tongue, but Rose's plea for him to keep her and Mark's love a secret, prevented him from giving one. Mildred never made a threat she wasn't willing to keep.

"That's what I thought." Lux jerked away from his touch.

"Not because I don't want to," he added quickly. "But because there are other factors I must take into consideration. Why don't we take a walk, and I can try to explain better."

She shook her head forcibly. "Not necessary. You see, I get it," she said. "I really do. You know why I do? Because there are things I also must take into consideration as well. Which is why I asked to meet with you tonight." She opened her purse and pulled out a wrapped pastry and pushed it toward him.

"What is this?"

"It's the antidote to your curse. Eat it, and your heart will be freed from its bondage."

Her words caused his head to spin. "I don't understand."

"Ms. Birdie told me about your curse and recruited my help to break it."

"Why would she involve you when she damn well knows…"

"Knows that the woman who brings the antidote must be in love with you," Doc said when he sputtered to a stop. "And the woman must give you the antidote while knowing that by giving it, she will never receive your love in return."

"Then you do love me?" Joy swept through him. He wasn't the only one feeling the strong connection between them. "You're crazy if you think I'm going to consume the antidote knowing you love me. Mother and Father were happy even without the antidote—we can be as well."

"Scott, while I admit you own a small section of my heart, let me be clear as to why I'm choosing to give you the antidote," she said in her Dr. Stone voice. One all business. "You see, by doing so, I know it guarantees you won't love me back. And that's what I desire."

"You want me rendered forever incapable of loving you?" He was so confused.

"Yes. That way, I won't have to worry about doing something stupid—like lowering my standards when it comes to the type of man I want to spend the rest of my life with."

Pain ripped through him like a white-hot poker to the heart. "That makes no fucking sense. You love me, but you don't want me? Is it because of Rose? Because I've told you—"

"It's because you're not the right man for me," Doc said coldly.

Trying to find the calm he needed, he exhaled hard, but didn't succeed. Too many emotions were detonating inside of him. Anger, fear, hurt, more fear. "You seriously don't want my heart, because I don't meet your preconceived notions of the perfect man? Bloody hell, if it means that much to you, I'll start wearing corduroy jackets and attending lectures on college campuses."

"It's more than that." Her lips trembled, and she bit down on them.

He reached for her hands again. "Doc, please—"

She yanked her hands away. "You're not the type of man who will ever be happy with just one woman. It's not in your DNA. I know that. You know that."

"I know nothing of the sort, and you know nothing about me as a boyfriend. All you know about me is what *Naked Runway* has allowed you to know."

She scowled. "What does that mean?"

"It means I'm under a nondisclosure clause with them. I've not been allowed to mention my bride in waiting—"

"That's a very convenient NDA."

"And my contract with *Naked Runway* requires me to date a different woman every week."

"In other words, between your NDA and your contract, you were given a license to be a serial dater. Always the flirt, never the deep stuff. Eat the damn cookie, already."

He thrust the love knot back at her. "I don't want this. I want to love you even if you don't want to love me back."

She shook her head. "That's the stupidest thing I've ever heard. When I leave here tonight, I'm walking away from you forever. I'll go on remaining rake-dates per our agreement with Frankie, and then I'll never look back at this episode in my life."

Bollocks. "Who are you going on dates with? Have you already made the dates?"

"It doesn't matter who, and yes, they're made. I'm serious about not wanting you. Now, eat the cookie. Go back to Shiretopia, tell your father the curse is broken, and then do whatever it is you and your bride-to-be decide to do from there."

He slammed his palm on the table, causing those around them to glance their way. He took a breath and leaned toward her. "Doc, please change your mind."

"Scott, I don't know what you're feeling, but we both know it's not love."

"It's not nothing," he muttered.

"Have you even taken a good look at me tonight? This isn't what you fell in love with. You fell for the false eyelash wearing, big hair, tight pants woman. You and I both know that's not the real me. The real me is girl next door at best."

"The real you is a person who doesn't think I'm good enough for her," he said quietly.

"Scott, I want a man who is a homebody. One who doesn't blink when I tell him I want to learn to knit."

Scott blinked. Wasn't that a pastime for grandmothers?

She rolled her eyes. "And one who attends conferences on things like the Annual Meeting of the Linguistic Society."

"Doc, if you want to learn to knit, I'm down with that. Hell, I'll even learn. And if you want a conference goer, let's do it. Let's go to one together. In fact, there's one coming up in a month in Vegas I was to attend for a column. It's called the: Geeky Kink Event. Come with me."

The mention of kink caused her to blush, and he pushed on, wanting to keep her off balance until he could talk some sense into her. "Do you think this professor you dream of will do half the things to your body I did last night?"

"You're not going to change my mind," she said. "Anyone can learn to be good at sex. I'm taking the safe path to a happy ever after. And the safe path is a man with all the markers of relationship security."

His phone dinged, and he glanced at it. His time was up. For Mark's sake, he had to get on the plane and return to Shiretopia. He took one last shot at knocking Lux off balance in the hopes of making her see sense. "I never saw the delightful woman who busted my balls from day one to be a coward."

"If it makes you feel better to call me a coward, I can live with that." She pushed the cookie toward him. "Please, eat the cookie before you leave."

"You're sure you won't change your mind?" Scott asked.

"You're not the man I want to love," Doc said without a moment of hesitation.

Anger and hurt fired through him. "Fine." He shoved the cookie in his mouth and stood. "I hope Corduroy makes you happy."

Tears welled in Lux's eyes. She fumbled with her purse and pulled out some type of box and a program and handed them to him. "Here. I found the recipe for the love knots inside this music chest. It's written on the back of that showbill. I believe the box was made by a Shire-topian woodworker. Consider it my wedding gift to you and your betrothed."

He took the item with one hand, wrapped his other around the back of her neck and pulled her in for a hard kiss. "Goodbye, Doc."

CHAPTER 23

TWO HOURS LATER, THE plane took off with no paparazzi on the ground snapping images of them.

Settled in a comfy seat, Scott closed his eyes and focused on the moment. Shouldn't he be feeling absolutely nothing for Doc by now?

The woman he thought was the one for him didn't want him. Without an ounce of uncertainty, she'd labeled him not good enough.

"Are you excited to finally be able to fall in love some day?" Rose asked. "Perhaps, even with me if we're forced to get married and stay married?"

"That's the thing. I don't feel any different than I did before I ate the cookie. I don't know what cockamamie story Ms. Birdie told Doc, but that bloody pastry wasn't the antidote."

Rose let out a soft sigh. "Maybe it just takes a while to activate."

"Maybe."

"I'm sorry about Lux not wanting you," Rose said. "From everything you've told me, she balanced you out."

"The problem is I don't balance her out. Or more to the point, she doesn't want balanced out by me," Scott said, his words sounding bitter even to his own ears. "Doc wants the scales of her future tipped heavily to the safe side."

Rose leaned forward and patted him on the knee. "Not every woman is brave enough to love the wrong man."

"What are you saying? Do you see Mark as the wrong man for you? I thought you loved him."

Rose nodded. "He's wrong in the sense he's not you, and my destiny has always been to marry you. I knew the moment I felt an inkling of love for Mark, I should bolt. That loving him would break my heart."

"But you didn't. You weren't a coward. Neither of you were. You both chose to follow the path of potential heartbreak, anyway. Just like Father and Mum."

"We did."

"Why?" If he understood, perhaps he could convince Doc to do the same. Then again, why would he ever beg a woman to see him as good enough? What sort of foundation was that with which to start a marriage?

"Because I'm a romantic," Rose said, giving him a soft smile. "I truly believed love would conquer all, and Mark and I would have our happy ending."

He scoffed. "And therein lies the problem. Doc is a pragmatist. Every decision she makes is based on facts and probabilities."

Rose picked up the jewelry box he had handed her the moment they'd met at the airport and turned it over in her hands. "I wonder if a descendent of the wicked witch has been moving this and its contents from one location to another all these years."

"Probably," he muttered, still thinking of Doc.

Rose chuckled. "Wouldn't it be wild if you know the current witch in charge of the box and just don't know it?"

"I'm sure that would be a possibility if the container had actually held the antidote. But it didn't." Scott understood why Doc had believed she'd found the antidote. A recipe for love knots found on the back of a piece of paper that originated in Shiretopia had been a perfect red herring.

"I think Lux giving you the antidote was actually an act of love wrapped in words that made her able to do it," Rose said.

"What?"

"It took an act of courage on her part to give you the antidote knowing you wouldn't love her back. She told herself the lie to make it easier to do the selfless deed."

"I appreciate your trying to spin it into something romantic, but we both know that would never actually happen. A person who loved me would have been happy with part of me versus none of me."

"Not true. A smidge of me has always loved you, and I would happily give up any chance of your ever loving me back—even knowing we're probably going to end up married—if it meant your being out from under this damn curse."

"You love me?"

"Don't get your ego too inflated. It never grew into anything more than puppy love. But sure. Of course, I love you. You're quite lovable."

He huffed out a sigh. Why had he never picked up on that? "I'm certain if I were capable, I'd have the same kind of love for you. As it is, I think of you as a kid sister. AKA, a pain in the ass," he teased.

She wound the knob and opened the musical box. A beautiful song spilled into the cabin. One they both recognized. The Shiretopian Wedding Anthem.

Scott scowled. Of course, that's what it would play.

Rose smiled softly and sang the lyrics. Her voice so beautiful he would have sworn an angel lived inside of her. Peace fell over Scott even as the plane hit turbulence. He laid his head back, closed his eyes, and soaked up the moment.

When the singing faded away so did the rocking of the plane. Scott opened his eyes and glanced at Rose and felt...a weird emptiness.

This is how eating the cookie should have made him feel toward Doc. Not one of his best friends. What in the hell was going on? Was this depression settling in? Doc had done a show once on how those going through depression often struggled to feel the happy emotions. And how the negative emotions were amplified.

"Are you okay?" Rose asked. "You're so pale."

About to respond, a new emotion engulfed him. One he'd never experienced. One that conjured stars and images of Doc's face tilted up in laughter. He closed his eyes to rid himself of the picture. Told himself to forget the woman who didn't want him.

Something painful shot through him.

He snapped opened his eyes and glanced around the cabin. "I'm not okay," he answered. "I think I'm having a mental breakdown."

"Are you thinking about Lux?" Rose asked.

He nodded. Thoughts of never seeing Doc again, of her marrying her professor, of her spending a lazy Sunday afternoon knitting with anyone other than him caused a wave of emotion to well inside of him. Emotions he had no idea how to handle.

Was this what love felt like? This had to be love. Not just soul love but mind and body as well. But how could that be? The cookie hadn't worked. If it had worked, he'd not love Doc. It would be her, not Rose he felt an emptiness toward. Unless—

Claustrophobia grabbed him by the throat, making it hard to breathe. He frantically glanced around as his brain spun what-ifs.

What if the curse was defective?

What if it had mutated over the years?

What if what they thought they knew about the curse was wrong?

What if the one who loved and gave the antidote was the one who would become free of love? Lux had given him the antidote, thus she'd quit loving him.

And what if the one under the curse would be able to love, but in doing so would lose the one they loved forever, and thus, giving the wicked witch her ultimate revenge? That would be him. He'd been under the curse. He was the one who could now love the one who would never love him in return.

A revenge with no antidote.

It wasn't like a wicked witch could be trusted to tell the truth.

Rakeish

CHAPTER 24

O NE MONTH AGO, Lux had said her forever goodbye to Scott.

Since then, she'd completed the Win a Rake in Eight Days challenge by going on dates with guys from the Flirtation Gala, without Scott there to coach her.

The first date had been with the idiot who had asked her to be his mistress.

The second with John. Or, as Scott called him, Corduroy.

The first date had lasted all of one hour before Lux had left him sitting in a bar cleaning up the Bloody Mary she'd poured over his head—that, after he'd reached out and pinched her nipple on a whim because that's what filthy rich guys do. Asshole.

On the second date, instead of leaning in for a goodnight kiss, John had pulled out his phone and shared with her his latest Instagram post. In it, he'd declared his official love for Dr. Luxury Stone.

Thus, Frankie had claimed victory for *Naked Runway*, and the fashion magazine had spun the story, painting Lux's new beau as a rake in sheep's clothing. A rake who'd approached her as a fumbling professor in order to win her over.

It was a narrative that Lux had found both amusing and frustrating.

Date three with John had happened only after he'd promised to tone down the whole insta-love thing.

Much to Lux's delight, John had not only kept his word on that, but he'd also thrown himself into getting to know her. Hell, he'd slowed things down so much, he'd yet to even pressure her for sex.

Tonight was date eleven with John. He'd brought her to a small Italian bistro.

"Have I mentioned how lovely you look tonight?" He topped off her wine.

"A couple of times," Lux responded, her fingers tracing the stem of her wine glass, pulling her thoughts back to the present.

The light from the candle flickered across her date's thoughtful expression, highlighting the premature gray in his hair. John, a renowned figure in academia, exuded a kindness she'd always sought in the man of her forever romance.

She reached out and placed her hand on his. "I get the feeling you want to say something but aren't sure if you should."

"You're not wrong," he said ruefully.

"I promise not to overreact." The night he'd shown her the Instagram post, she'd slammed her door in his face and refused to return any of his calls for three days. Then she'd realized it wasn't him she was mad at. It was herself, and she'd answered his next call. They'd talked, she'd set her terms about premature declarations of love, he'd agreed, and they'd made up. "And I won't stomp out in a temper."

He sat back and chuckled good-naturedly.

She liked that about him. It was one of the many things she liked about him. Sure, he wasn't anywhere near as handsome as Scott, and his body—what she could feel of it when he hugged her good night—was softer than the rake's. And his kisses didn't produce butterflies in her stomach. But those things didn't matter. What mattered was he was safe.

"I've been offered a position at Harvard." The slight tilt to his chin told her just how excited he was about the opportunity. And why shouldn't he be?

"Wow," she said, a tiny bit of envy causing her voice to pitch high. "That's incredible."

"I agree," he said in what she'd come to think of as his trademark lack of humility. That was something he had in common with the rakes of Manhattan.

"Why would you be afraid to tell me that?"

"In my discussions with the committee," John said. "Your name came up as my probable future fiancée."

"Oh." They were back to that again. Damn.

"They're quite keen on having me join their faculty and are willing to create a position for you as well." John continued to watch her closely. "It's a rare chance, Luxury. A dual appointment at Harvard."

Harvard was the dream for many in their field, a pinnacle of academic success. Yet having the offer tangled with his mention of their probable future marriage tied a knot in her stomach.

Telling herself not to overreact, she paused and checked for any flickers of excitement at the idea of someday saying yes to him. Any glimmers that her heart understood the assignment. Fall in love with a safety-net guy.

There were none.

And that aside, the idea of securing a position at Harvard—as a sweetening of the pot for John to accept his offered position—left her feeling undervalued, her achievements reduced to mere leverage.

"Harvard is impressive," Lux conceded, her voice steady despite the contradictory emotions she felt. "But I'm not comfortable making a career move just to be part of someone else's negotiation."

John's eyebrows rose slightly at her response, a mixture of surprise and admiration flickering in his eyes. "That, my dear Luxury, is why I was nervous to bring up the topic. But no matter how you get your foot in the Ivy League door, it's a strategic move. You'd be part of one of the most esteemed academic communities in the world. And it would certainly help put the whole Scott Landshire debacle behind you."

Lux gave him a tight smile. Was her social media presence what had provoked him to apply at Harvard? A desire to remove the woman he wanted to marry away from the place where everyone knew her as Scott Landshire's foe?

"Thank you for considering me, John, but I must decline," Lux said, her words measured. "If I were in love with you, it would be different. I'd jump at your offer. But don't let me stop you from taking the position. In fact, I insist you go."

His lips tightened ever so slightly. "Without you?"

She nodded.

John shook his head. "I never stood a chance against him, did I?"

"There is no him. My saying no to you has nothing to do with Scott."

John motioned for the check. "Then I guess this is it."

"I'm sorry, but you deserve a woman who is as crazy about you as you are about them." And she deserved a man who would fight harder than John had just done to get her to change her mind. Like Scott had. Only not Scott.

Two hours later, Lux, wearing pajamas and a clay mask on her face, sat in her apartment preparing for her final radio show. One she'd entitled: Hypnosis for the Broken-Hearted.

Unfortunately, her scattered thoughts made it impossible to compile her show notes.

Not that she was surprised. It was hard to concentrate when show note number one had the words written on it: Admit you fell in love with the Rake of Manhattan. Note two: Go public with how the Mr. Insta-Love relationship had gone. Note three: Moving forward.

What would moving forward look like?

Her gut told her to try hypnosis, thus the title. Only her heart rebelled at the idea of being stripped of its memory of loving Scott.

It didn't help that her thoughts kept drifting to the broadcast of Monday Musings she had done right after Scott had left. It had been a tumultuous episode, filled with raw emotions and candid revelations. She had publicly admitted she'd been wrong about Scott as a person, dispelling the misconceptions she had once fervently broadcast.

In that same episode, she had spoken of John—Frankie had insisted she do so. It had been a bittersweet situation to find herself in. While she appreciated having a wonderful man like John crazy for her, her time with Scott was a melody that refused to quietly fade into the night.

Lux's fingers tapped a rhythmic beat on her desk. Monday's broadcast would be her opportunity to share her growth and her realizations one last time. It would be her moment to step out of the shadow of *RAKEish* and *Naked Runway*, to forge her own path, independent of the narratives others had woven around her.

Had she grown? Were there any startling new realizations for her to share? She was not the same woman who had started that show—she was someone stronger, wiser, and, for the first time in a very long time, ready to embrace her feminine side.

The question that remained: would she ever trust her heart on an unchartered path when it came to love? Or would she always be the woman who looked for the safe route?

Which left her with a decision. Yay or nay—hypnosis for the broken hearted.

As she was about to flip a coin, a knock at her door interrupted the moment. It was times like these, she wished her building had a doorman.

For a hot second, she allowed herself to imagine that it was Scott knocking at her door. And when she opened it, he would tell her he had a broken heart—not penis—and would she please help him fix it. That was how the dream that started it all had been analyzed. In her sleep, Lux's brain had conjured a man like him wanting a woman like her to ease the truth of her reality and the whole dating app debacle.

CHAPTER 25

S COTT STOOD RIGIDLY AT the altar, his hands clasped so tightly he was losing feeling in his fingers. The chapel, adorned with the finest silks and flowers, felt less like a venue for a joyous union and more like the grand stage for his personal tragedy. He could hear the soft rustling of the guests, the quiet anticipation of the crowd waiting for the grand event to unfold.

Behind him stood his best friend, Mark, anxiety and distress emanating from him and coating Scott in misery and regret. If ever there was a man who did not want to be a best man, it was Mark. But to not have him stand up with Scott would have caused talk because everyone in Shiretopia knew they'd been best friends since preschool.

Their plan for Scott to flee Shiretopia, thus allowing Mark and Rose more time to find a way for their happy ever after, had failed. Not that

Mark or Rose blamed him. They'd all known their plan was thin; they just hadn't realized how thin.

Scott turned and glanced at his friend, who gave him a tight smile.

The solemn notes of the wedding march reverberated through the chapel, each chord resonating with a sense of finality in Scott's heart. As he watched Rose, a vision in white, glide down the aisle on her father's arm, the reality of the moment hit him with the force of a tidal wave. The veil delicately draped over her face did little to conceal her tear-stained cheeks, a poignant reminder of their heart-wrenching conversation just moments ago.

As the priest's solemn voice filled the hallowed space, the age-old question hanging in the air, "If anyone here knows any reason why these two should not be wed, speak now or forever hold your peace," a weighty silence enveloped the room.

Scott's pulse quickened, a rush of adrenaline flooding his system. He'd forgotten about this pivotal moment in the ceremony. If only they had thought ahead, planted someone in the crowd to voice an objection...

His eyes darted desperately across the sea of faces, searching for a savior, a chance, a miracle. He couldn't help but think of Ms. Birdie, whose fearless spirit would have boldly challenged the royal decree. Unfortunately, she was not in attendance and could not come to his rescue. A twist of fate had delayed her arrival.

Beside him, Rose's quiet sniffles pierced the silence, a subtle re-minder of their shared plight. Scott reached out, his fingers intertwin-ing with hers in a silent promise of solidarity. They had agreed to a temporary alliance—a marriage in name only, a facade to weather the storm.

In the quiet aftermath of their union, they would seek their mutual freedom.

Rose's fingers tightened around his, her watery smile barely visible through the veil. Scott, ever the gentleman, discreetly handed her his handkerchief, a small act of kindness in their shared charade.

The priest's voice, grave and unwavering, brought Scott back to the present. Each word seemed to echo from a great distance, his thoughts adrift in a sea of memories. Memories of Doc—her vibrant laugh, the fierce spark in her eyes, her unyielding spirit. She had been a constant challenge, a thorn in his side, and yet, in removing that thorn, it had embedded itself irreversibly in his heart.

Now, as the moment to recite his vows drew near, a sense of suffocating panic set in. His mother's words echoed in his mind, a mantra for him to always follow his true North. Yet, how could he have ever chosen to go back for Doc and rekindle her love when his best friend's freedom hung in the balance, a pawn in this royal game?

The priest turned to Scott. "Scott, repeat after me. I, Scott," he began, initiating the binding vows.

Scott's throat tightened, his voice a mere whisper lost in the grandeur of the moment. He knew the weight of the words he was about to utter, the invisible chains they would forge. "I, Scott," he echoed, his voice barely audible, a reluctant echo in the hushed chapel.

"Take thee, Rose," the priest continued, oblivious to the turmoil churning within Scott.

"Take thee, Rose," Scott repeated mechanically, each word a heavy stone in his heart. He was playing his part in a script written by others, a script that betrayed his true feelings.

"To be my lawfully wedded wife," the priest concluded the phrase, a final step toward sealing a fate Scott never wanted.

Suddenly, a soft, pain-filled sound escaped from Rose, a note of distress that resonated with Scott's own inner turmoil. It was a sound that shattered the façade, a crack in the perfect image of the royal wedding.

That very sound seemed to trigger something in Mark. With a sudden burst of resolve, he stepped forward, his voice cutting through the tense air. "Stop. I can't stand by and watch this happen."

The priest, taken aback, turned to Mark. "What is the problem, my child?" he asked, his expression a mix of confusion and concern.

"I'm in love with Rose." Mark's confession hung in the air like a thunderclap.

The chapel, once a scene of royal decorum, erupted into a cacophony of whispers and gasps. Guests turned to one another, their expressions a mixture of shock and intrigue.

"He's lying," Scott said. There was no way he would allow Mark to take the heat. If anyone was to be painted the villain, it would be him. "He's just saying that to get me out of this wedding. The truth is, I'm in love with another woman. Madly in love. That is why Rose is crying."

Mildred, the wicked queen, stood with a regal yet cold demeanor. With a dismissive wave of her hand toward Mark, she commanded, "Take him away."

The guards began to advance toward Mark, but before they could lay a hand on him, Rose's voice, strong and unwavering, pierced through the chaos. "I would rather face death than marry a man in love with another!" Her declaration echoed through the chapel, a fierce testament to her own heart's truth, and silenced the room with its intensity.

The Queen, undeterred, fixed all of them with a cold, unyielding stare. "It is the will of the King that this union take place. None of your feelings matter when weighed against duty and tradition." This was Mildred's ultimate revenge against Scott's mother. To show no mercy for her son. For Scott.

Scott's temper took over. The absurdity of it all—a wedding where both the bride and the groom's hearts belonged elsewhere—was overwhelmingly clear. "As the future King of Shiretopia," he said, speaking directly to Mildred, "I declare you wrong." He then glanced at those in attendance. "The desires of Shiretopia's future king shall not be dismissed so easily."

"Future kings have no say in current matters of the country," Mildred said coldly. She turned toward her husband. "Tell them I'm correct, King Landshire. Tell them this wedding will go through as planned."

"Father?" Scott said. "Will you have me marry a woman whom I feel nothing for? A woman whom all of Shiretopia now knows is in love with my best friend?"

The King, his voice, seasoned with age, resonated with a quiet authority. "We are not barbarians, intent on forcing unions upon those unwilling. This should never have reached such a point," he acknowledged, casting a sympathetic glance at Scott and Rose. "If neither wishes to proceed with this marriage, it can be halted, provided there is proof that the curse afflicting the Landshire lineage has indeed been broken, thus allowing my son to know the emotion love."

"Father, is my word not adequate?" Scott asked.

"The time for your marriage is upon us, my son. If there is a woman who holds your heart, let her take Rose's place," the King decreed.

"That can be arranged, but I must first return to Manhattan to win her heart," Scott protested.

"I planned for such an outburst during this ceremony," Father said. "As such, I've arranged for you to win her heart here and now in front of all of Shiretopia." He gestured toward the chapel doors. "Let her in."

As the doors swung open, Doc stood there, looking outrageously out of place yet strikingly beautiful. Her emerald eyes were wide with shock, her blonde hair tousled as if she had been caught in a whirlwind. She was clad in mismatched pajamas—the bottoms had images of books on them, the top a mismatched, oversized T-shirt—one of his. On her feet, mismatched fuzzy slippers. One pink. One black. Yet even in this disheveled state, there was an undeniable charm about her that made Scott's heart trip all over itself with the urge to escape and run to her side.

Doc's eyes darted around the chapel, taking in the opulent setting, the expectant faces, and Scott standing at the altar. "You kidnapped me from my apartment to witness your wedding?" The absurdity of her attire in the midst of the grandeur of a royal wedding struck a note of humor amidst the tension, eliciting a few stifled chuckles from the crowd.

A scoffing noise from the queen drew Scott's eyes toward her.

"You can't seriously be considering allowing her as the next queen of Shiretopia!" Mildred said to the King. "She looks no more fit than that shrew—"

"Enough," the king bellowed.

The queen's words trailed off into a venomous hiss as she glared at Doc, her disdain palpable.

Doc glared back. "I'll have you know I was very comfortable in the privacy of my home until two men showed up and brought me here against my will." She paused and gave a proper huff of exasperation. "So, excuse my lack of royal attire. They didn't even let me pack my Jimmy Choos."

Scott's heart swelled with admiration as Doc faced the queen's contempt with fiery determination. Despite her bewildering and abrupt arrival, clad in pajamas that were a stark contrast to the regal setting, she exuded a strength that defied her casual appearance.

"You are perfectly perfect as you are," Scott told Doc.

A murmur of approval, mixed with a few suppressed smiles, rippled through the assembly. Scott couldn't quash a wave of pride. Doc, with her unapologetic authenticity, had captivated the room, earning admiration from everyone present, including himself.

Scott's gaze shifted to his father, who stood silently, observing Doc with an expression that bordered on respect. "Father?" Scott prompted, seeking his response.

The king seemed to emerge from a contemplative state, nodding slowly. "Indeed," he said, his voice resonating with a newfound acknowledgment. "The future queen's mettle is not measured by her dress, but by her character." His words, affirming Doc's worthiness, were in sharp contrast to the queen's superficial judgments.

"Could someone please tell me why I'm here?" Doc's voice cut through the tension.

Scott's attention was drawn back to Doc, who stood defiantly amidst the chapel's opulence. She'd loved him once; he'd do whatever it took to win her heart again. "Dr. Luxury Stone, a part of my body is broken, I need for you to please put it back together."

Her eyes widened, and her gaze swung down his body and then back up to his eyes and too late he realized his folly. But before he could correct her misunderstanding, she spoke.

"Hell's fudging bells. I thought...but my analysis...it must have been wrong. Gah. I warned you, my nightmares come true. I mean, of course, in my dream you came to me, but it stands to reason—with such a medical condition you're in no shape to travel, and thus my need to come to you. How did it happen? How did you break your—"

A guffaw came from Mark. He knew.

A snicker came from Rose. She knew.

"Scott," the king said, cutting off Doc's babbling, a hint of amusement in his voice. He knew. "You've got ten minutes."

CHAPTER 26

Lux's heart thudded erratically as she stood in the grand chapel, a bewildering mix of opulence and chaos swirling around in her. Scott's mention of a broken body part reverberated in her head, her eyes darting involuntarily down his frame before snapping to his face. According to her dream interpretation, it had been a broken heart he'd brought to her in hopes she could mend it. But...given the antidote, that was no longer viable...so then...it must truly be—

"If he's saying I have ten minutes to fix your broken penis, that's not going to be enough time," she blurted out. "I might be a doctor, but I'm not that kind of doctor. I'm not a penis doctor. I'm a brain doctor, and despite your brain seemingly residing in your penis since puberty, I don't have the foggiest idea how to repair a broken...you know. *Penis.*" She gestured vaguely. "I told you my nightmares come true. You should have believed me. But no, you just had to insist on my telling you about your impending broken penis before breakfast!"

Scott's face turned a shade of red that could rival the finest of rubies. "For the love of all that's sacred, will you stop saying broken penis?"

"Sure," she said. *Penis. Penis. Penis.* "I can see how my saying broken penis is traumatizing. My apologies. No more mentions of...your penile predicament. But—"

Laughter emanating from the altar interrupted her sentence. Rose was now in the comforting embrace of another man, presumably from the wedding party, and the two of them were laughing. Lux glanced back at Scott. She had the very real feeling a soap opera was unfolding right before her eyes.

Scott's expression had shifted from embarrassment to amusement. "If you're quite finished, let me assure you and—all Shiretopia—that my penis is just fine. My penis is magnificent. I have the healthiest penis one could ever possibly hope for. It's my heart that is broken."

"Oh." She grappled to make sense of what he'd said. "Oh," she echoed again as realization struck, releasing a sudden urge to either run or kick somebody. "So...this isn't about your penis at all?"

He smirked. "Maybe a little bit. It doesn't seem to be interested in anyone but you."

In the short time between her removing any chance of him ever loving her, he'd fallen in love with another and had gotten his heart broken in the process. Had he found himself in love with Rose, only to learn she didn't love him back? Had Lux just walked in on him being dumped at the altar? She glanced back at the woman in question. All signs pointed to yes.

But what did any of that have to do with her being hauled unceremoniously from her warm home to Shiretopia?

Unless the king was pissed she'd broken the curse, consequently shattering his son's heart.

"I am a citizen of the United States," she declared, her voice firm, trying to grasp at any semblance of control in this absurd situation. "I have rights. If you've dragged me here—"

Before she could continue her indignant proclamation, Scott reached out, his hand encircling her arm. With a gentle yet urgent tug, he guided her away from the prying eyes of the chapel and into the privacy of a small dressing room.

"Doc," he began, his voice unsteady but resolute. "Before you say anything else, let me explain. The antidote to the curse didn't work the way we were led to believe it would. Instead of me not loving you, I love you greatly. Which is why, if you've been wondering, you were so easily able to stop loving me."

"You love me?"

He nodded. "So much it broke my heart not to have you love me back."

"That can't be."

"I can assure you I'm telling you the truth."

"The truth doesn't make it less scary."

"I know you're more interested in a safe choice, but if you'll gift me the chance to revive your love, I promise to never stop loving you and never stop proving to you that it is possible to reform a rake."

"Scott, will you shut up and let me talk?" Lux said when he paused for a breath.

"Yes, dear."

"I didn't stop loving you. I love you so much I was considering hypnosis to get over it."

"But how can that be?" Scott said.

"I don't know. It was your curse. Your antidote. What happened after you ate the love knot?"

"I got on the plane, gave Rose the box you gave me, she sang the words to the music..."

"What? What happened next?"

"There was unexpected turbulence and when I opened my eyes, I had a strange sense of emptiness toward her."

Lux gasped. "Do you think the singing of the anthem was the actual antidote? That the recipe was a red herring?"

"God, why didn't I think of that possibility? I just assumed my sudden nothingness toward her was all tied up in my brain rebelling against my being forced to marry her. I assumed my emotions would return. I even shared what I was feeling—or more like not feeling—with her."

"And what did she say?" Lux asked.

He smiled ever so slightly. "Rose is a born optimist. She said she'd won me over once with her wit and charm and lack of taste in friends, and she'd do it again. She forbade me to give it another thought."

"And how did that make you feel toward her?" Lux asked, putting on her psychologist hat?

He rolled his eyes. "Doc, are you analyzing me? Now is not the—"

"Shut up and answer the question." She tossed in a smile to soften her stern tone.

He sighed. "It made me like her."

"So, you went from nothingness to like?"

He nodded, a thoughtful expression on his face. "Yeah."

"Then maybe she's right. Maybe she will win you back. Which leads me to this question, and please just give me a freaking honest answer. Do you really love me? Or is this a scheme to get out of marrying Rose so she can marry another?"

"Not a scheme. Now it's my turn to ask the questions," he said earnestly. "Doc, do you see yourself ever seeing me as good enough?"

Lux's breath hitched as she shook her head. "Do you see yourself ever being satisfied with just one woman?"

"Absolutely." Scott reached out, taking her hands in his. "I know this is sudden, and I know—on paper—I meet none of your qualifications. I know you're so certain I'm wrong for you, you gave me what you thought was the antidote to the curse as a protective measure for your own heart."

"And with good reason," she mumbled. "Pretty words of love don't change the man you are. A rake not capable of living life as a one-woman-man...of that, I'm certain."

"About that," he said. "I've recently learned something about certainty. It's a mental sensation, Doc. It's not evidence of fact."

She processed his words. What if, in all her certainty he was wrong for her, she'd been wrong? Just like she'd been wrong about the advice he'd given in his column and had had to admit that to her audience.

He stepped closer, the space between them charged with unspoken emotions. "Life, it turns out, is full of surprises. What we're certain about one day can change the next. And I'm standing here, asking you to reconsider what you think you know about me, about us."

"I—"

"Wait. Let me finish. There are things you don't know. Things you deserve to know." His eyes searched hers. "I'm not the same man who first arrived in Manhattan. I've grown, I've changed. While working for *Naked Runway*, I wasn't able to reveal that to you or anyone else because my contract with them was to lead the life of a rake to up my ratings. But most of what you were certain I was doing because that's how it appeared in the news was all smoke and mirrors. Not truth."

"You didn't bring the twins to your place?"

"I did, and then they immediately slipped out the back."

"That night when I was standing outside the bar, and you arrived in a limo and exited, and chose ten beautiful women—"

"The women were all part of an advertising campaign."

"Scott. I'm a hot mess. I'm not glamorous. I don't want to be glamorous. I want a man who will love me when I'm old and wrinkled and no longer eye-candy capable."

"Darling, don't you understand? I love all of you, but especially what's inside of you. I won't deny I find you sexy as hell, but that's not why I love you. It's just a bonus."

"Wait. I just realized something. You're standing here asking me to fix your broken heart. Aren't you?"

He nodded.

She grinned. "You know what that means? It means, my nightmare has come true."

"The hell it did?"

"Well, the analyzed version did."

He gave her a measured look. "And what was that?"

"The penis symbolized your heart, since that's where the heart of most men resides. So, you didn't bring me your penis to fix but instead your broken heart. And I dreamed your heart got broken because that would be poetic justice for a man who lived his life as an unapologetic rake."

"You little minx. You could have put that version out to the public a long time ago."

She giggled. "Where would the fun in that have been?"

A smile tugged his lips.

"Scott," she said, her expression sobering. "What did your father mean when he said you had ten minutes?"

"My best friend is in love with Rose and she, him. The King has declared I must get married today. It will either be to her or to you...the woman I love."

She blinked. "Today?"

"I know I'm not good enough for you, but I promise to work every day for the rest of my life to change that fact."

Lux couldn't explain it, but right then, she saw Scott for the man he was, not the man she'd branded him to be in her mind. When her heart whispered, *we love him,* she didn't try to shut it down. She embraced its wisdom. A tear rolled down her cheek. "It's I who should work every day to deserve you. I can't believe I told you that you weren't good enough. Scott, I love you like you're my last breath."

He pumped his fist in the air as if he were a man who'd just won a freaking trophy. Or a trophy wife. "You've just made me the happiest man in the universe."

"The Rake of Manhattan. A closet romantic. That's a plot twist no one saw coming...especially not me."

As they stood there, hand in hand, the reality of what would soon unfold hit her—she was about to get married in a royal chapel, in her pajamas, to a man who had just upended every notion she had about love and certainty.

And she wouldn't have it any other way.

Scott leaned in, his lips brushing against hers in a kiss that sealed their promise—a promise of a new beginning, a journey of love that they would embark on together, rewriting their story one page at a time.

Epilogue

THREE MONTHS AFTER LUX and Scott's impromptu wedding in the grand chapel of Shiretopia—while she wore mismatched pajamas and he a tuxedo—their life had settled into a delightful rhythm, swinging between the vibrant energy of Manhattan and the serene majesty of his country. Scott's future as the King of Shiretopia was secured, but until it was imminent, he was allowed to live the life of a royal with dual citizenship. His column with *Naked Runway* would come to an end with the next issue.

Tonight, Manhattan buzzed with the celebration of their union, hosted by *Naked Runway* and the ever-spirited Ms. Birdie. The venue, a stunning fusion of European elegance and Manhattan's modern flair, was abuzz with excitement and laughter.

As Lux mingled with the eclectic mix of guests, she caught sight of Scott across the room, sharing a laugh with a group of friends. Two of them being Mark and Rose. Rose, as it turned out, had been right. She'd won back Scott's affection in absolutely no time at all, which probably had the wicked witch who'd cursed the clan twitching in her dusty remains.

Lux met Scott's gaze, and a silent exchange of happiness passed between them.

Amidst the revelry, Lux watched as Ms. Birdie approached, her eyes sparkling with mischief. "Lux, darling, I've got a surprise for you," she announced with her characteristic flair.

"I find that hard to imagine," Lux said, grinning. "You're normally not one for surprises."

"I'd like to introduce you to Molly Thorn," Ms. Birdie replied, her lips twitching. "The friend I told you about with contacts in the second veil."

"Ms. Thorn, it is so nice to meet you," Lux said, shaking hands with the woman.

Once Lux had agreed to go to work for Ms. Birdie as the CEO of the Fairy Godmother Project, life had gotten even more interesting than marrying a rakish prince. At first, she'd resisted the idea of leaving academia, but Ms. Birdie had made an excellent case for why she should. Mainly, Lux would be able to put her psychology degree to use as she helped people experiencing life's struggles. And since Lux had just come out on the bright end of a life struggle, she could relate to those going through something hard.

"I insist you call me Molly," the spirit whisperer said. "After all, we'll be working closely together for the next several weeks."

Lux glanced at Ms. Birdie. "Is that so? I wasn't aware I'd been given an assignment. I thought my job was to oversee all the on-going missions." The position allowed Lux to know about all of those who'd been helped so far by Ms. Birdie's group of merry busybodies. For instance, Isabella had once been an assignment of the FGP, and Scott had been known to help the organization on occasion.

"That was the plan, but Molly just called in a favor," Ms. Birdie said, looking quite amused with the situation.

"And what does that have to do with the FGP?" Lux asked.

"Well, in order to understand, you're going to need to know what it is Molly does for a living," Ms. Birdie said.

"You two look like you're in cahoots on something big?" Scott came up behind Lux and slid his arms around her waist, pulling her into him. "Do I even want to know?"

Ms. Birdie gave him a warm smile. "Your wife was just about to be given the details of her debut assignment as the CEO of The Fairy Godmother Project."

"It's not to talk me into taking on the task of starting a Fairy Godfather Project, is it?" he asked. "Because I've told you, I need more time to consider."

"I would not bore her with such an easy assignment." With that, Ms. Birdie turned to Lux. "Lux, why don't we table this conversation until tomorrow, and you two love birds go dance?"

"You don't have to twist my arm," Scott said, tugging Lux toward the dance floor.

"Have I told you tonight how great your ass looks in those pants?" she asked him, leaning to the side and ogling his butt.

"Not as great as yours looks in that dress." He pulled her into his arms and nipped her earlobe. "Now, tell me, Doc. Who is your first FGP assignment and what is her greatest need?"

"I have no idea," Lux admitted. "But whoever it is, they are somehow connected to Molly Thorn, who can communicate with spirits."

"God help us all." He chuckled as he twirled her out and back into his arms.

Lux leaned into Scott's embrace, her heart beating in tandem with the rhythm of his. "Honestly," she mused, glancing up at him. "I can't wait to tackle whatever the Fairy Godmother Project throws at me. I think I'm really going to like my new career."

Scott dropped a tender kiss on her mouth. "Whatever it is," he murmured, "you'll shine, and Ms. Birdie's nonprofit will have another win to add to its large tally."

"With the spirit world now in her arsenal," Lux mused, "I see that list quickly overflowing."

He laughed. "Between curses, superstitions, spirits, and fairy godmothers, we're definitely never going to be one of those boring couples."

"That we're not," she agreed, smiling from an overwhelming sense of pure happiness.

They stopped dancing and glanced around.

"Don't look now," Scott murmured, "but the Glam Team are over by the bar smiling at us like proud parents."

Lux turned and glanced at her friends. "They are looking rather smug." She gave them a jaunty wave before refocusing her attention on her husband.

Scott raised a hand and fingered one of the dangling emerald earrings he'd gifted her earlier this evening. "Did you ever think our story would be one of love, laughter, and unexpected adventures?"

She touched the matching pendant at her throat and gave him a wicked grin. "You mean as opposed to a story of a fair maiden and a prince with a broken—"

His lips crashed down on hers, silencing her sassy reply.

"Ewww. Get a room already," Ziggy said in the background. "I'm blushing over here, and red is not my color."

"You heard the order," Scott said, scooping her up in his arms, and turning to stride away like a man off to battle.

She batted her eyelashes. "Why Prince Landshire, are you whisking me away to do nefarious things?"

"Absolutely," he said in a sexy, growly voice that had her swooning with anticipation.

"Then, by all means, carry on." She rested her head against the strong shoulder of her very own dashing prince—a living testament to the fairy tale that even undreamt dreams can, and do, come true.

Don't miss the next book in the Naked Runway Series

BOOK BOYFRIENDish

(Releases July 23)

What if Book Boyfriends weren't fictional?

Professional Day Dreamer Sophie E. Clark had gotten the last laugh.

Those who'd told her she'd never make money daydreaming could bite her curvaceous derriere because she had just landed the most daydreamiest of daydream gigs with Naked Runway. Of course, if you wanted to get technical about it, for tax purposes and whatnot, they had her listed as a columnist. But her current assignment was to—drum roll please—search out Manhattan men who could stack up to the winners of this year's Swooniest of Book Boyfriends contest.

Former Navy SEAL operative Stone Blackthorn is on the injured list at the security firm he co-owns with his brothers. When a family member calls in a favor, he reluctantly agrees to become an undercover bodyguard—as in he'd play the part of a cinnamon roll boyfriend—for a fluff reporter. A no-action assignment if ever there was one.

Little did he know, his client—the president of a romance book club—would rile up members of motorcycle gangs, mafia sorts, etc., in her quest to find real men who were the living-breathing equivalent of those fictional ones her club drooled over at weekly meetings.

Coming out of this assignment unscathed didn't look favorable for either of them.

Download BOOK BOYFRIENDish now.

Disclaimer Continued

The long answer...

As I mentioned in my dedication, I started writing this book when my dad went into the hospital. There were many days I took my laptop with me and would write while I sat with him. On one such day, I added the broken penis dream to the story line. Doing so made me chuckle at a time when chuckles were few and far between. Dad asked me why I was smiling, and I told him it was because of a story line I'd just written.

Unfortunately, Dad never came home. We lost him on June 23rd, 2023. After his death, I had a really hard time finishing this book. I have more deleted words in the deleted file than I have in the completed manuscript. One of the things I never deleted, even though I knew in my gut my editor would tell me it needed to go, was the broken penis dream. I just couldn't. It reminded me of my last days with my Dad.

So there you have it, the story behind why I ignored my editor's advice and left the *inappropriate thread* in RAKEish. My hope is it gave you a few chuckles.

Lisa Wells

P.S. Once I explained to my editor the why of the thread, she backed me one hundred percent in keeping it in the story.

About Author

Welcome to the whimsical world of Lisa Wells, a place where the paranormal waltzes with the everyday and contemporary romance sizzles with a humor that could lighten even the gloomiest of days. Nestled in the heart of Missouri, Lisa writes with a fervor that steams up the room—whether it be your eyeglasses or Kindle screen, nothing is safe from the heat radiating off her pages.

Lisa's own life is as full-flavored as her writing, with a taste for the finest dark chocolate, the richest red wine, and the most swoon-worthy book boyfriends—a trifecta of treats that inspire her storytelling. She's a maestro of indulgence, her writing days punctuated by the triumph of jeans that zip smoothly on miraculous mornings—a testament to life's simple pleasures (and the occasional indulgence that makes those jeans a bit snug).

In Lisa's tales, love is always in the air—whether it's tinged with the supernatural or wrapped in the warmth of real-world wonder. Donning her mom jeans with pride, she invites you to escape into stories where laughter blooms, passion ignites, and the possibility of a happy ending is just a page away. So settle in, pour yourself a glass of your best-loved beverage, and prepare to be delighted by the steamy romances of Lisa Wells—where every story is a love letter to those who believe in the magic of "What if?"

To stay up-to-date on book releases and news about this author: Lisa Wells Romance Author Newsletter

Website

Newsletter

Facebook:

Instagram

BookBub:

TikTok: